Marion Casey

Admiral Hornblower
in the West Indies

Admiral Hornblower in the West Indies

BY

C. S. Forester

LITTLE, BROWN AND COMPANY

Boston   Toronto

*Admiral Hornblower
in the West Indies*

1

REAR ADMIRAL LORD HORNBLOWER, for all his proud appointment as commander-in-chief of His Majesty's ships and vessels in the West Indies, paid his official visit to New Orleans in H.M. schooner *Crab*, mounting only two six-pounders and with a crew of no more than sixteen men, not counting supernumeraries.

His Britannic Majesty's consul-general at New Orleans, Mr. Cloudesley Sharpe, remarked on the fact.

"I hardly expected to see your lordship in so diminutive a craft," he said, looking round him. He had driven down in his carriage to the pier against which *Crab* was lying, and had sent his liveried footman to the gangway to announce him, and it had been something of an anticlimax to be received by the trilling of the only two bos'n's calls that *Crab* could muster, and to find on the quarterdeck to receive him, besides the admiral and his flag lieutenant, a mere lieutenant in command.

"The exigencies of the service, sir," explained Hornblower. "But if I may lead the way below, I can offer you whatever hospitality this temporary flagship of mine affords."

Mr. Sharpe—surely there never was a name that accorded so ill with its possessor's figure, for he was a fat man, a mountain of puffy flesh—squeezed himself into a chair at the table in the pleasant little cabin, and replied to Hornblower's suggestion of breakfast with the statement that he had already broken his fast. He obviously had the gravest doubts as to the quality of any breakfast that could be served in this little ship. Gerard, the flag lieutenant, made himself inconspicuous in a corner of the cabin, notebook and pencil on his knee, while Hornblower reopened the conversation.

"*Phoebe* was struck by lightning off Morant Cape," said Hornblower. "She was the ship I had planned to come in. *Clorinda* was already in dock, refitting. And *Roebuck*'s off Curaçao, keeping an eye on the Dutchmen—there's a brisk trade in arms with Venezuela at present."

"Well I know that," said Sharpe.

"Those are my three frigates," said Hornblower. "With the arrangements all made I judged it better to come in this schooner rather than not to come at all."

"How are the mighty fallen!" was Mr. Sharpe's comment. "Your lordship, a commander-in-chief, with no more than three frigates and half a dozen sloops and schooners."

"Fourteen sloops and schooners, sir," corrected Hornblower. "They are very desirable craft for the duties I have to perform."

"No doubt, my lord," said Sharpe. "But I can remember the days when the commander-in-chief on the West India Station disposed of a squadron of ships of the line."

"That was in time of war, sir," explained Hornblower, recalling the oral comments of the First Sea Lord in the interview when he had been offered this command. "The House of Commons would sooner allow the Royal Navy to rot at its moorings than reimpose the income tax."

"At any rate, your lordship has arrived," said Sharpe. "Your lordship exchanged salutes with Fort St. Philip?"

"Gun for gun, as your despatch informed me had been arranged."

"Excellent!" said Sharpe.

It had been a strange little formality; all hands on board *Crab* had lined the rail very properly during the salute, and the officers had stood at attention on the quarterdeck, but "all hands" amounted to very little, with four men manning the saluting gun, and one at the signal halyards, and one at the helm. It had poured with rain, too; Hornblower's glittering uniform had clung damply around him.

"Your lordship made use of the services of a steam tug?"

"Yes, by George!" exclaimed Hornblower.

"A remarkable experience for your lordship, apparently?"

"Indeed, yes," said Hornblower. "I—"

He held himself back from giving utterance to all his thoughts on that subject; they would lead to too many exciting irrelevancies. But a steam tug had brought *Crab* against the hundred miles of current from the sea to New Orleans between dawn and dusk, arriving at the very minute the tug captain had predicted. And here was New Orleans, crowded not merely with ocean-going sailing ships but also with a fleet of long narrow steamers, manoeuvring out into the stream and against piers with a facility—thanks to their two paddle wheels—that even *Crab* with her handy fore-and-aft rig could not attempt to emulate. And with a thrash of those paddle wheels they would go flying upstream with a rapidity almost unbelievable.

"Steam has laid open a continent, my lord," said Sharpe, echoing Hornblower's thoughts. "A veritable empire. Thousands and thousands of miles of navigable waterways. The population of the Mississippi Valley will be counted in millions within a few years."

Hornblower remembered discussions at home, when he was a half-pay officer awaiting his promotion to flag rank, when the "steam kettles" had been mentioned. Even the possibility of ocean-going ships propelled by steam had been suggested, and had been properly laughed to scorn—it would mean the ruin of good seamanship. Hornblower had not been quite so sure on the point, but he had been careful to keep his opinions to himself, having no desire to be regarded as a dangerous crank. He did not want to be drawn into any similar discussions now, not even with a mere civilian.

"What intelligence do you have for me, sir?" he asked.

"A considerable amount, my lord." Mr. Sharpe produced a fold of papers from his tail pocket.

"Here are the latest advices from New Granada—more recent I expect than anything you have had. The insurgents—"

Mr. Sharpe entered into a rapid exposition of the military and political situation in Central America. The Spanish colonies were entering into the final stage of their struggle for independence.

"It cannot be long before His Majesty's government recognizes that independence," said Sharpe. "And our minister in Washington informs me that the government of the United States meditates a similar recognition. It remains to be seen what the Holy Alliance will have to say on that score, my lord."

Europe under the rule of absolute monarchy would turn a jaundiced eye upon the establishment of a whole new series of republics, no doubt. But it hardly mattered what Europe had to say, as long as the Royal Navy—even the depleted peacetime navy—controlled the seas and the two English-speaking governments continued in amity.

"Cuba shows small signs of restlessness," went on Sharpe, "and I have information of the issue of further letters of marque by the Spanish government to vessels sailing from Havana."

Letters of marque were one of the principal sources of Hornblower's troubles. They were being issued by insurgent and national-ist governments alike, to prey upon ships flying the old flags and the new, and the bearers of letters of marque turned pirates in the twin-kling of an eye in the absence of legitimate prizes and efficient prize courts. Thirteen of Hornblower's fourteen small craft were scattered over the Caribbean keeping an eye on the activities of the privateers.

"I have prepared duplicates of my reports for your lordship's in-formation," concluded Sharpe. "I have them here to give to your lordship, along with copies of the complaints of the master mariners concerned."

"Thank you, sir," said Hornblower, while Gerard took the papers into his charge.

"Now for the slave trade, with your lordship's permission," went on Sharpe, opening a fresh series of papers.

The slave trade was as acute a question as piracy, even more acute in some ways, because the Anti-Slavery Society in England commanded a great deal of powerful and vocal support in both Houses of Parliament, and would raise an even more violent to-do about a cargo of slaves run into Havana or Rio de Janeiro than a shipping company pestered by privateers.

"At this moment, my lord," said Sharpe, "a raw hand newly brought from the Slave Coast is selling for eighty pounds in the Ha-vana barracoons, and he costs no more than a pound in trade goods at Whydah. Those profits are tempting, my lord."

"Naturally," said Hornblower.

"I have reason to believe that ships of both British and American registry are engaged in the traffic, my lord."

"So have I."

The First Sea Lord had tapped ominously on the table in that interview when touching on this part of his instructions to Horn-blower. Under the new law, British subjects who engaged in the slave trade could be hanged and their ships seized. But care would be necessary in dealing with ships flying American colours. If they refused to heave-to on the high seas for examination, the utmost tact would have to be employed. To shoot away an American spar or to kill an American citizen would mean trouble. America had gone to war with England only nine years before over matters very similar.

"We want no trouble, my lord," said Sharpe. He had a pair of hard intelligent grey eyes deep set in his puffy face.

"I am aware of that, sir."

"And in this connection, my lord, I must employ special emphasis in calling your lordship's attention to a vessel making ready for sea here in New Orleans."

"Which ship is this?"

"She is visible from the deck, my lord. In fact—" Sharpe struggled out of his chair and walked to the cabin window. "Yes, there she is. What do you make of her, my lord?"

Hornblower looked out from beside Sharpe. He saw a beautiful ship of eight hundred tons or more. Her fine lines, the lofty rake of her masts, the wide spread of her yards were all clear indications of speed, for which some sacrifice of cargo-carrying capacity had been made. She was flush-decked, with six painted gunports along each side. American shipbuilders had always evinced a tendency toward building fast ships, but this was an advanced example of the type.

"Are there guns behind those ports?" asked Hornblower.

"Twelve-pounders, my lord."

Even in these days of peace, it was not unusual for merchant vessels to carry guns, whether for voyages in the West Indies or the East, but this was a heavier armament than usual.

"She was built as a privateer," said Hornblower.

"Quite right, my lord. She's the *Daring;* she was built during the war and made one voyage and took six prizes from us before the Treaty of Ghent. And now, my lord?"

"She could be a slaver."

"Your lordship is right again, of course."

That heavy armament would be desirable in a slaver anchoring up a West African river, liable to a treacherous attack; she could easily have a slave deck with that flush build; her speed would minimize deaths among the slaves during the middle passage; her lack of capacity for bulk cargo would be unimportant in a slaver.

"Is she a slaver?" asked Hornblower.

"Apparently not, my lord, despite her appearance. She is being chartered to carry a great many men, all the same."

"I would like you to explain further, if you please, Mr. Sharpe."

"I can only tell your lordship the facts as disclosed to me. She is under charter to a French general, Count Cambronne."

"Cambronne? Cambronne? The man who commanded the Imperial Guard at Waterloo?"

"That's the man, my lord."

"The man who said, 'The Old Guard dies, but does not surrender'?"

"Yes, my lord, although report says he actually used a ruder expression. He was wounded and taken prisoner, but he did not die."

"So I have heard. But what does he want with this ship?"

"It is all open and aboveboard, apparently. After the war, Boney's Old Guard formed an organization for mutual aid. In 1816 they decided to become colonists. Your lordship must have heard something about the project?"

"Hardly anything."

"They came out and seized an area of land on the coast of Texas, the province of Mexico adjacent to this state of Louisiana."

"I have heard about it, but that is the extent of my knowledge."

"It was easy enough to start, with Mexico in the throes of her revolt against Spain. There was no opposition to them, as you understand, my lord. But it was not so easy to continue. I cannot imagine that soldiers of the Old Guard would ever make good agriculturists. And on that pestilential coast—it is a series of dreary lagoons, with hardly an inhabitant."

"The scheme failed?"

"As your lordship might expect. Half of them died of malaria and yellow fever, and half of the rest simply starved. Cambronne has come out from France to carry the survivors home, five hundred of them. The government of the United States never liked the project, as your lordship can imagine, and now the insurgent government is strong enough to take exception to the presence on the shores of Mexico of a large body of trained soldiers, however peaceable their intentions. Your lordship can see Cambronne's story could be perfectly true."

"Yes."

An eight-hundred-ton ship equipped as a slaver could pack five hundred soldiers on board and feed them during a long passage.

"Cambronne is stocking her largely with rice and water—slave rations, my lord, but the best adapted to the purpose for that very reason."

The slave trade had had long experience of how to keep alive a close-packed body of men.

"If Cambronne is going to take them back to France, I should do nothing to hinder him," said Hornblower. "Rather on the contrary."

"Exactly, my lord."

Sharpe's grey eyes met Hornblower's in an expressionless stare. The presence of five hundred trained soldiers afloat in the Gulf of Mexico was very much the concern of the British admiral commanding-in-chief, when the shores of the Gulf and of the Caribbean were in as much of a turmoil as at present. Bolívar and the other Spanish-American insurgents would pay a high price for their services in the present war. Or someone might be meditating the conquest of Haiti or a piratical descent upon Havana. Any sort of filibustering expedition was possible. The actual Bourbon government in France might be looking for a pie in which to put a finger, for that matter, a chance to snap up a colony and confront the English-speaking powers with a *fait accompli.*

"I'll keep my eye on them until they are safely out of the way," said Hornblower.

"I have called your lordship's attention officially to the matter," said Sharpe.

It would be one more drain upon Hornblower's limited resources for the policing of the Caribbean; he already was wondering which of his few craft he could detach to observe the Gulf Coast.

"And now, my lord," said Sharpe, "it is my duty to discuss the details of your lordship's stay here in New Orleans. I have arranged a program of official calls for your lordship. Does your lordship speak French?"

"Yes," said Hornblower, fighting down the urge to say, "My lordship does."

"That is excellent, because French is commonly spoken among good society here. Your lordship will, of course, be calling upon the naval authorities here, and upon the governor. There is an evening reception planned for your lordship. My carriage is, of course, at your lordship's disposition."

"That is extremely kind of you, sir."

"No kindness at all, my lord. It is a great pleasure to me to assist in making your lordship's visit to New Orleans as enjoyable as possible. I have here a list of the prominent people your lordship will meet, along with brief notes regarding them. Perhaps it might be as well if I explain it to your lordship's flag lieutenant?"

"Certainly," said Hornblower; he was able now to relax his attention a little; Gerard was a good flag lieutenant and had supported his commander-in-chief very satisfactorily during the ten months that Hornblower had held command. He supplied some of the social flair that Hornblower was too indifferent to acquire. The business was rapidly settled.

"Very well, then, my lord," said Sharpe. "Now I can take my leave. I will have the pleasure of seeing your lordship again at the governor's house."

"I am deeply obliged to you, sir."

This city of New Orleans was an enchanting place. Hornblower was bubbling internally with excitement at the prospect of exploring it. Nor was he the only one, as appeared as soon as Sharpe had taken his leave, when Lieutenant Harcourt, captain of the *Crab*, intercepted Hornblower on the quarterdeck.

"Pardon, my lord," he said, saluting. "Are there any orders for me?"

There could be no doubt about what Harcourt had in mind. Forward of the mainmast most of the crew of *Crab* were congregated, looking eagerly aft; in a tiny ship like this, everyone was aware of everyone else's business, and discipline ran on lines different from those in a big ship.

"Can you trust your men to be steady on shore, Mr. Harcourt?" asked Hornblower.

"Yes, my lord."

Hornblower looked forward again. The hands looked remarkably smart; they had been labouring on making new clothes for themselves all the way from Kingston, from the moment when it was announced that *Crab* would have the astonishing distinction of flying the admiral's flag. They were wearing neat blue frock jumpers and white ducks and shady straw hats; Hornblower saw their self-conscious poses as he glanced toward them—they knew perfectly well what was being discussed. These were peacetime sailors, voluntarily enlisted; Hornblower had had twenty years of wartime service with pressed crews who could never be trusted not to desert, and even now he had consciously to adjust his mind to the change.

"If you could give me notice of when you intend to sail, sir—I mean, my lord—" said Harcourt.

"Until dawn tomorrow in any case," said Hornblower, coming to a sudden decision; his day was full until then.

"Aye aye, my lord."

Would the grogshops of New Orleans' water-front be any different from the grogshops of Kingston or Port of Spain?

"Now perhaps I can have my breakfast, Mr. Gerard," said Hornblower. "Unless you have any objection?"

"Aye aye, my lord," answered Gerard, carefully ignoring the sarcasm. He had long learned that his admiral objected to nothing in the world as much as having to be active before breakfast.

It was after breakfast that a Negro, trotting barefooted along the pier, came bearing on his head a basket of fruit, which he handed in at the gangway at the moment when Hornblower was about to start off on his official round of calls.

"There's a note with it, my lord," said Gerard. "Shall I open it?"

"Yes."

"It is from Mr. Sharpe," reported Gerard, after breaking the seal, and then, some seconds later, "I think you had better read this yourself, my lord."

Hornblower took the thing impatiently. The note read:

MY LORD:

I have imposed upon myself the pleasure of sending some fruit to your lordship.

It is my duty to inform your lordship that I have just received information that the freight which Count Cambronne brought out here from France, and which has been lying in bond in charge of the United States customs service, will shortly be transferred by lighter through the agency of a bonded carrier to the *Daring*. As your lordship will, of course, understand, this is an indication that the *Daring* will be sailing soon. My information is that the amount of bonded freight is very considerable, and I am endeavouring to discover in what it consists. Perhaps your lordship might, from your lordship's coign of vantage, find an opportunity of observing the nature of this freight.

I am, with great respect,

> Your lordship's humble and
> obedient servant,
> CLOUDESLEY SHARPE,
> H.B.M.'s Consul General at New Orleans

Now what could Cambronne have possibly brought from France in large amount that could be legitimately needed for the purpose he had avowed when he chartered the *Daring?* Not personal effects, certainly. Not food or liquor—he could pick those up cheaply in New Orleans. Then what? Warm-weather clothing would be a possible explanation. Those guardsmen might well need it when returning to France from the Gulf of Mexico. It was possible. But a French general, with five hundred men of the Imperial Guard at his disposal, would bear the closest watching when the Caribbean was in such a turmoil. It would be a great help to know what kind of freight he was shipping.

"Mr. Harcourt!"

"Sir—my lord!"

"I would like your company in the cabin for a moment, if you please."

The young lieutenant stood at attention in the cabin a little apprehensively, waiting to hear what his admiral had to say.

"This isn't a reprimand, Mr. Harcourt," said Hornblower testily. "Not even an admonition."

"Thank you, my lord," said Harcourt, relaxing.

Hornblower took him to the cabin window and pointed out through it, just as Sharpe had done previously.

"That's the *Daring*," he said. "An ex-privateer, now under charter to a French general."

Harcourt looked his astonishment.

"That is the case," went on Hornblower. "And today she will be taking on some cargo out of bond. It will be brought round to her out of bond by lighter."

"Yes, my lord."

"I want to know as much about that cargo as possible."

"Yes, my lord."

"Naturally, I do not want the world to know that I am interested. I want nobody to know unnecessarily."

"Yes, my lord. I could use a telescope from here and see a good deal, with luck."

"Very true. You can take note of whether it is bales or boxes or bags. How many there are of each. From the tackle employed, you can guess at the weights. You can do all that."

"Aye aye, my lord."

"Make careful note of all you see."

"Aye aye, my lord."

Hornblower fixed his eyes on his youthful flag lieutenant's face, trying to estimate his discretion. He remembered so well the emphatic words of the First Sea Lord regarding the necessity for the utmost tenderness regarding American susceptibilities. Hornblower decided the young man could be trusted.

"Now, Mr. Harcourt," he said, "pay special attention to what I have to say. The more I know about that cargo the better. But don't go at it like a bull at a gate. Should an opportunity present itself for finding out what it is, you must seize upon it. I can't imagine what that opportunity may be, but opportunities come to those who are ready for them."

Long, long ago, Barbara had said to him that good fortune is the portion of those who merit it.

"I understand, my lord."

"If the slightest hint of this gets out—if the Americans or the French get to know what you are doing—you will be sorry you were ever born, Mr. Harcourt."

"Yes, my lord."

"I've no use for a dashing young officer in this connection, Mr. Harcourt. I want someone with ingenuity, someone with cunning. You are sure you understand?"

"Yes, my lord."

Hornblower at last took his eyes from Harcourt's face. He himself had been a dashing young officer once. Now he had far more sympathy than ever before with the older men who had entrusted him with enterprises. A senior officer had perforce to trust his juniors, while still carrying the ultimate responsibility. If Harcourt should blunder, if he should be guilty of some indiscretion leading to a diplomatic protest, it would certainly be true that he might wish he had never been born; Hornblower would see to that. But Hornblower would be wishing he himself had never been born, too. But there was no useful purpose to be served in pointing that out.

"That is all, then, Mr. Harcourt."

"Aye aye, sir."

"Come on, Mr. Gerard. We're late already."

⸫　　⸫　　⸫

The upholstery of Mr. Sharpe's carriage was of green satin, and the carriage was admirably sprung, so that, although it lurched and swayed over the uneven street surfaces, it did not jolt or jerk. Yet after five minutes of lurching and swaying—the carriage had been standing for some time in the hot May sun—Hornblower felt himself turning as green as the upholstery. The Rue Royale, the Place d'Armes, the cathedral received hardly a glance from him. He welcomed the halts despite the fact that each halt meant a formal meeting with strangers—the kind of meeting he disliked most heartily. He stood and gulped in the humid air during the blessed moments between descending from the carriage and entering in under the ornate porticoes that stood to welcome him. It had never occurred to him before that an admiral's full-dress uniform might with advantage be made of something thinner than broadcloth, and he had worn his broad red ribbon and his glittering star far too often by now to feel the slightest pleasure in displaying it.

At the naval headquarters he drank an excellent Madeira; the general gave him a heavy Marsala; at the governor's mansion he was given a tall drink which had been iced—presumably with ice sent down during the winter from New England and preserved in an ice house until nearly at midsummer it was more precious than gold—extraordinarily, to the point where actual frost was visible on the tumbler. The delicious cold contents of that tumbler disappeared rapidly, and the tumbler was as rapidly refilled.

He checked himself abruptly when he found himself talking a little too loudly and dogmatically regarding some point of trivial importance. He was glad to catch Gerard's eye and withdraw as gracefully as he could; he was also glad that Gerard seemed perfectly cool and sober and had charge of the card case, dropping the necessary number of cards into the silver trays that the Negro butlers held out to receive them. By the time he reached Sharpe's house he was glad to see a friendly face—friendly even though it was only that morning that he had first set eyes on it.

"It is an hour before the guests are due to arrive, my lord," said Sharpe. "Would your lordship care for a short rest?"

"I would indeed," said Hornblower.

Mr. Sharpe's house had a contrivance which merited much attention. It was a douche bath—Hornblower knew only the French name for it. It was in a corner of the bathroom, floored and walled with the most excellent teak; from the ceiling hung an apparatus of perforated zinc, and from this hung a bronze chain. When Hornblower stood under this apparatus and pulled the chain, a deluge of delicious cold water came streaming down on him from some unseen reservoir above. It was as refreshing as ever it had been to stand under the wash-deck pump on the deck of a ship at sea, with the additional advantage of employing fresh water; and in his present condition, after his experiences of the day, it was doubly refreshing. Hornblower stood under the raining water for a long time, reviving with every second. He made a mental note to install a similar contrivance at Smallbridge House if ever he found himself at home again.

A Negro valet in livery stood by with towels to save him from the reheating exertion of drying himself, and while he was being dabbed, a knock at the door heralded Gerard's entrance.

"I sent to the ship for a fresh shirt for you, my lord," he said.

Gerard was really displaying intelligence; Hornblower put on the fresh shirt with gratitude, but it was with distaste that he tightened his stock and pulled on his heavy uniform coat again. He hung the red ribbon over his shoulder, adjusted his star, and was ready to face the next situation.

The darkness of evening was descending, but it had not brought much relief from the heat; on the contrary, the drawing room of Mr. Sharpe's house was brightly lit with wax candles that made it feel like an oven. Sharpe was awaiting him, wearing a black coat; his ruffled shirt made his bulky form appear larger than ever. Mrs. Sharpe, sweeping in in turquoise blue, was of much the same size; she curtseyed deeply in response to Hornblower's bow when Sharpe presented him, and made him welcome to the house in a French whose soft tang rang pleasantly on Hornblower's ears.

"A little refreshment, my lord?" asked Sharpe.

"Not at present, thank you, sir," said Hornblower hastily.

"We are expecting twenty-eight guests besides your lordship and Mr. Gerard," said Sharpe. "Some of them your lordship already met during your lordship's official calls today. In addition there are—"

Hornblower did his best to keep the list of names in his mind with mental labels attached. Gerard, who came in and found himself a secluded chair, listened intently.

"And there will be Cambronne, of course," said Sharpe.

"Indeed?"

"I could hardly give a dinner party of this magnitude without inviting the most distinguished foreign visitor, after your lordship, present in this city."

"Of course not," agreed Hornblower.

Yet six years of peace had hardly stilled the prejudices established during twenty years of war. There was something a little unnatural about the prospect of meeting a French general on friendly terms, especially the late commander-in-chief of Bonaparte's Imperial Guard, and the meeting might be a little strained because Bonaparte was under lock and key in St. Helena and complaining bitterly about it.

"The French consul-general will accompany him," said Sharpe. "And there will be the Dutch consul-general, the Swedish—"

The list seemed interminable; there was only just time to complete it before the first of the guests was announced. Substantial citizens and their substantial wives; the naval and military officers whom he had already met, and their ladies; the diplomatic officers; soon even that vast drawing room was crowded, men bowing and women curtseying. Hornblower straightened up from a bow to find Sharpe at his elbow again.

"I have the honour of making two distinguished figures acquainted with each other," he said in French. "*Son Excellence Contre-Amiral milord Hornblower, Chevalier de l'Ordre Militaire du Bain. Son Excellence le Lieutenant Général le Comte de Cambronne, Grand Cordon de la Légion d'Honneur.*"

Hornblower could not help being impressed, even at this moment, at the neat way in which Sharpe had evaded the thorny question of whom to introduce to whom, a French general and count, and an English admiral and peer. Cambronne was an immensely tall beanpole of a man. Across one lean cheek and the beaky nose ran a purple scar—perhaps the wound he had received at Waterloo; perhaps a wound received at Austerlitz or Jena or any other of the battles in which the French army had overthrown nations. He was wearing a blue uniform covered with gold lace, girt about with the red watered-silk ribbon of the Legion of Honor, a vast plaque of gold on his left breast.

"Enchanted to make your acquaintance, sir," said Hornblower in his best French.

"No more enchanted than I am to make yours, milord," replied Cambronne. He had a cold green-grey eye with a twinkle in it; a grey cat's-whisker moustache adorned his upper lip.

"The Baroness de Vautour," said Sharpe. "The Baron de Vautour, His Most Christian Majesty's consul-general."

Hornblower bowed and said again that he was enchanted. His Most Christian Majesty was Louis XVIII of France, using the papal title conferred on his house centuries earlier.

"The count is being mischievous," said Vautour. He indicated Cambronne's star. "He is wearing the Grand Eagle, given him during the last regime. Officially the Grand Cordon has been substituted, as our host very properly said."

Vautour called attention to his own star, a more modest affair. Cambronne's displayed an immense eagle of gold, the badge of the now-defunct French Empire.

"I won this on the field of battle," said Cambronne.

"Don Alphonso de Versage," said Sharpe. "His Most Catholic Majesty's consul-general."

This was the representative of Spain, then. A word or two with him regarding this pending cession of Florida might be informative, but Hornblower had hardly time to exchange formal courtesies before another presentation was being made. It was some time before Hornblower had a breathing space, and could look round the pretty scene in the candlelight, with the uniforms and the broadcloth coats, the bare arms and shoulders of the women in their bright gowns and flashing jewelry, and the two Sharpes moving unobtrusively through the throng, marshalling their guests in order of precedence. The entrance of the governor and his lady was the signal for the announcement of dinner.

The dining room was as vast as the drawing room; the table with covers for thirty-two stood comfortably in it, with ample room all round for the numerous footmen. The candlelight was more subdued here, but it glittered impressively on the silver which crowded the long table. Hornblower, seated between the governor's lady and Mrs. Sharpe, reminded himself that he must be alert and careful regarding his table manners; it was the more necessary to be alert because he had to speak French on one side of him and English on the other. He looked dubiously at the six different wine glasses that stood at each place—the sherry was already being poured into the first of the glasses. He could see Cambronne seated between two pretty girls and obviously making himself pleasant to both of them. He did not look as if he had a care in the world; if he was meditating a filibustering expedition, it did not weigh very heavily on his mind.

A steaming plate of turtle soup arrived, thick with gobbets of green fat. This was to be a dinner served in the Continental fashion which had come in after Waterloo, with no hodgepodge of dishes set out on the table for the guests to help themselves. He spooned cautiously at the hot soup and applied himself to making small talk with his dinner partners.

Dish succeeded dish, and soon he had to face in the hot room the delicate question of etiquette as to whether it was more ungentlemanly to mop the sweat from his face or to leave it there, flowing and visible; his discomfort decided him in the end to mop, furtively. Now Sharpe was catching his eye, and he had to rise to his feet, striving to make his stupefied brain work while the buzz of conversation died down. He raised his glass.

"The President of the United States," he said; he had been about to continue, idiotically, "Long may he reign." He checked himself with a jerk and went on, "Long may the great nation of which he is President enjoy prosperity and the international amity of which this gathering is symbolic."

The toast was drunk with acclaim, with nothing said about the fact that over half the continent Spaniards and Spanish-Americans were busy killing one another. He sat down and mopped again. Now Cambronne was on his feet.

"His Britannic Majesty George the Fourth, King of Great Britain and Ireland."

The toast was drunk, and now it was Hornblower's turn again, as evidenced by Sharpe's glance. He stood up, glass in hand, and began the long list: "His Most Christian Majesty. His Most Catholic Majesty. His Most Faithful Majesty." That disposed of France and Spain and Portugal. "His Majesty the King of the Netherlands."

For the life of him he could not remember who came next. But Gerard caught his despairing eye and gave a significant jerk of his thumb.

"His Majesty the King of Sweden," gulped Hornblower. "His Majesty the King of Prussia."

A reassuring nod from Gerard told him that he had now included all the nations represented, and he plucked the rest of his speech out from the whirlpool of his mind.

"Long may their majesties reign, in increasing honour and glory."

Well, that was over, and he could sit down again. But now the governor was on his feet, speaking in rhetorical phrases, and it broke in upon Hornblower's dulled intelligence that his own health was the next to be drunk. He tried to listen. He was aware of keen glances shot at him from around the table when the governor alluded to the defence of this city of New Orleans from the "misguided hordes" who had assailed it in vain—the allusion was perhaps inevitable even though it was over six years since the battle—and he tried to force a smile. At long last the governor reached his end.

"His lordship, Admiral Hornblower, and I couple with his name a toast to the British navy."

Hornblower climbed back upon his feet as the approving murmur of the company died down.

"Thank you for this unexpected honour," he said, and gulped as he sought for further words. "And to have my name coupled with that of the great navy in which it has been my privilege to serve so long is an additional honour for which to thank you."

The ladies were all rising, now that he had sat down, and he stood again while they withdrew. The highly trained footmen swept the table clear of its accessories in a trice, and the men gathered at one end of the table as the decanter was put into circulation. The glasses were filled as Sharpe brought one of the merchants present into the conversation with a question about the cotton crop. It was safe ground from which to make brief and cautious sorties upon the much more debatable ground of world conditions. But only a few minutes later the butler came in and murmured something to Sharpe, who turned to convey the news he brought to the French consul-general. Vautour rose to his feet with an expression of dismay.

"Perhaps you will accept my excuses, sir," he said. "I much regret the necessity."

"No more than I regret it, Baron," said Sharpe. "I trust it is only a slight indisposition."

"I trust so," said Vautour.

"The Baroness finds herself indisposed," explained Sharpe to the company. "I am sure you gentlemen will all join me in hoping, as I said, that the indisposition is slight, and regretting that it involves the loss to us of the Baron's charming company."

There was a sympathetic murmur, and Vautour turned to Cambronne.

"Shall I send back the carriage for you, Count?" he asked.

Cambronne pulled at his cat's-whisker moustache. "Perhaps it might be better if I came with you," he said. "Much as I regret leaving this delightful assembly."

The two Frenchmen took their leave, after polite farewells.

"It is a great pleasure having made your acquaintance, milord," said Cambronne, bowing to Hornblower. The stiffness of his bow was mitigated by the twinkle in his eye.

"It has been a profound experience to meet so distinguished a soldier of the late empire," replied Hornblower.

The Frenchmen were escorted out of the room by Sharpe, voluble in his regrets.

"Your glasses need refilling, gentlemen," said Sharpe on his return.

There was nothing Hornblower disliked more than drinking large glasses of port in a hot and humid room, even though he now found himself free to discuss the Florida question with the Spanish consul-general. He was glad when Sharpe made the move to rejoin the ladies. Somewhere within earshot of the drawing room a string orchestra was playing, but luckily in a subdued manner, so that Hornblower was spared much of the irritation that he usually suffered when he was compelled to listen to music with his tone-deaf ear.

He found himself sitting next to one of the pretty young women beside whom Cambronne had been sitting at dinner. In reply to her questions, he was forced to admit that on this, his first day, he had seen almost nothing of the city of New Orleans, but the admission led to a discussion of other places he had visited. Two cups of coffee, poured for him by a footman passing round the drawing room, cleared his head a little; the young woman was attentive and listened well, and nodded sympathetically when the conversation revealed that Hornblower had left behind, at the call of duty, a wife and a ten-year-old son in England.

Gradually the night wore on, and at last the governor and his lady rose to their feet and the party was over. There were the last few weary minutes of awkward conversation as the carriages were announced one by one, and then Sharpe returned to the drawing room after escorting the last of the guests to the door.

"A successful evening, I fancy. I trust your lordship agrees with me," he said, and turned to his wife. "But I must ask you, my dear, to remember to reprimand Grover about the soufflé."

The entry of the butler with another murmured message prevented Mrs. Sharpe's reply.

"Your lordship's pardon for a moment," said Sharpe. He wore an expression of dismay and hastened out of the room, leaving Hornblower and Gerard to begin polite words of thanks to his hostess for his pleasant evening.

"Cambronne's stolen a march on us!" exclaimed Sharpe, returning with a rapid waddle. "*Daring* left her mooring three hours ago! Cambronne must have gone on board her the moment he left here." He swung round on his wife. "Was the Baroness really ill?" he demanded of her.

"She seemed decidedly faint," replied Mrs. Sharpe.

"It must have been all a plant," said Sharpe. "She was acting. Cambronne put the Vautours up to it because he wanted a chance to get clear away."

"What do you think he means to do?" asked Hornblower.

"God knows. But I expect he was disconcerted by the arrival of a

King's ship here. His leaving in this fashion means he's up to no good. San Domingo—Cartagena—where'll he take that Imperial Guard of his?"

"I'll get after him in any case," said Hornblower, rising to his feet.

"You'll find it hard to overtake him," said Sharpe—the fact that he said "you" and not "your lordship" was a proof of his agitation. "He has taken two tugs—the *Lightning* and the *Star*—and with the new lighthouses on the river a galloping horse wouldn't overtake him before he reaches the pass. He'll be clear out to sea by daylight. I don't know if we can find a tug for you tonight in any case, my lord."

"I'll start after him, all the same," said Hornblower.

"I've ordered the carriage round, my lord," said Sharpe. . . . "Forgive us, my dear, if we leave without ceremony."

Mrs. Sharpe received the hasty bows of the three men; the butler was waiting with their hats; the carriage stood at the door and they scrambled in.

"Cambronne's bonded freight went on board at nightfall," said Sharpe. "My man is meeting me at your ship with his report."

"That may help us make up our minds," said Hornblower.

The carriage lurched along the pitch-dark streets.

"May I make a suggestion, my lord?" asked Gerard.

"Yes. What is it?"

"Whatever scheme Cambronne has in mind, my lord, Vautour is party to it. And he is a servant of the French government."

"You're right. The Bourbons want a finger in every pie," agreed Sharpe thoughtfully. "They take every opportunity to assert themselves. Anyone would think it was them that we beat at Waterloo and not Boney."

The sound of the horses' hoofs changed suddenly as the carriage reached the pier. They stopped, and Sharpe had the door open before the footman could leap down from the box, but as the three men scrambled out, he stood beside the door, hat in hand, his dark face illuminated by the carriage lamps.

"Wait!" snapped Sharpe.

They almost ran along the pier to where the glimmer of a lamp revealed the gangway; the two hands of the anchor watch stood at attention in the darkness as they hastened on board.

"Mr. Harcourt!" shouted Hornblower as soon as his foot touched the deck; this was no time to stand on ceremony. There was a light in the companion and Harcourt was there.

"Here, my lord."

Hornblower pushed his way into the after cabin; a lighted lantern dangled from the deck beam, and Gerard brought in another one.

"What's your report, Mr. Harcourt?"

"The *Daring* sailed at five bells in the first watch, my lord," said Harcourt. "She had two tugs with her."

"I know. What else?"

"The lighter with the freight came alongside her early in the second dogwatch. Just after dark, my lord."

A short dark man came unobtrusively into the cabin as he spoke, and remained in the background.

"Well?"

"This gentleman, whom Mr. Sharpe sent, kept watch as well as me on what they took on board, my lord."

"What was it?"

"I kept count as they swayed it up, my lord. They had lights in the mizzen stay."

"Well?"

Harcourt had a piece of paper in his hand, and he proceeded to read from it:

"There were twenty-five wooden cases, my lord." Harcourt went on just in time to forestall an exasperated exclamation from Hornblower. "I recognized those cases, my lord. They are the usual ones in which muskets are shipped, twenty-four stand of arms in each case."

"Six hundred muskets and bayonets," put in Gerard, calculating rapidly.

"I guessed as much," said Sharpe.

"What else?" demanded Hornblower.

"There were twelve large bales, my lord. Oblong ones; and twenty other bales, long narrow ones."

"Couldn't you guess—"

"Would you hear the report of the hand I sent, my lord?"

"Very well."

"Come down here, Jones!" yelled Harcourt up the companion, and then turned back to Hornblower. "Jones is a good swimmer, my lord. I sent him and another hand off in the quarter boat, and Jones swam to the lighter. . . . Tell his lordship what you found, Jones."

Jones was a skinny, stunted young man, who came in blinking at

the lights, ill at ease in this distinguished company. When he opened
his mouth he spoke with the accent of Seven Dials.

"Uniforms, they was, in them big bales, sir."

"How do you know?"

"I swum to the side of the lighter, sir. I could reach over an' feel
'em, sir."

"Did anyone see you?" This was from Sharpe.

"No, sir. No one didn't see me at all, sir. They was all busy swayin'
up the cases. Uniforms, they was, in the bales, like I said, sir. What
I could feel through the sacking was buttons, sir. Not flat buttons,
sir, like yours, sir. Round buttons, like bullets, sir, rows of 'em, on
each coat. An' I thought I could feel hembroidery, too—gold lace,
p'raps, sir. Uniforms, they was, sir, I'm sure of it."

The dark man came forward at this moment; in his hands was a
limp something that looked like a drowned black cat. Jones pointed
to the object before he went on.

"I couldn't guess for the life of me what was in the other bales, sir,
the long ones. So I outs with my knife—"

"You're sure no one saw you?"

"Certain sure, sir. I outs with my knife an' cuts the stitching at
the end. They'll think it come apart in the handlin', sir. An' I takes
the end one out an' I swims with it back to the quarter boat, sir."

The dark man held it forward for inspection, and Hornblower took
it gingerly, a black soggy mass of hair, but his fingers encountered
metal as he turned it in his hands.

"Heagles, sir," said Jones.

There was a brass chain and a big brass badge—the same displayed
eagle as he had seen that evening on Cambronne's chest. What he
held in his hands was a bearskin uniform cap, soaked with its recent
immersion and adorned with the brass finery.

"Is that what the Imperial Guard wore, my lord?" suggested
Gerard.

"Yes," said Hornblower.

He had seen prints for sale often enough purporting to illustrate
the last stand of the Guard at Waterloo. In London now the Guards
sported bearskin caps not unlike this that he held in his hand; they
had been awarded to the Guards in recognition of their overthrow
of the Imperial Guard at the crisis of the battle. "Then we know all
we need to know," said Sharpe.

"I must try to catch him," said Hornblower. . . . "Call all hands, Mr. Harcourt."

"Aye aye, my lord."

After the automatic reply, Harcourt opened his mouth again to speak, but he could make no sound come from it.

"I remember," said Hornblower, his cup of unhappiness filling to the brim. "I said I would not need the hands before morning."

"Yes, my lord. But they'll not be far. I'll send along the water-front and find 'em. I'll have 'em back here in an hour."

"Thank you, Mr. Harcourt. Do your best. . . . Mr. Sharpe, we shall need to be towed as far as the pass. Will you send and order a steam tug for us?"

Sharpe looked over at the dark man who had brought in the bear-skin cap.

"Doubt if there'll be one before noon," said the dark man. "*Daring* took two—and I know now why she did. The *President Madison's* laid up. *Toueur's* gone up to Baton Rouge with flatboats. *Ecrevisse* —the one that brought this ship up—went down again in the after-noon. I think *Temeraire's* on her way up. We might be able to get her to turn round as soon as she arrives. And that's all there are."

"Noon," said Hornblower. "Thirteen hours' start. *Daring'll* be at sea before we leave here."

"And she's one of the fastest ships built," said Sharpe. "She logged fifteen knots when she was being chased by *Tenedos* during the war."

"What's the Mexican port where she'll take the soldiers on board?"

"It's only a village on a lagoon, Corpus Christi, my lord. Five hun-dred miles and a fair wind."

Hornblower could picture the *Daring*, with her beautiful lines and enormous spread of canvas, booming along before the trade wind. The little *Crab*, in whose cabin he stood, was not intended for fast ocean runs. She had been built and rigged small and handy, to work in and out of obscure inlets, doing the police work of the West In-dian archipelago. On the run to Corpus Christi, *Daring* would cer-tainly gain several hours, a day or more, perhaps, to add to the thirteen hours' lead she already enjoyed. It would not take long to march or to ferry five hundred disciplined men on board, and then she would sail again. Where?

Hornblower's weary brain baulked at the contemplation of the immensely complex political situation in the lands within easy run of Corpus Christi. If he could guess, he might be able to anticipate *Daring*'s arrival at the danger point; if he merely pursued her to Corpus Christi, he would almost certainly arrive there to find her already gone, soldiers and all, having vanished out into the trackless sea or whatever errand of mischief she meditated.

"*Daring*'s an American ship, my lord," said Sharpe, to add to his troubles.

That was an important point, a very important point. *Daring* had an ostensibly legal errand, and she flew the Stars and Stripes. He could think of no excuse for taking her into port for examination. His instructions had been very strict regarding his treatment of the American flag. No more than nine years ago America had gone boldly to war against the greatest maritime power in the world on account of the Royal Navy's attitude toward the American mercantile marine.

"She's armed, and she'll be full of men, my lord," said Gerard.

That was another important point, and a very positive point at that. With her twelve-pounders and five hundred disciplined soldiers —and her large American crew as well—she could laugh at anything *Crab* could threaten with her six-pounders and her crew of sixteen. *Daring* would be within her rights to refuse to obey any signals from *Crab,* and *Crab* could do nothing to compel obedience.

Shoot away a spar? Not so easy with a six-pounder, and even if no one were to be killed by accident, there would be a terrible diplomatic storm if he were to fire on the Stars and Stripes. Could he shadow her, so at least to be on hand when her real purpose was revealed? No; impossible. Anywhere out at sea *Daring* had only to spread her wings to a fair wind to leave *Crab* below the horizon in an afternoon, and then *Daring* could resume her true course unpursued.

Sweating in the stifling night, Hornblower felt like a lassoed wild animal. At every moment some fresh coil was being wound about him to render him more helpless. He was tempted, like a wild animal, to lose all self-control, to lapse into mad panic, to fling away all his strength in an explosion of rage. He had sometimes seen, during his long professional career, senior officers giving vent to explosions of that sort. But it would not help.

He looked round at the circle of faces in the lamplight; the faces wore the sober expressions of men who were witnessing a failure, men who were aware that they were in the presence of an admiral who had made a woeful hash of the first important business he had encountered. That in itself could drive him insane with fury.

Pride came to help him. He would not sink to human weaknesses in the sight of these men.

"I shall sail in any case," he said coldly, "as soon as I have a crew and a steam tug."

"May I ask what your lordship intends to do?" asked Sharpe.

Hornblower had to think quickly to make a reasonable answer to this question; he had no idea. All he knew was that he was not going to give up without a struggle; no crisis was ever alleviated by wasting time.

"I shall employ what time I have here in the composition of orders for my squadron," he said. "My flag lieutenant will write them at my dictation, and I shall ask you, Mr. Sharpe, to undertake the distribution of them by all the means you find available."

"Very good, my lord."

Hornblower remembered at that moment something he should have done already. It was not too late; this part of his duty he must still carry out. And it would at least disguise the anguish he felt.

"Mr. Harcourt," he said, "I have to commend you greatly on the excellent way in which you executed my orders. You carried out the task of observing *Daring* in most exemplary fashion. You can be sure I shall call the attention of Their Lordships to your behaviour."

"Thank you, my lord."

"And this man Jones," went on Hornblower. "No seaman could have acted with more intelligence. You made a good selection, Mr. Harcourt, and Jones justified it. I have it in mind to reward him. I can give him an acting rating and confirm it as soon as possible."

"Thank you, my lord. He has been rated before and disrated."

"Drink? Is that why he was denied shore leave?"

"I'm afraid so, my lord."

"Then what do you recommend?"

Harcourt was at a loss.

"You could say to his face what you've already said to me, my lord. You could shake his hand."

Hornblower laughed.

"And be known through the navy as the meanest admiral who ever flew a flag? No. A golden guinea at least. Two guineas. I'll give them to him myself, and I shall request you to give him three days' leave as soon as we see Kingston again. Let him have his debauch, if that is the only way in which we can reward him. I have to consider the feelings of the whole squadron."

"Aye aye, my lord."

"Now, Mr. Gerard, I'll begin the writing of those orders."

It was indeed noon before *Crab* cast off and was taken in tow by the tug *Temeraire;* it was significant of Hornblower's state of mind that he never gave a thought to the implication of that glorious name. The interval before sailing, all the long, stifling morning, was taken up by the dictation of orders, to be dispersed to every ship of his squadron. An infinity of copies was necessary. Sharpe would send them under seal by every British ship leaving New Orleans for the West Indies, in the hope that should one of them encounter a King's ship his orders would be passed on without the delay of being sent to Kingston and then transmitted through official channels. Every ship of the West India squadron was to keep a sharp lookout for the American ship *Daring.* Every ship was to inquire her business, and was to ascertain, if possible, whether *Daring* had troops on board; but—Hornblower sweated more feverishly than ever as he worded this—captains of H.M.'s vessels were reminded of that passage in the commander-in-chief's original instructions regarding behaviour toward the American flag. If troops were not on board, an effort was to be made to ascertain where they had been landed; if they were, *Daring* was to be kept in sight until they should be landed. Captains were to exercise a wide discretion regarding any interference with *Daring's* operations.

Seeing that these orders would not leave New Orleans until tomorrow, and would travel by slow merchant ships, it was hardly likely that they would reach any ship of the squadron before *Daring* had done whatever she planned to do. Yet it was necessary to take every possible precaution.

Hornblower signed twenty copies of his orders with a sweating hand, saw them sealed, and handed them over to Sharpe. They shook hands before Sharpe went down the gangway.

"Cambronne will head for Port-au-Prince or Havana, in my opinion, my lord," said Sharpe.

The two places were not more than a thousand miles apart.

"Might it not be Cartagena or La Guaira?" asked Hornblower with elaborate irony. Those places were about a thousand miles apart as well, and more than a thousand miles from Havana.

"It well might be," said Sharpe, the irony quite wasted on him. Yet it could not be said that he was unsympathetic regarding Hornblower's difficulties, for he went on, "The very best of good fortune, my lord, in any case. I am certain your lordship will command success."

Crab cast off, and *Temeraire* had her in tow, smoke and sparks belching from her funnels, much to Harcourt's indignation. He was afraid not only of fire but of stains on his spotless deck; he had the hands at work pumping up water from overside, continuously soaking deck and rigging.

"Breakfast, my lord?" said Gerard at Hornblower's elbow.

Breakfast? It was one o'clock in the afternoon. He had not been to bed. He had drunk far too much last night, and he had had a busy morning, an anxious morning, and he was as desperately anxious at this moment. His first reaction was to say no; then he remembered how he had complained yesterday—only yesterday? It seemed more like a week ago—about his delayed breakfast. He would not allow his agitation to be so obvious.

"Of course. It could have been served more promptly, Mr. Gerard," he said, hoping he was displaying the irascibility of a man who had not broken his fast.

"Aye aye, my lord," said Gerard. He had been Hornblower's flag lieutenant for several months now, and knew nearly as much about Hornblower's moods as a wife might have done. He knew, too, of Hornblower's kindly interior. He had received his appointment as the son of an old friend, at a moment when admirals' sons and dukes' sons had yearned to serve as flag lieutenant to the fabulous Hornblower.

Hornblower forced himself to eat his fruit and his boiled eggs, to drink his coffee despite the heat. He whiled away a considerable time before he came on deck again, and during that period he had actually contrived to forget his problems—at least nearly to forget them. But they returned in full force as soon as he came on deck again. So harassing were they that he could feel no interest in this still unusual method of navigating a river, no interest in the low banks that were going by so fast alongside. This hurried departure from New Orleans was only a gesture of despair, after all. He could not hope to catch the *Daring*. She would bring off whatever coup she had in mind almost under his very nose and leave him the laughingstock of the world—of his world, at least. This would be the last command he would ever hold.

Hornblower looked back over the years of half pay he had endured since Waterloo. They had been dignified and happy years, one would think, with a seat in the Lords and a position of influence in the county, a loving wife and a growing son, but he had not been living the right life, even so. The five years after Waterloo until at last the course of nature brought his promotion to flag rank had been fretful years; he had realized it only when he knew the intense joy of his appointment to the West Indies. Now all the years to come until he went down into the grave would be as dreary as those five —more dreary, because they would be unrelieved by the hope of future employment at sea.

Here he was, pitying himself, he said to himself bitterly, when what he should be doing was working out the problems set him. What was it Cambronne had in mind? If he could head him off, arrive triumphantly at the place where Cambronne intended to strike his blow, he could retrieve his reputation. He might be able, with great good fortune, to intervene decisively. But there was turmoil everywhere through Spanish America, and through the West Indies as well, save for the British colonies. One place was as likely as another; in any case, it would be extremely doubtful if he would have any excuse to interfere—Cambronne probably held a commission from Bolívar or some other leader; but, on the other hand, the precautions Cambronne had taken seemed to imply that he would at least prefer that the Royal Navy would not have a chance to intervene. Intervene? With a crew of sixteen, not counting supernumeraries, and with nothing larger than a six-pounder? Rubbish. He was a fool. But he must think, think, think.

"It will be sunset before we sight St. Philip, my lord," reported Harcourt, saluting.

"Very well, Mr. Harcourt."

There would be no salutes fired, then. He would make his departure from the United States with his tail between his legs, so to speak. There could hardly fail to be comment about the briefness of his visit. Sharpe might do his best to explain why he had left so hurriedly, but any explanation would be unsatisfactory. In every way this command for which he had yearned was turning out to be a ridiculous fiasco.

Even this visit, to which he had looked forward so eagerly, was a disappointment. He had seen almost nothing of New Orleans, of America, or of the Americans. He could take no interest in this vast Mississippi. His problems deprived him of interest in his surroundings, and his surroundings distracted him from a proper attention to his problems. This fantastic method of progression, for instance— *Crab* was going through the water at a good five knots, and there was the current as well. Quite a breeze was blowing past him in consequence; it was extraordinary to be going ahead with the wind dead foul, without a heel or a pitch, with the standing rigging uttering a faint note and yet not a creak from the running rigging.

"Your dinner is served, my lord," said Gerard, appearing on deck again.

Darkness was closing in round the *Crab* as Hornblower went below, but the cabin was hot and stuffy.

"Scotch broth, my lord," said Giles, putting a steaming plate before him.

Hornblower dipped his spoon perfunctorily into the plate, tried to swallow a few mouthfuls, and laid his spoon down again. Giles poured him a glass of wine; he wanted neither wine nor soup, yet he must not display human weaknesses. He forced himself to take a little more of the soup, enough to preserve appearances.

"Chicken Marengo, my lord," said Giles, putting another plate before him.

Appearances were more easily preserved with chicken; Hornblower haggled the joints apart, ate a couple of mouthfuls, and laid down his knife and fork. They would report to him from the deck if the miracle had happened—if *Daring's* two steam tugs had broken down or if *Daring* had run aground and they were passing her triumphantly. Absurd hope. He was a fool.

Giles cleared the table, reset it with cheese dish and cheese plate, and poured a glass of port. A sliver of cheese, a sip of port, and dinner might be considered over. Giles set out the silver spirit lamp, the silver coffeepot, the porcelain cup—Barbara's last present to him. Somehow there was comfort in coffee despite his misery; the only comfort in a black world.

On deck again it was quite dark. On the starboard bow gleamed a light, moving steadily aft to the starboard beam; that must be one of the lighthouses installed by the Americans to make the navigation of the Mississippi as convenient by night as by day. It was one more proof of the importance of this developing commerce—the fact that as many as six steam tugs were being constantly employed was a further proof.

"If you please, my lord," said Harcourt in the darkness beside him. "We are approaching the pass. What orders, my lord?"

What could he do? He could only play a losing game out to the bitter end. He could only follow *Daring*, far, far astern of her, in the hope of a miracle, a fortunate accident. The odds were a hundred to one that by the time he reached Corpus Christi the bird would be flown, completely vanished. Yet perhaps the Mexican authorities, if there were any, or local gossip, if he could pick up any, might afford him some indication of the next destination of the Imperial Guard.

"As soon as we are at sea set a course for Corpus Christi, if you please, Mr. Harcourt."

"Aye aye, my lord. Corpus Christi."

"Study your sailing directions for the Gulf of Mexico, Mr. Harcourt, for the pass into the lagoon there."

"Aye aye, my lord."

That was done, then; the decision was taken. Yet he stayed up on deck, trying to wrestle with the problem in all its vague and maddening complexity.

He felt rain on his face and soon it was falling in torrents, roaring on the deck, soaking his best uniform. His cocked hat weighed on his head like lead with the accumulation of water in the brim. He was about to take shelter below when his mind began to follow an old train of thought, and he stayed. Gerard loomed up in the darkness with his sou'wester and oilskins, but he paid no attention to him. Was it possible that all this was a false alarm? That Cambronne had nothing else in mind than to take back the Guard to France? No, of course not. He would not have taken six hundred muskets on board in that case, nor bales of uniforms, and there would have been no need for a hurried and clandestine departure.

"If you please, my lord," said Gerard, standing insistently by with his oilskins.

Hornblower remembered how, before he left England, Barbara had taken Gerard to one side and had talked to him long and earnestly. No doubt she had been telling him of the need to see that he did not get wet and that he had his meals regularly.

"Too late now, Mr. Gerard," he said, with a grin. "I'm soaked through."

"Then please, my lord, go below and shift your clothes."

There was genuine anxiety in Gerard's voice, a real concern. The rain was roaring on Gerard's oilskins in the darkness like the nitre crusher of a powder mill.

"Oh, very well," said Hornblower.

He made his way down the little companion, Gerard following him.

"Giles!" called Gerard sharply; Hornblower's servant appeared at once. "Put out dry clothes for his lordship."

Giles began to bustle round the little cabin, kneeling on the deck to fish a fresh shirt out of the chest. Half a gallon of water cascaded down beside him as Hornblower took off his hat.

"See that his lordship's things are properly dried," ordered Gerard.

"Aye aye, sir," said Giles, with sufficient restrained patience in his tone to make Gerard aware that it was an unnecessary order. Hornblower knew that both these men were fond of him. So far, their affection had survived his failure—for how long?

"Very well," he said in momentary irritation. "I can look after myself now."

He stood alone in the cabin, stooping under the deck beams. Unbuttoning his soaking uniform coat, he realized he was still wearing his ribbon and star; the ribbon, as he passed it over his head, was soaking wet, too. Ribbon and star mocked at his failure, just at the very moment when he was sneering at himself for hoping again that *Daring* might have gone aground somewhere during her passage down the river.

A tap at the door brought Gerard back into the cabin.

"I said I could look after myself," snapped Hornblower.

"Message from Mr. Harcourt, my lord," said Gerard, unabashed. "The tug will be casting off soon. The wind is fair, a strong breeze, east by north."

"Very well."

A strong breeze, a fair wind, would be all in *Daring*'s favor. *Crab* might have stood a chance of overhauling her in fluky contrary airs. Fate had done everything possible to load the dice against him.

Giles had taken the opportunity to slip back into the cabin. He took the wet coat from Hornblower's hand.

"Didn't I tell you to get out?" blared Hornblower cruelly.

"Aye aye, my lord," replied Giles imperturbably. "What about this —this cap, my lord?"

He had picked up the bearskin cap of the Imperial Guard, which was still lying in the locker.

"Oh, take it away!" roared Hornblower.

He had kicked off his shoes and was beginning to peel off his stockings when the thought struck him; he remained stooping to consider it.

A bearskin cap—bales and bales of bearskin caps. Why? Muskets and bayonets he could understand. Uniforms, too, perhaps. But who in their sane senses would outfit a regiment for service in tropical America with bearskin caps? He straightened up slowly, and stood still again, thinking deeply. Even uniform coats with buttons and embroidery would be out of place among the ragged ranks of Bolívar's hordes; bearskin caps would be quite absurd.

"Giles!" he roared; and, when Giles appeared round the door, "Bring that cap back to me!"

He took it into his hands again; within him surged the feeling that he held in his hands the clue to the mystery. There was the heavy chain of lacquered brass, the brazen Imperial eagle. Cambronne was a fighting soldier of twenty years' experience in the field; he would never expect men wearing things like this to wage war in the pestilential swamps of Central America or the stifling canebrakes of the West Indies. Then—The Imperial Guard in their uniforms and bearskins, already historic, would be associated in everyone's mind with the Bonapartist tradition, even now making itself felt as a political force. A Bonapartist movement? In Mexico? Impossible. In France, then?

Within his wet clothes Hornblower felt a sudden surge of warmth as his blood ran hot with the knowledge that he had guessed the solution. St. Helena! Bonaparte was there, a prisoner, an exile in one of the loneliest islands in the world. Five hundred disciplined troops arriving by surprise out of a ship flying American colours would set him free.

And then? There were few ships in the world faster than the *Daring*. Sailing for France, she would arrive there before any warning could reach the civilized world. Bonaparte would land with his Guard—oh, the purpose of the uniforms and bearskins was quite plain. Everyone would remember the glories of the empire. The French army would flock to his standard as it had done once before when he returned from Elba. The Bourbons had already outworn their welcome—Sharpe had remarked how they were acting as international busybodies in the hope of dazzling the people with a successful foreign policy. Bonaparte would march again to Paris without opposition. Then the world would be in a turmoil once more. Europe would experience again the bloody cycle of defeat and victory.

After Elba a campaign of a hundred days had been needed to overthrow Bonaparte at Waterloo, but a hundred thousand men had died during those hundred days, millions and millions of money had been expended. This time it might not even be as easy as that. Bonaparte might find allies in the disturbed state of Europe. There might be twenty more years of war, leaving Europe in ruins. Hornblower had fought through twenty years of war; he felt physically sick at the thought of their repetition. The prospect was so monstrous that he went back through the deductions he had been making, but he could not avoid reaching the same conclusion.

Cambronne was a Bonapartist; no man who had been commander-in-chief of the Imperial Guard could be anything else. It was even indicated by a trifle—he had worn the Bonapartist Grand Eagle of the Legion of Honor instead of the Bourbon Grand Cordon which had been substituted for it. He had done that with Vautour's knowledge and agreement. Vautour was a servant of the Bourbons, but he must be a traitorous one; the whole business of chartering the *Daring* and sending her fatal freight on board could have been carried out only with the connivance of the French authorities—presumably France was riddled with a fresh Bonapartist conspiracy. The Baroness's behaviour was further proof.

Central America and the West Indies might be in a turmoil, but there was no particular strategic point there—as he well knew, after so much wondering about it—inviting an invasion by the Imperial Guard in uniforms and bearskins. It must be St. Helena, and then France. He could have no doubt about it now. Now the lives of millions, the peace of the whole world, depended on the decisions he had to make at this moment.

There was a rush of feet on the deck just above his head. He heard ropes slapping down upon it, orders being given, loud creakings. The cabin suddenly leaned over sideways with the setting of sail, catching him completely unaware, so that he staggered and dropped the bearskin cap, which lay unnoticed at his feet. *Crab* rose to an even keel again. The deck under his feet felt suddenly lively, as if the breath of life had been breathed into it. They were at sea; they were heading for Corpus Christi. With the wind east by north, *Crab* would be running wing-and-wing, possibly. Now he had to think fast, with every second of value. He could not afford to run to leeward in this fashion if he was going to change his plans.

And he knew he was going to change them. He had yearned so desperately for a chance to guess whither *Daring* would head after calling at Corpus Christi. Now he could intervene. Now he had a chance to preserve the peace of the world. With his eyes, unseeing, focussed upon an infinite distance, he stood in the swaying cabin calling up into his mental sight the charts of the Gulf of Mexico and the Caribbean. The northeast trades blew across them, not quite as reliably at this time of year as during the winter, but constantly enough to be a calculable factor. A ship bound for the South Atlantic —for St. Helena—from Corpus Christi would be bound to take the Yucatán Channel. Then—especially if her business was such as not to invite attention—she would head for the shoulder of South America, down the centre of the Caribbean, with scores of miles of open sea on either beam. But she would have to pass through the chain of the Antilles before breaking through into the Atlantic.

There were a hundred passages available, but only one obvious one, only one route that would be considered for a moment by a captain bound for St. Helena and with the trade winds to contend with. He would round Galera Point, the northernmost extremity of Trinidad. He would give it as wide a berth as possible, but he could not give it a very wide berth because to the northward of Galera Point lay the island of Tobago, and the Tobago Channel between the two was no more than—Hornblower could not be sure—exactly— certainly no more than fifty miles wide. In favourable conditions a single ship could patrol that channel and make certain that nothing passed through unsighted. It was a typical example of maritime strategy on a tiny scale. Sea power made its influence felt all over the wide oceans, but it was in the narrow seas, at the focal points, that the decisive moments occurred.

The Yucatán Channel would not be nearly as suitable as the Tobago Channel, for the former was more than a hundred miles wide. *Crab* would get there first; that could be taken for granted, seeing that *Daring* would have two sides of a triangle to cover, call- ing at Corpus Christi, and with a long beat to windward as a result. It would be best to employ the advantage so gained to hasten to the Tobago Channel. There would be just time to anticipate *Daring* there—just time—and there was a substantial chance that on the way he might meet some ship of his squadron, to take her along with him. A frigate, now. That would give him all the force he needed. He made his resolve at that moment, conscious as he did so of his quickened heart beat.

"Giles!" shouted Hornblower.

Giles reappeared, and, within the wide discretion of a spoiled servant, displayed shocked disapproval at the sight of him still in his wet shirt and ducks.

"My compliments to Mr. Harcourt, and I would be glad to see him here as quickly as is convenient to him."

That was very quickly, naturally, when an admiral needed the presence of a lieutenant.

"Mr. Harcourt, I have decided on a change of plan. There is no time to be lost. Kindly set a course for Cape San Antonio."

"Cape San Antonio. Aye aye, sir."

Harcourt was a good officer. There was neither surprise nor doubt in his voice as he heard the surprising order.

"When we are on the new course I will explain what I intend to do, if you will have the goodness to report to me with the charts, Mr. Harcourt. Bring Mr. Gerard with you."

"Aye aye, sir."

Now he could take off his wet shirt and trousers, and dab himself dry with a towel. Somehow the little cabin did not seem so oppressively hot; perhaps because they were out at sea, perhaps because he had reached a decision. He was putting on his trousers at the moment when Harcourt had the helm put down. *Crab* came round like a top, with lusty arms hauling in on the sheets. She lay far over to starboard, with the wind abeam, and Hornblower, one leg in his trousers, after a frantic hop, trying to preserve his balance, fell on his nose across his cot with his legs in the air. He struggled to his feet again; *Crab* still heeled over to starboard, farther and then less, as each roller of the beam sea passed under her, each roll taking Hornblower by surprise as he tried to put his other leg into his trousers, so that he sat down twice, abruptly, on his cot before he managed it.

It was as well that Harcourt and Gerard re-entered the cabin only after he had succeeded. They listened soberly while Hornblower told them of his deductions regarding *Daring's* plans and of his intention to intercept her at the Tobago Channel; Harcourt took his dividers and measured off the distances, and nodded when he had finished.

"We can gain four days on her to San Antonio, my lord," he said. "That means we'll be three days ahead of her there."

Three days should be just enough start for *Crab* in the long, long race down the length of the Caribbean.

"Could we call at Kingston on our way, my lord?" asked Gerard.

It was tempting to consider it, but Hornblower shook his head. It would be no use calling at headquarters, telling the news, possibly picking up reinforcements, if *Daring* slipped past them as they were doing so.

"It would take too long to work in," he said. "Even if we had the sea breeze. And there would be delay while we were there. We've nothing to spare as it is."

"I suppose not, my lord," agreed Gerard grudgingly. He was playing the part of the staff officer, whose duty it was to be critical of any suggested plan. "Then what do we do when we meet her?"

Hornblower met Gerard's eyes with a steady glance; Gerard was asking the question that had been already asked and left unanswered.

"I am forming plans to meet that situation," said Hornblower, and there was a rasping tone in his voice which forbade Gerard to press the matter.

"There's not more than twenty miles of navigable water in the Tobago Channel, my lord," said Harcourt, still busy with his dividers.

"Then she can hardly pass us unobserved, even by night," said Hornblower. "I think, gentlemen, that we are acting on the best possible plan. Perhaps the only possible plan."

"Yes, my lord," said Harcourt; his imagination was hard at work. "If Boney once gets loose again—"

He could not go on. He could not face that appalling possibility.

"We have to see to it that he does not, gentlemen. And now that we have done all that we can, it would be sensible if we took some rest. I don't think any one of us has had any sleep for a considerable time."

That was true. Now that he had made up his mind upon a course of action, now that he was committed to it, for good or ill, Hornblower felt his eyelids drooping and sleep overcoming him.

He lay down on his cot after his officers had left him. With the wind on the port beam and the cot against the bulkhead to starboard, he could relax completely with no fear of rolling out. He closed his eyes. Already he had begun to form the answer to the question Gerard had asked. The answer was a hideous one, something horrible to contemplate. But it seemed to be inevitable. He had his duty to do, and now he could be sure that he was doing it to the best of his ability.

With his conscience clear, with a reassuring certainty that he was using the best of his judgment, the inevitability of the rest of the future reinforced his need for sleep. He slept until dawn; he even dozed for a few minutes after that, before he began to think clearly enough again in the daylight for that horrible thought to begin to nag at him again.

That was how the *Crab* began her historic race to the Tobago Channel, over a distance nearly as great as the Atlantic is wide, with the brave trade wind laying her over as she thrashed along. All hands on board knew that she was engaged in a race, for in a little ship like *Crab* nothing could be kept secret; and all hands entered into the spirit of the race with the enthusiasm to be expected of them. Sympathetic eyes were turned toward the lonely figure of the admiral standing braced on the tiny quarterdeck with the wind singing round him. Everyone knew the chances he was taking; everyone thought that he deserved to win; and no one could guess at his real torment over the certainty that was crystallizing in his mind that this was the end of his career, whether he should win the race or lose it.

No one on board begrudged the constant labor involved in getting every yard of speed out of *Crab*, the continual hauling in and letting out of the sheets as the sails were trimmed to the least variation of the wind, the lightening and urgent shortening of canvas at the last possible moment as squalls came hurtling down upon them, the instant resetting as the squalls passed on their way.

All hands constituted themselves as unofficial lookouts; there was really no need for the admiral to have offered a golden guinea to the man who should first sight *Daring*—there was always the chance of an encounter even before reaching the Tobago Channel. Nobody minded wet shirts and wet beds as the spray burst over *Crab*'s bows in dazzling rainbows and found its way below through the deck as the overdriven schooner worked her seams open in the heavy swell. The hourly casting of the log, the daily calculation of the ship's run were eagerly anticipated by men who usually displayed all the fatalistic indifference of the hardened sailor toward these matters.

"I am shortening the water allowance, my lord," said Harcourt to Hornblower the first morning out.

"To how much?" Hornblower asked the question trying to appear as if he were really interested in the answer, so that his misery over something else should not be apparent.

"To half a gallon, my lord."

Two quarts of fresh water a day per man—that would be hardship for men laboring hard in the tropics.

"You are quite right, Mr. Harcourt," said Hornblower.

Every possible precaution must be taken. It was impossible to predict how long the voyage would last, or how long they would have to remain on patrol without refilling their water casks; it would be absurd if they were driven prematurely into port as a result of thoughtless extravagance.

"I'll instruct Giles," went on Hornblower, "to draw the same ration for me."

Harcourt blinked a little at that; his small experience with admirals led him to think they led a life of maximum luxury. He had not thought sufficiently far into the problem to realize that if Giles had a free hand as regarded drinking water for his admiral, Giles and perhaps all Giles's friends would also have all the drinking water they needed. And there was no smile on Hornblower's face as he spoke; Hornblower wore the same bleak and friendless expression that he had displayed toward everyone since reaching his decision when they went to sea.

They sighted Cape San Antonio one afternoon, and knew they were through the Yucatán Channel; not only did this give them a fresh departure, but they knew that from now on it would not be extremely unlikely for them to sight *Daring* at any moment; they were pursuing very much the same course as she would be taking, from this point onward.

Two nights later they passed Grand Cayman; they did not sight it, but they heard the roar of the surf on one of the outlying reefs. That was a proof of how closely Harcourt was cutting his corners; Hornblower felt that he would have given Grand Cayman a wider berth than that. It was a moment when he chafed more than usual at the convention which prohibited an admiral from interfering in the management of his flagship.

The following night they picked up soundings on the Pedro Bank, and knew that Jamaica and Kingston were a scant hundred miles to windward of them. From this new departure Harcourt could set a fresh course, direct for the Tobago Channel, but he could not hold it. The trade wind took it into its head to veer round south of east, as was not surprising with midsummer approaching, and it blew dead foul. Harcourt laid *Crab* on the starboard tack—never voluntarily would any captain worth his salt yield a yard to the southward in the Caribbean—and clawed his way as close to the wind as *Crab* would lie.

"I see you've taken in the tops'ls, Mr. Harcourt," remarked Hornblower, venturing on ticklish ground

"Yes, my lord." In response to his admiral's continued inquiring glance, Harcourt condescended to explain further. "A beamy schooner like this isn't intended to sail on her side, my lord. We make less leeway under moderate sail like this, my lord, as long as we're close-hauled with a strong breeze."

"You know your own ship best, of course, Mr. Harcourt," said Hornblower grudgingly.

It was hard to believe that *Crab* was making better progress without her magnificent square topsails spread to the breeze. He could be sure that *Daring* would have every stitch of canvas spread—perhaps a single reef. *Crab* thrashed on her way, once or twice shipping it green over her starboard bow; those were the moments when it was necessary for every man to grab and hold on.

At dawn next morning there was land right ahead, a blue line on the horizon—the mountains of Haiti. Harcourt held on until noon, raising them farther and farther out of the water, and then he went about. Hornblower approved—in an hour or two the land breeze might set in and there was Beata Point to weather.

It was maddening that on this tack they would actually be losing a little ground, for it was perfectly possible that *Daring*, wherever she was, might have the wind a point or two more in her favor and could be able to hold her course direct. And it was quite remarkable to see the foremast hands raising wetted fingers to test the wind, and studying the windward horizon, and criticizing the way the quartermaster at the tiller struggled to gain every yard to windward that he could.

For a day and a half the wind blew foul; in the middle of the second night, Hornblower, lying sleepless in his cot, was roused by the call for all hands. He sat up and reached for his dressing gown while feet came running above his head. *Crab* was leaping madly.

"All hands shorten sail!"

"Three reefs in the mains'l!" Harcourt's voice was pealing out as Hornblower reached the deck.

The wind blew the tails of Hornblower's dressing gown and night-shirt up round him as he stood out of the way by the taffrail; darkness was roaring all round him. A midsummer squall had come hurtling at them in the night, but someone had had a weather eye lifting and had been prepared for it. Out of the southward had come the squall.

"Let her pay off!" shouted Harcourt. "Hands to the sheets!"

Crab came round in a welter of confused water, plunged, and then steadied. Now she was flying along in the darkness, belying her unlovely name. She was gaining precious distance to the north-ward; an invaluable squall this was, as long as it permitted them to hold this course. The roaring night was hurrying by; Hornblower's dressing gown was whipping about his legs. It was impossible not to feel exhilarated to stand thus, compelling the elements to work in their favour, cheating the wind that thought to take them by surprise.

"Well done, Mr. Harcourt!" shouted Hornblower into the wind as Harcourt came and stood beside him in the darkness.

"Thank you, sir—my lord. Two hours of this is what we need."

Fate granted them an hour and a half at any rate, before the squall died away and the trade wind pigheadedly resumed its former direction of east by south. But next morning at breakfast Giles was able to report good news.

"Wind's backing to the nor'rard, my lord," he said—Giles was as interested as everyone else in the vessel's progress.

"Excellent," said Hornblower; it was only some seconds later that the dull pain grew up again inside him. That wind would bear him more swiftly to his fate.

As the day wore on, the trade wind displayed some of its mid-summer freakishness. It died away, died away more and more, until it blew only in fitful puffs, so that there were intervals when *Crab* drifted idly over the glassy blue sea, turning her head to all points of the compass in turn, while the vertical sun blazed down upon a deck in whose seams the pitch melted. Flying fish left fleeting dark tracks upon the enamel surface of the sea. No one cared; every eye was scanning the horizon for the first hint of the next cat's-paw of wind creeping toward them. Perhaps, not too far away in this moody

Caribbean, *Daring* was holding her course with all sail set and drawing.

The day ended and the night went by, and still the trade wind did not blow; only occasionally would a puff send *Crab* ghosting along momentarily toward the Tobago Channel. The sun blazed down, and men limited to two quarts of water a day were thirsty, thirsty all the time.

They had seen very few sails, and the ones they saw were of no use in furthering Hornblower's plans. An island schooner bound to Belize, a Dutchman homeward bound from Curaçao, no one to whom Hornblower could entrust a letter, and no ship of his own squadron— that was something almost beyond the bounds of possibility. Hornblower could only wait, as the days went by, in grim, bleak patience.

At last the freakish wind blew again, from one point north of east, and they were able to hold their course, with topsails set again, heading steadily for the Antilles, reeling off as much as six knots hour after hour. Now as they approached the islands they saw more sails, but they were only interisland sloops trading between the Leeward Islands and Trinidad. A square-rigger seen on the horizon roused momentary excitement, but she was not the *Daring*. She flew the red and gold of Spain—a Spanish frigate heading for the Venezuelan coast, presumably to deal with the insurgents. The voyage was nearly completed; Hornblower heard the cry of land from the masthead lookout, and it was only a moment before Gerard came into the cabin.

"Grenada in sight, my lord."

"Very well."

Now they were entering the waters where they could really expect to meet *Daring;* now the direction of the wind was of more importance than ever. It was blowing from the northeast now, and that was helpful. It extinguished the very faint possibility that *Daring* might pass to the northward of Tobago instead of through the Tobago Channel.

"*Daring's* bound to make the same landfall, my lord," said Gerard, "and by daylight if she can."

"We can hope for it, at least," said Hornblower.

If *Daring* had been as long out of sight of land as had *Crab*, in the fluky winds and unpredictable currents of the Caribbean, her captain would certainly take all precautions in his approach.

"I think, Mr. Harcourt," said Hornblower, "that we can safely hold our course for Point Galera."

"Aye aye, my lord."

Now was the worst period of waiting, of wondering whether the whole voyage might not prove to be a fool's errand, patrolling, beating up to within sight of Trinidad and then going about and reaching past Tobago again toward Grenada. Waiting was bad; if the voyage should not turn out to be a fool's errand, it meant something that Hornblower, and Hornblower alone, knew to be worse. Gerard raised the question again.

"How do you propose to stop him, my lord?"

"There may be means," answered Hornblower, trying to keep the harshness out of his voice that would betray his anxiety.

It was on a blue and gold, blazing day, with *Crab* ghosting along before only the faintest breeze, that the masthead lookout hailed the deck with the news of the sighting.

"Sail ho! Dead to loo'ard, sir!"

A sail might be anything, but at long intervals, as *Crab* crept closer, the successive reports made it more and more likely that the strange sail was *Daring*. Three masts—even that first supplementary report made it reasonably sure, for not many big ships plied out into the South Atlantic from the Caribbean. All sail set, even skysails, and stu'ns'ls to the royals. That did not mean quite so much.

"She looks like an American, sir!"

The skysails had already hinted strongly in the same direction. Then Harcourt went up to the mainmast head with his own glass, and came down again with his eyes shining with excitement.

"That's *Daring*, my lord. I'm sure of it."

Ten miles apart they lay, on the brilliant blue of the sea with the brilliant blue of the sky above them, and on the far horizon a smudge of land. *Crab* had won her race by twenty-five hours. *Daring* was "boxing the compass," swinging idly in all directions under her pyramids of sails in the absence of all wind; *Crab* carried her way for a while longer, and then she, too, fell motionless under the blazing sun. All eyes turned on the admiral, standing stiffly, with his hands locked behind him, gazing at the distant white rectangles that indicated where lay his fate. The schooner's big mainsail flapped idly, flapped again, and then the boom began to swing over.

"Hands to the sheets!" yelled Harcourt.

The air was so light that they could not even feel it on their sweat-

ing faces, but it sufficed to push the booms out, and a moment later
the helmsman could feel the rudder take hold just enough to give
him control. With *Crab*'s bowsprit pointed straight at *Daring*, the
breath of wind was coming in over the starboard quarter, almost
dead astern, almost dead foul for *Daring* if ever it should reach her,
but she was still becalmed. The breath of wind increased until they
could feel it, until they could hear under the bows the music of the
schooner's progress through the water, and then it died away
abruptly, leaving *Crab* to wallow on the swell. Then it breathed
again, over the port quarter this time, and then it drew farther aft,
so that the topsails were braced square and the foresail could be
hauled over to the port side, and *Crab* ran wing-and-wing for ten
blessed minutes until the wind dropped again, to a dead, flaming
calm. Then they could see *Daring* catch a wind, see her trim her
sails, but only momentarily, only long enough to reveal her intentions
before she lay once more helpless. Despite her vast sail area, her
greater dead weight made her less susceptible to these very faint
airs.

"Thank God for that," said Gerard, glass to his eye, as he watched
her swing idly again. "I think she aims to pass us beyond cannon
shot, my lord."

"I shouldn't be surprised at that," agreed Hornblower.

Another breath, another slight closing of the gap, another dead
calm.

"Mr. Harcourt, perhaps it would be best if you let the men have
their dinners now."

"Aye aye, my lord."

Salt beef and pease pudding under a noonday sun in the tropics—
who could have any appetite for that, especially with the excitement of watching for a wind? And in the middle of dinner, hands
were sent again to the sheets and braces to take advantage of another
breath of wind.

"At what time will you have your dinner, my lord?" asked Giles.

"Not now," was all the answer Hornblower would give him, glass
to eye.

"He's hoisted his colours, my lord," pointed out Gerard. "American
colours."

The Stars and Stripes, regarding which he had been expressly
ordered to be particularly tender. But he could be nothing else in any

case, seeing that *Daring* mounted twelve-pounders and was full of men.

Now both vessels had a wind, but *Crab* was creeping bravely along at a full two knots, and *Daring*, trying to head to the south-ward close-hauled, was hardly moving; now she was not moving at all, turning aimlessly in a breeze too faint to give her steerage way.

"I can see very few people on her deck, my lord," said Harcourt; the eye with which he had been staring through his glass was water-ing with the glare of sun and sea.

"She'd keep 'em below out of sight," said Gerard.

That was so likely as to be certain. Whatever *Daring*, and Cam-bronne, thought of *Crab*'s intentions, it would be safest to conceal the fact that she had five hundred men on board while heading for the South Atlantic.

And between her and that South Atlantic lay *Crab*, the frailest barrier imaginable. Let *Daring* once pass through the channel out into the open sea and nothing could be done to stop her. No ship could hope to overtake her. She would reach St. Helena to strike her blow there, and no possible warning could be given. It was now or never, and it was Hornblower's fault that matters had reached such a pass. He had been utterly fooled in New Orleans. He had allowed Cambronne to steal a march on him. Now he had to make any sacrifice that circumstances demanded of him, any sacrifice whatever, to redeem the peace of the world. *Crab* could do nothing to stop *Daring*. It could be done only by his own personal exertions.

"Mr. Harcourt," said Hornblower, in his harsh expressionless monotone, "I'll have the quarter boat cleared away ready to lower, if you please. Have a full boat's crew told off to double-bank the oars."

"Aye aye, my lord."

"Who'll go in her, my lord?" asked Gerard.

"I will," said Hornblower.

The mainsail flapped, the boom came creaking inboard, swung out again, swung in. The breeze was dying away again. For a few minutes more *Crab* held her course, and then the bowsprit began to turn away from *Daring*.

"Can't keep her on her course, sir," reported the quartermaster.

Hornblower swept his gaze round the horizon in the blazing after-noon. There was no sign of a further breeze. The decisive moment had come, and he snapped his telescope shut.

"I'll take that boat now, Mr. Harcourt."

"Let me come, too, my lord," said Gerard, a note of protest in his voice.

"No," said Hornblower.

In case a breeze should get up during the next half hour, he wanted no useless weight in the boat while crossing the two-mile gap.

"Put your backs into it," said Hornblower to the boat's crew as they shoved off. The oar blades dipped in the blue, blue water, shining gold against the blue. The boat rounded *Crab*'s stern, with anxious eyes looking down on them; Hornblower brought the tiller over and pointed straight for *Daring*. They soared up a gentle swell, and down again, up again and down again; with each rise and fall, *Crab* was perceptibly smaller and *Daring* perceptibly larger, lovely in the afternoon light, during what Hornblower told himself were the last hours of his professional life. They drew nearer and nearer to *Daring*, until at last a hail came, borne by the heated air.

"Boat ahoy!"

"Coming aboard!" hailed Hornblower back again. He stood up in the sternsheets so that his gold-laced admiral's uniform was in plain sight.

"Keep off!" hailed the voice, but Hornblower held his course.

There could be no international incident made out of this—an unarmed boat's crew taking an admiral alone on board a becalmed ship. He directed the boat toward the mizzen chains.

"Keep off!" hailed the voice, an American voice.

Hornblower swung the boat in. "In oars!" he ordered.

With the way she carried, the boat surged toward the ship; Hornblower timed his movements to the best of his ability, knowing his own clumsiness. He leaped for the chains, got one shoe full of water, but held on and dragged himself up.

"Lie off and wait for me!" he ordered the boat's crew, and then turned to swing himself over onto the deck of the ship.

The tall thin man with a cigar in his mouth must be the American captain; the burly fellow beside him, one of the mates. The guns were cast off, although not run out, and the American seamen were standing round them ready to open fire.

"Did you hear me say keep off, mister?" asked the captain.

"I must apologize for this intrusion, sir," said Hornblower. "I am

Rear Admiral Lord Hornblower, of His Britannic Majesty's service, and I have the most urgent business with Count Cambronne."

For a moment on the sunlit deck they stood and looked at each other, and then Hornblower saw Cambronne approaching.

"Ah, Count," said Hornblower, and then made himself speak French. "It is a pleasure to meet *Monsieur le Comte* again."

He took off his cocked hat and held it over his breast and doubled himself in a bow which he knew to be ungainly.

"And to what do I owe this pleasure, milord?" asked Cambronne. He was standing very stiff and straight, his cat's-whisker moustache bristling out on either side.

"I have come to bring you the very worst of news, I regret to say," said Hornblower. Through many sleepless nights he had rehearsed these speeches to himself. Now he was forcing himself to make them naturally. "And I have come also to do you a service, Count."

"What do you wish to say, milord?"

"Bad news."

"Well?"

"It is with the deepest regret, Count, that I have to inform you of the death of your Emperor."

"No!"

"The Emperor Napoleon died at St. Helena last month. I offer you my sympathy, Count."

Hornblower told the lie with every effort to appear like a man speaking the truth.

"It cannot be true!"

"I assure you that it is, Count."

A muscle in the Count's cheek twitched restlessly beside the purple scar. His hard, slightly protruding eyes bored into Hornblower's like gimlets.

"I received the news two days back in Port of Spain," said Hornblower. "In consequence, I cancelled the arrangements I had made for the arrest of this ship."

Cambronne could not guess that *Crab* had not made so quick a passage as he indicated.

"I do not believe you," said Cambronne, nevertheless. It was just the sort of tale that might be told to halt *Daring* in her passage.

"Sir!" said Hornblower haughtily. He drew himself up even stiffer, acting as well as he could the part of the man of honour whose word was being impugned. The pose was almost successful.

"You must understand the importance of what you are saying, milord," said Cambronne, with the faintest hint of apology in his voice. But then he said the fatal dreaded words that Hornblower had been expecting, "Milord, do you give me your word of honour as a gentleman that what you say is true?"

"My word of honour as a gentleman," said Hornblower.

He had anticipated this moment in misery for days and days. He was ready for it. He compelled himself to make his answer in the manner of a man of honour. He made himself say it steadily and sincerely, as if it did not break his heart to say it. He had been sure that Cambronne would ask him for his word of honour.

It was the last sacrifice he could make. In twenty years of war he had freely risked his life for his country. He had endured danger, anxiety, hardship. He had never, until now, been asked to give his honour. This was the further price he had to pay. It was through his own fault that the peace of the world was in peril. It was fitting that he should pay the price. And the honour of one man was a small price to pay for the peace of the world, to save his country from the renewal of the deadly perils she had so narrowly survived for twenty years. In those happy years of the past, returning to his country after an arduous campaign, he had looked about him and he had breathed English air and he had told himself, with fatuous patriotism, that England was worth fighting for, was worth dying for. England was worth a man's honour, too. Oh, it was true. But it was heart-rending, it was far, far worse than death that it should be his honour that had to be sacrificed.

A little group of officers had appeared on deck and were standing grouped on either side of Cambronne, listening to every word; to one side stood the American captain and his mate. Facing them, alone, his gaudy uniform flashing in the sun, stood Hornblower, waiting. The officer on Cambronne's right spoke next. He was some kind of adjutant or staff officer clearly, of the breed that Hornblower hated. Of course, he had to repeat the question, to turn the iron in the wound.

"Your word of honour, milord?"

"My word of honour," repeated Hornblower, still steadily, still like a man of honour.

No one could disbelieve the word of honour of a British admiral, of a man who had held His Majesty's commission for more than twenty years. He went on now with the arguments he had rehearsed.

"This exploit of yours can be forgotten now, Count," he said. "With the Emperor's death, all hope of reconstituting the empire is at an end. No one need know of what you had intended. You, and these gentlemen, and the Imperial Guard below decks can remain uncompromised with the regime that rules France. You can carry them all home, as you had said you would do, and on the way you can drop your warlike stores quietly overboard. It is for this reason that I have visited you like this, alone. My country, your country do not desire any new incident to imperil the amity of the world. No one need know; this incident can remain a secret between us."

Cambronne heard what he said, and listened to it, but the first news he had heard was of such moving importance that he could speak of nothing else.

"The Emperor is dead!" he said.

"I have already assured you of my sympathy, Count," said Hornblower. "I offer it to these gentlemen as well. My very deepest sympathy."

The American captain broke into the murmurs of Cambronne's staff.

"There's a cat's-paw of wind coming towards us," he said. "We'll be under way again in five minutes. Are you coming with us, mister, or are you going over the side?"

"Wait," said Cambronne; he seemingly had some English.

He turned to his staff and they plunged into debate. When they all spoke at once, Hornblower's French was inadequate to follow the conversation in detail. But he could see they were all convinced. He might have been pleased, if there had been any pleasure left in the world for him.

Someone walked across the deck and shouted down the hatchway, and next moment the Imperial Guard began to pour up on deck. The Old Guard, Bonaparte's Old Guard; they were all in full uniform, apparently in readiness for battle if *Crab* had been foolish enough to risk one. There were five hundred of them in their plumes and bearskins, muskets in hand. A shouted order formed them up on deck, line behind line, gaunt, whiskered men who had marched into every capital in Europe save London alone. They carried their muskets and stood at rigid attention; only a few of them did not look straight to their front, but darted curious glances at the British admiral.

The tears were running down Cambronne's scarred cheeks as he turned and spoke to them. He told them the news in broken sentences, for he could hardly speak for sorrow. They growled like beasts as he spoke. They were thinking of their Emperor dying in his island prison under the harsh treatment of his English gaolers; the looks that were turned upon Hornblower now showed hatred instead of curiosity, but Cambronne caught their attention again as he went on to speak of the future. He spoke of France and peace.

"The Emperor is dead!" he said again, as if he were saying that the world had come to an end.

The ranks were ragged now; emotion had broken down even the iron discipline of the Old Guard. Cambronne drew his sword, raising the hilt to his lips in the beautiful gesture of the salute; the steel flashed in the light of the sinking sun.

"I drew this sword for the Emperor," said Cambronne. "I shall never draw it again."

He took the blade in both hands close to the hilt and put it across his lifted knee. With a convulsive effort of his lean, powerful body, he snapped the blade across, and, turning, he flung the fragments into the sea. The sound that came from the Old Guard was like a long-drawn moan. One man took his musket by the muzzle, swung the butt over his head, and brought it crashing down on the deck, breaking the weapon at the small of the butt. Others followed his example. The muskets rained overside.

The American captain was regarding the scene apparently unmoved, as if nothing more would ever surprise him, but the unlit cigar in his mouth was now much shorter, and he must have chewed off the end. He approached Hornblower obviously to ask the explanation of the scene, but the French adjutant interposed.

"France," said the adjutant. "We go to France."

"France?" repeated the captain. "Not—"

He did not say the words "St. Helena," but they were implicit in his expression.

"France," repeated the adjutant heavily.

Cambronne came towards them, stiffer and straighter than ever as he mastered his emotion.

"I will intrude no further on your sorrow, Count," said Hornblower. "Remember always you have the sympathy of an Englishman."

Cambronne would remember those words later, when he found he had been tricked by a dishonourable Englishman, but they had to be said at this moment, all the same.

"I will remember," said Cambronne. He was forcing himself to observe the necessary formalities. "I must thank you, milord, for your courtesy and consideration."

"I have done my duty towards the world," said Hornblower.

He would not hold out his hand. Cambronne later would feel contaminated if he touched him. He came stiffly to attention and raised his hand instead in salute.

"Good-bye, Count," he said. "I hope we shall meet again in happier circumstances."

"Good-bye, milord," said Cambronne heavily.

Hornblower climbed into the mizzen chains and the boat pulled in to him, and he fell rather than climbed into the sternsheets.

"Give way," he said. No one could feel as utterly exhausted as he felt. No one could feel as utterly unhappy.

They were waiting for him eagerly on board *Crab*—Harcourt and Gerard and the others. He still had to preserve an unmoved countenance as he went on board. He still had duties to do.

"You can let *Daring* go past, Mr. Harcourt," he said. "It is all arranged."

"Arranged, my lord?" This was from Gerard.

"Cambronne has given up the attempt. They are going quietly to France."

"France? To France? My lord—"

"You heard what I said."

They looked across the strip of sea, purple now in the dying day; *Daring* was bracing round her yards to catch the faint breeze that was blowing.

"Your orders are to let them pass, my lord?" persisted Gerard.

"Yes, damn you," said Hornblower, and instantly regretted the flash of rage and bad language. He turned to the other. "Mr. Harcourt, we can now proceed into Port of Spain. I presume that even if the wind is fair you will prefer not to risk the Dragon's Mouth by night. You have my permission to wait until daylight."

"Aye aye, my lord."

Even then they would not leave him in peace as he turned to go below.

"Dinner, my lord?" asked Gerard. "I'll give orders for it at once."

Hopeless to snarl back that he wanted no dinner; the discussion that would have ensued would have been worse than going through the form of eating dinner. Even so, it meant that on entering his cabin he could not do as he wanted and fall on his cot with his face in his hands and abandon himself to his misery. He had to sit up stiff and square while Giles laid and served and cleared away, while the tropical sunset flamed in the sky and black night swooped down upon the little ship on the purple sea. Only then, after Giles's last "Good night, my lord," could he think again, and work back through all the horror of his thoughts.

He had ceased to be a gentleman. He was disgraced. Everything was at an end. He would have to resign his command; he would have to resign his commission. How would he ever face Barbara? When little Richard grew up and could understand what had happened, how would he ever be able to meet his eyes? And Barbara's aristocratic family would sneer knowingly to one another. And never again would he walk a quarterdeck, and never again step on board with his hand to his hat and the bos'n's calls shrilling in salute. Never again; his professional life was at an end—everything was at an end. He had made the sacrifice deliberately and cold-bloodedly, but that did not make it any less horrible.

His thoughts moved into the other half of the circle. He could have done nothing else. If he had turned aside to Kingston or Port of Spain, *Daring* would have slipped past him, as her time of arrival off Tobago proved, and any additional strength he might have brought with him—if any, as was not likely—would have been useless.

If he had stayed at Kingston and sent a despatch to London? If he had done that, he might at least have covered himself with the authorities. But it would have been unavailing. How much time would elapse between the arrival of his letter in London and the arrival of *Daring* on the coast of France with Bonaparte on board? Two weeks? Very likely less than that. The clerks at the Admiralty would have treated his despatch at first as coming from a madman. There would be delay in its reaching the First Lord's hands, delay in its being laid before the Cabinet, delay while action was being debated, delay while the French ambassador was informed, delay while joint action was being agreed upon.

And what action, if any—if the Cabinet did not dismiss his letter as that of an unbalanced alarmist? The peacetime navy of England could never have been got to sea in time and in sufficient numbers to cover the whole coast of France, so as to make it impossible for *Daring* to land her deadly cargo. And the mere inevitable leakage of the news that Bonaparte was at sea and expected to land would throw France into immediate revolution—no doubt about that, and Italy was in a turmoil too.

By writing to London, he would have covered himself, as he had already decided, from the censure of the government. But it was not the measure of a man's duty to avoid blame. He had a positive duty to do, and he had done it in the only way possible. Nothing else would have stopped Cambronne. Nothing else. He had seen where his duty lay. He had seen what the price would be, and now he was paying it. He had bought the peace of the world at the price of his own honour. He had ceased to be a gentleman—his thoughts completed the other half of the circle.

His mind plunged on, struggling desperately, like a man in utter darkness waist-deep in a slough. It would not be long before the world knew of his dishonour. Cambronne would talk, and so would the other Frenchmen. The world would hear soon of a British admiral giving his plighted word in the certain knowledge that he was telling a lie. Before then he would have left the service, resigned his command and his commission. That must be done at once; his contaminated flag must fly no longer; he must give no further orders to gentlemen.

In Port of Spain there was the governor of Trinidad. Tomorrow he would tell him that the West India squadron no longer had a commander-in-chief. The governor could take all the necessary official action in circularizing the squadron and informing the government—just as if yellow fever or apoplexy had taken off the commander-in-chief. In this way anarchy would be reduced to a minimum and a change of command arranged as simply as possible; that was the last service he could perform for his country, the very last.

The governor would think he was mad, of course—he might be in a strait jacket tomorrow unless he confessed his shame. And then the governor would pity him; the first of the pity, the first of the contempt, he would have to face for the rest of his life. Barbara, Richard

—the lost soul plunged on through the stinking slough, through the dark night.

At the end of that dark night, a knock at the door brought in Gerard. The message he was bearing died on his lips as he looked at Hornblower's face, white under the tan, and at his hollow eyes.

"Are you quite well, my lord?" he asked anxiously.

"Quite well. What is it?"

"Mr. Harcourt's respects, my lord, and we are off the Dragon's Mouth. The wind is fair at nor'nor'east and we can make the passage as soon as day breaks, in half an hour, my lord. We'll drop anchor in Port of Spain by two bells in the forenoon watch, my lord."

"Thank you, Mr. Gerard." The words came slowly and coldly as he forced himself to utter them. "My compliments to Mr. Harcourt and that will do very well."

"Aye aye, my lord. This will be the first appearance of your flag in Port of Spain, and a salute will be fired."

"Very well."

"The governor by virtue of his appointment takes precedence of you, my lord. Your lordship must therefore pay the first call. Shall I make a signal to that effect?"

"Thank you, Mr. Gerard. I would be obliged if you would."

The horror still had to be gone through and endured. He had to make himself spick and span; he could not appear on deck unshaven and dirty and untidy. He had to shave and endure Giles's conversation.

"Fresh water, my lord," said Giles, bringing in a steaming can. "Cap'n's given permission, seeing that we'll be watering today."

There might once have been sheer sensuous pleasure in shaving in fresh water, but now there was none. There might have been pleasure in standing on deck watching *Crab* make the passage of the Dragon's Mouth, in looking about him at new lands, in entering a new port, but now there was none. There might have been pleasure once in fresh linen, even in a crisp new neckcloth, even in his ribbon and star and gold-hilted sword. There might have been pleasure in hearing the thirteen guns of his salute fired and answered, but there was none now; there was only the agony of knowing that never again would a salute be fired for him, never again would the whole ship stand at attention for him as he went over the side. He had to hold himself stiff and straight, so as not to droop like a weakling in his misery. He even had to blink hard to keep the tears from overflowing down his cheeks as if he were a sentimental Frenchman. The blazing blue sky overhead might have been black for all he knew.

The governor was a ponderous major general, with a red ribbon and a star too. He went rigidly through the formalities of the reception, and then unbent as soon as they were alone together.

"Delighted to have this visit from you, my lord," he said. "Please sit down. I think you will find that chair comfortable. I have some sherry which I think you will find tolerable. May I pour your lordship a glass?"

He did not wait for an answer, but busied himself with the decanter and glasses.

"By the way, my lord, have you heard the news? Boney's dead."

Hornblower had not sat down. He had intended to refuse the sherry; the governor would not care to drink with a man who had lost his honour. Now he sat down with a jerk and automatically took the glass offered him. The sound he made in reply to the governor's news was only a croak.

"Yes," went on the governor. "He died three weeks back, in St. Helena. They've buried him there, and that's the last of him. Well— are you quite well, my lord?"

"Quite well, thank you," said Hornblower.

The cool twilit room was swimming round him. As he came back to sanity he thought of Saint Elizabeth of Hungary. She, disobeying her husband's commands, had been carrying food to the poor—an apron full of bread—when her husband saw her.

"What have you in your apron?" he demanded.

"Roses," lied Saint Elizabeth.

"Show me," said her husband.

Saint Elizabeth showed him—and her apron was full of roses.

Life could begin anew, thought Hornblower.

2

HERE WHERE THE TRADE WINDS blew at their freshest, just within the tropics, in the wide unbroken Atlantic, was, as Hornblower decided at that moment, the finest stretch of water for a yachting excursion to be found anywhere on the globe. This was nothing more than a yachting excursion, to his mind. Only recently he had emerged from a profound spiritual experience during which the peace of the whole world had depended on his judgment; by comparison it seemed now as if the responsibilities of being commander-in-chief on the West Indian Station were mere nothings. He stood on the quarterdeck of His Britannic Majesty's frigate *Clorinda*, balancing easily as she reached to windward under moderate sail, and allowed the morning sunshine to stream down on him and the trade wind to blow round his ears. With the pitch and the roll as *Clorinda* shouldered against the sea the shadows of the weather-rigging swooped back and forth over the deck; when she took a roll to windward, towards the nearly level morning sun, the shadows of the ratlines of the mizzen shrouds flicked across his eyes in rapid succession, hypnotically adding to his feeling of well-being. To be a commander-in-chief, with nothing more to worry about than the suppression of the slave trade, the hunting down of piracy, and the policing of the Caribbean, was an experience more pleasant than any emperor, or even any poet, could ever know. The bare-legged seamen washing down the decks were laughing and joking; the level sun was calling up dazzling rainbows in the spray flung up by the weather-bow; and he could have breakfast at any moment that he wanted it—standing here on the quarterdeck he was finding additional pleasure in anticipation and wantonly postponing that moment.

The appearance of Captain Sir Thomas Fell on the quarterdeck took something away from the feeling of well-being. Sir Thomas was a gloomy lantern-jawed individual who would feel it his bounden duty to come and be polite to his admiral, and who would never have the sensitivity to be aware when his presence was undesired.

"Good morning, my lord," said the captain, touching his hat.

"Good morning, Sir Thomas," replied Hornblower, returning the salute.

"A fine fresh morning, my lord."

"Yes, indeed."

Sir Thomas was looking over his ship with a captain's eye, along the decks, up aloft, and then turning aft to observe where, right astern, a smudgy line on the horizon marked the position of the hills of Puerto Rico. Hornblower suddenly realized that he wanted his breakfast more than anything on earth; and simultaneously he realized that he now could not gratify that desire as instantaneously as a commander-in-chief should be able to. There were limitations of politeness that constrained even a commander-in-chief—or that constrained him, at least. He could not turn away and go below without exchanging a few more sentences with Fell.

"Maybe we'll catch something today, my lord," said Fell; instinctively with the words the eyes of both men turned aloft to where a lookout sat perched up at the dizzy height of the main topgallant masthead.

"Let's hope we do," said Hornblower, and, because he had never succeeded in liking Fell, and because the last thing he wanted to do was to enter into a technical discussion before breakfast, he blundered on so as to conceal these feelings. "It's likely enough."

"The Spaniards will want to run every cargo they can before the convention's signed," said Fell.

"So we decided," agreed Hornblower. Rehashing old decisions before breakfast was not to his taste, but it was typical of Fell to do that.

"And this is the landfall they'd make," went on Fell remorselessly, glancing astern again at Puerto Rico on the horizon.

"Yes," said Hornblower. Another minute or two of this pointless conversation and he would be free to escape below.

Fell took the speaking trumpet and directed it upwards.

"Masthead, there! Keep a good lookout or I'll know the reason why!"

"Aye aye, sir!" came the reply.

"Head money, my lord," said Fell, in apologetic explanation.

"We all find it useful," answered Hornblower politely.

Head money was paid by the British government for slaves freed

on the high seas to the Royal Naval ships concerned in the capture
of the slaves, and divided among the ships' company like any other
prize money. It was a small fund compared with the gigantic sums
acquired during the great wars, but at five pounds a head a big capture could bring in a substantial sum to the ship making the capture.
And of that substantial sum one-quarter went to the captain. On the
other hand, one-eighth went to the admiral commanding, wherever
he happened to be. Hornblower with twenty ships at sea under his
command was entitled to one-eighth of all their head money. It was
a system of division which explained how during the great wars the
admirals commanding the Channel Fleet or in the Mediterranean
became millionaires, like Lord Keith.

"No one could find it more useful than I, my lord," said Fell.

"Maybe," said Hornblower.

Hornblower knew vaguely that Fell was in difficulties about
money. He had had many years of half pay since Waterloo, and
even now as captain of a fifth-rate his pay and allowances were less
than twenty pounds a month—lucky though he was, in peacetime,
to have command even of a fifth-rate. He had had experience himself of being a poor captain, of wearing cotton stockings instead of
silk, and brass epaulettes instead of gold. But he had no desire whatever to discuss the Tables of Personal Pay before breakfast.

"Lady Fell, my lord," went on Fell persistently, "has a position to
maintain in the world."

She was an extravagant woman, so Hornblower had heard.

"Let's hope we have some luck today, then," said Hornblower, still
thinking about breakfast.

It was a melodramatic coincidence that at that very moment a hail
came down from the masthead.

"Sail ho! Sail right to wind'ard!"

"Perhaps that's what we're waiting for, Sir Thomas," said Hornblower.

"As likely as not, my lord. Masthead, there! How's the sail heading? Mr. Sefton, bring the ship to the wind."

Hornblower backed away to the weather-rail. He felt he could
never grow used to his situation as admiral, and having to stand by
and be no more than an interested spectator while the ship he was
in was being handled at decisive moments. It was quite painful to
be a spectator, but it would be more painful still to go below and

remain in ignorance of what was going on—and much more painful than to postpone breakfast again.

"Deck, there! She's a two-master. Heading straight down for us. All sail to the royals. Captain, sir, she's a schooner! A big schooner, sir. Still running down for us."

Young Gerard, the flag lieutenant, had come running on deck, at the first hail from the masthead, to his place beside his admiral.

"A tops'l schooner," he said. "A big one. She could be what we're looking for, my lord."

"Plenty of other things she could be," said Hornblower, doing his best to conceal his absurd excitement.

Gerard had his telescope pointing to windward.

"There she is! Coming down fast, right enough. Look at the rake of those masts! Look at the cut of those tops'ls! My lord, she's no Island schooner."

It would not be a very remarkable coincidence if she should be a slaver; he had brought *Clorinda* here to the windward of San Juan in the full expectation that slave cargoes would be hurrying here. Spain was meditating joining in the suppression of the slave trade, and every slaver would be tempted to run cargoes and take advantage of enhanced prices before the prohibition should take effect. The main slave market for the Spanish colonies was at Havana, a thousand miles to leeward, but it could be looked upon as certain that Spanish slavers, making their passage from the Slave Coast, would touch first at Puerto Rico to refill with water if not to dispose of part of their cargo. It had only been logical to station *Clorinda* to intercept them.

Hornblower took the telescope and trained it on the fast-nearing schooner. He saw what Gerard had spoken about. Hull up now, he could see how heavily sparred she was, and how built for speed. With those fine lines it would only pay for her to carry highly perishable cargo—human cargo. As he looked he saw the rectangles of her square sails narrow vertically; the small distance between her masts widened greatly. She was wheeling away from the waiting *Clorinda* —a final proof, if any was needed, that she was what she appeared to be. Laying herself on the starboard tack, she proceeded to keep at a safe distance, and to increase that distance as fast as possible.

"Mr. Sefton!" shouted Fell. "Fill the main tops'l! After her, on the starboard tack! Set the royals!"

In an orderly and disciplined rush some of the hands hurried to

the braces while others scurried aloft to set more sail. It was only a
matter of moments before *Clorinda,* as close-hauled as she would lie,
was thrashing to windward in pursuit. With everything braced up
sharp, and carrying every inch of sail that the brisk trade wind
would allow, she lay steeply over, plunging through the sea, each
wave in turn bursting on her weather-bow with the spray flying aft
in sheets, and the taut weather-rigging shrieking in the wind. It was
a remarkable transition from the quiet that had reigned not so long
ago.

"Hoist the colours," ordered Fell. "Let's see what she says she is."

Through the telescope Hornblower watched the schooner hoist
her colours in reply—the red and yellow of Spain.

"You see, my lord?" asked Fell.

"Pardon, Cap'n," interposed Sefton, the officer of the watch. "I
know who she is. I saw her twice last commission. She's the *Estrella.*"

"The *Australia?*" exclaimed Fell, mishearing Sefton's Spanish pro-
nunciation.

"The *Estrella,* sir. The *Estrella del Sur*—the *Star of the South,* sir."

"I know about her, then," said Hornblower. "Her captain's Gomez
—runs four hundred slaves every passage, if he doesn't lose too
many."

"Four hundred!" repeated Fell.

Hornblower saw a momentary calculating look pass over Fell's
face. Five pounds a head meant two thousand pounds; a quarter of
that was five hundred pounds. Two years' pay at one swoop. Fell
darted glances aloft and overside.

"Keep your luff, there!" he shouted at the helmsman. "Mr. Sefton!
Hands to the bowlines, there, for'rard."

"She's weathering on us," said Gerard, the glass to his eye.

It was really only to be expected that a well-designed schooner
would work to windward more efficiently than even the best of
square-rigged frigates.

"She's forereaching on us, too," said Hornblower, gauging the distances and angles. She was not only lying closer to the wind but
travelling faster through the water. Very little faster, it was true—
a knot or perhaps two knots—but enough to render her safe from
Clorinda's pursuit.

"I'll have her yet!" said Fell. "Mr. Sefton! Call all hands! Run out
the guns on the weather-side. Mr. James! Find Mr. Noakes. Tell him
to start the water. Hands to the pumps, Mr. Sefton! Pump her dry."

Hands came pouring up through the hatchways. With the gun-ports opened the guns' crews flung their weight on the gun tackles, inch by inch dragging the guns on the weather-side up the steep slope presented by the heeling deck. The rumble of the wooden wheels over the seams of the planking made a stirring sound; it had been the preliminary of many a desperate fight in the old days. Now the guns were merely being run out in order to keep the ship on a slightly more even keel, giving her a better grip on the water and minimizing leeway. Hornblower watched the pumps being manned; the hands threw their weight on the handles with a will, the rapid clank-clank proving how hard they were at work, pumping overside the twenty tons of drinking water which might be thought of as the life blood of a cruising ship. But the slight reduction of draught that would result might, combined with the running out of the weather-guns, add a few yards to her speed.

The call for all hands had brought Mr. Erasmus Spendlove on deck, Hornblower's secretary. He looked round him at the organized confusion on deck with that air of Olympian superiority which always delighted Hornblower. Spendlove cultivated a pose of unruffled calm that exasperated some and amused others. Yet he was a most efficient secretary, and Hornblower had never once regretted acting on the recommendation of Lord Exmouth and appointing him to his position.

"You see the vulgar herd all hard at work, Mr. Spendlove," said Hornblower.

"Truly they appear to be, my lord." He looked to windward at the *Estrella*. "I trust their labours will not be in vain."

Fell came bustling by, still looking up at the rigging and overside at the *Estrella*.

"Mr. Sefton! Call the carpenter. I'll have the wedges of the main-mast knocked loose. More play there may give us more speed."

Hornblower caught a change of expression on Spendlove's face, and their eyes met. Spendlove was a profound student of the theory of ship design, and Hornblower was a man with a lifetime of experience, and the glance they exchanged, brief as it was, was enough for each to know that the other thought the new plan unwise. Hornblower watched the mainshrouds on the weather-side taking the additional strain. It was as well that *Clorinda* was newly refitted.

"Can't say we're doing any better, my lord," said Gerard from behind his telescope.

The *Estrella* was perceptibly farther ahead and more to windward. If she wished, she would run *Clorinda* practically out of sight by noon. Hornblower observed an odd expression on Spendlove's face. He was testing the air with his nose, sniffing curiously at the wind as it blew past him. It occurred to Hornblower that once or twice he had been aware, without drawing any conclusions from the phenomenon, that the clean trade wind had momentarily been tainted with a hint of a horrible stench. He himself tried the air again, and caught another musky whiff. He knew what it was— twenty years ago he had smelt the same stench when a Spanish galley crowded with galley slaves had passed to windward. The trade wind, blowing straight from the *Estrella* to the *Clorinda*, was bearing with it the reek from the crowded slave ship, tainting the air over the clean blue sea far to leeward of her.

"We can be sure she's carrying a full cargo," he said.

Fell was still endeavouring to improve *Clorinda*'s sailing qualities. "Mr. Sefton! Set the hands to work carrying shot up to wind'ard."

"She's altering course!" Half a dozen voices made the announcement at the same moment.

"Belay that order, Mr. Sefton!"

Fell's telescope, like all the others, was trained on the *Estrella*. She had put her helm up a little, and was boldly turning to cross *Clorinda*'s bows.

"Damned insolence!" exclaimed Fell.

Everyone watched anxiously as the two ships proceeded headlong on converging courses.

"She'll pass us out of range," decided Gerard; the certainty became more apparent with every second of delay.

"Hands to the braces!" roared Fell. "Quartermaster! Starboard your helm! Handsomely! Handsomely! Steady as you go!"

"Two points off the wind," said Hornblower. "We stand more chance now."

Clorinda's bows were now pointed to intercept the *Estrella* at a far distant point, several miles ahead. Moreover, lying a little off the wind as both ships now were, it seemed probable that *Estrella*'s fore-and-aft rig and fine lines might not convey so great an advantage.

"Take a bearing, Gerard," ordered Hornblower.

Gerard went to the binnacle and read the bearing carefully.

"My impression," said Spendlove, gazing over the blue, blue water, "is that she's still forereaching on us."

"If that's the case," said Hornblower, "then all we can hope for is that she carries something away."

"We can at least hope for it, my lord," said Spendlove. The glance he directed upwards was indicative of his fear that it would be the *Clorinda* whose gear would give way. *Clorinda* now had wind and sea very nearly abeam. She was lying over very steeply under every inch of canvas she could carry, and lifting unwillingly to the seas which came rolling in upon her, swirling in through her open gunports. Hornblower realized that he had not a dry stitch of clothing on him, and probably no one else on board had, either.

"My lord," said Gerard, "you've had no breakfast as yet."

Hornblower tried to conceal the discomfiture he felt at this reminder. He had forgotten all about breakfast, despite the cheerful anticipation with which he had once been looking forward to it.

"Quite right, Mr. Gerard," he said, jocular, but only clumsily so, thanks to being taken by surprise. "And what of it?"

"It's my duty to remind you, my lord," said Gerard. "Her ladyship—"

"Her ladyship told you to see that I took my meals regularly," replied Hornblower. "I am aware of that. But her ladyship, owing to her inexperience, made no allowance for encounters with fast-sailing slavers just at mealtimes."

"But can't I persuade you, my lord?"

The thought of breakfast, now that it had been reimplanted in his mind, was more attractive than ever. But it was hard to go below with a pursuit being so hotly conducted.

"Take that bearing again before I decide," he temporized.

Gerard walked to the binnacle again.

"Bearing's opening steadily, my lord," he reported. "She must be drawing ahead fast."

"Clearly so," said Spendlove, telescope trained out towards the *Estrella*. "And it looks—it looks as if she's hauling in on her sheets. Maybe—"

Hornblower had whipped his telescope to his eye on the instant.

"She's jibing over," he pronounced. "See how she comes round, by George!"

Estrella must have a bold captain and a well-trained crew. They had hauled in on her sheets and had stood ready at her topsail braces. Then, with the helm hard over, she had spun round on her heel. Her whole beautiful profile was now presented to Hornblower's telescope. She was headed to cross *Clorinda*'s bows from starboard to port, and not too far ahead, either.

"Damned insolence!" said Hornblower, but full of admiration for the daring and skill displayed.

Fell was standing close by, staring at the impertinent schooner. He was rigid, even though the wind was flapping his coattails round him. For a few seconds it seemed as if the two vessels were heading towards a common point, where they must meet. But the impression soon passed. Even without taking a compass bearing it became apparent that *Estrella* must pass comfortably ahead of the frigate.

"Run the guns in!" bellowed Fell. "Stand by to wear ship! Clear away the bow chasers, there!"

It might be just possible that the schooner would pass within range of the bow chasers, but to take a shot at her, at long range and on that heaving sea, would be a chancy business. Should they score a hit, it might as likely take effect in the hull, among the wretched slaves, as on the spars or rigging. Hornblower was prepared to restrain Fell from firing.

The guns were run in, and after another minute's examination of the situation Fell ordered the helm to be put a-starboard and the ship laid right before the wind. Hornblower through his telescope could see the schooner lying right over with the wind abeam, so far over that as she heaved she presented a streak of copper to his view, pinkish against the blue of the sea. Clearly she was drawing across the frigate's bows, as Fell tacitly acknowledged when he ordered a further turn of two points to port. Thanks to her two knots' superiority in speed, and thanks also to her superior handiness and weatherliness, the *Estrella* was literally making a circle round the *Clorinda*.

"She's built for speed, my lord," said Spendlove from behind his telescope.

So was *Clorinda*, but with a difference. *Clorinda* was a fighting ship, built to carry seventy tons of artillery, with forty tons of powder and shot in her magazines. It was no shame to her that she should be outsailed and outmanoeuvred by such a vessel as the *Estrella*.

"I fancy she'll make for San Juan, Sir Thomas," said Hornblower.

Fell's face bore an expression of helpless fury as he turned to his admiral; it was with an obvious effort that he restrained himself from pouring out his rage, presumably in a torrent of blasphemy.

"It's—it's—" he spluttered.

"It's enough to madden a saint," said Hornblower.

Clorinda had been ideally stationed, twenty miles to windward of San Juan; *Estrella* had run practically into her arms, so to speak, and had yet dodged neatly round her and had won for herself a clear run to the port.

"I'll see him damned, my lord!" said Fell. "Quartermaster!"

There was now the long run ahead to San Juan, one point off the wind, in what was practically a race with an even start. Fell laid a course for San Juan; it was obvious that *Estrella,* comfortably out of range on the starboard beam, was heading for the same point. Both ships had the wind practically abeam; this long run would be a final test of the sailing qualities of the two ships, as though they were a couple of yachts completing a triangular course in a race in the Solent. Hornblower reminded himself that earlier this morning he had compared the present voyage with a yachting excursion. But the expression on Fell's face showed that his flag captain by no means looked on it in the same light. Fell was in the deadliest earnest, and not from any philanthropic feelings about slavery, either. It was the head money he wanted.

"About that breakfast, my lord?" said Gerard.

An officer was touching his hat to Fell with the request that it might be considered noon.

"Make it so," said Fell. The welcome cry of "Up spirits" rang through the ship.

"Breakfast, my lord?" asked Gerard again.

"Let's wait and see how we do on this course," said Hornblower. He saw something of dismay in Gerard's face and laughed. "It's a question of your breakfast, I fancy, as well as mine. You've had nothing this morning?"

"No, my lord."

"I starve my young men, I see," said Hornblower, looking from Gerard to Spendlove; but the latter's expression was peculiarly unchanging, and Hornblower remembered all he knew about him. "I'll wager a guinea that Spendlove hasn't spent the morning fasting."

The suggestion was answered by a wide grin.

"I am no sailor, my lord," said Spendlove. "But I have learned one thing while I have been at sea, and that is to snatch at any meal that makes its appearance. Fairy gold vanishes no faster than the opportunity of eating food at sea."

"So, while your admiral has been starving, you have been walking this deck with a full belly? Shame on you."

"I feel that shame as deeply as the situation merits, my lord."

Spendlove obviously had all the tact that an admiral's secretary needed to have.

"Hands to the main brace!" bellowed Fell.

Clorinda was hurtling along over the blue sea with the wind abeam; it was her best point of sailing, and Fell was doing all he could to get the very best out of her. Hornblower looked over at *Estrella*.

"I fancy we're falling behind," he said.

"I think so too, my lord," said Gerard after a glance in the same direction. He walked over and took a bearing, and Fell glared at him with irritation before turning to Hornblower.

"I hope you will agree, my lord," he said, "that *Clorinda* has done all a ship can do?"

"Certainly, Sir Thomas," said Hornblower. Fell really meant to say that no fault could be found with his handling of the ship; and Hornblower, while convinced that he himself could have handled her better, had no doubt that in any case *Estrella* would have evaded capture.

"That schooner sails like a witch," said Fell. "Look at her now, my lord."

Estrella's lovely lines and magnificent sail plan were obvious even at this distance.

"She's a beautiful vessel," agreed Hornblower.

"She's headreaching on us for sure," announced Gerard from the binnacle. "And I think she's weathering on us too."

"And there goes five hundred pounds," said Fell bitterly. Assuredly he was in need of money. "Quartermaster! Bear up a point. Hands to the braces!"

He brought *Clorinda* a little closer to the wind and studied her behaviour before turning back to Hornblower.

"I'll not give up the chase until I'm compelled, my lord," he said.

"Quite right," agreed Hornblower.

There was something of resignation, something of despair, in Fell's expression. It was not only the thought of the lost money that troubled him, Hornblower realized. The report that Fell had tried to capture the *Estrella*, and had failed, almost ludicrously, would reach Their Lordships of the Admiralty, of course. Even if Hornblower's own report minimized the failure, it would still be a failure. That meant that Fell would never be employed again after his present two years' appointment had expired. For every captain with a command in the Royal Navy now there were twenty at least hungry for commands. The slightest lapse would be seized upon as reason for ending a man's career; it could not be otherwise. Fell was now looking forward apprehensively to spending the rest of his life on half pay. And Lady Fell was an expensive and ambitious woman. No wonder that Fell's usually red cheeks had a grey tinge.

The slight alteration of course Fell had ordered was really a final admission of defeat. *Clorinda* was retaining her windward position only at the cost of seeing *Estrella* draw more rapidly ahead.

"But I fear she'll beat us easily into San Juan," went on Fell with admirable stoicism. Right ahead the purple smear on the horizon that marked the hills of Puerto Rico was growing loftier and more defined. "What orders have you for me in that case, my lord?"

"What water have you left on board?" asked Hornblower in return.

"Five tons, my lord. Say six days at short allowance."

"Six days," repeated Hornblower, mostly to himself. It was a tiresome complication. The nearest British territory was a hundred miles to windward.

"I had to try the effect of lightening the ship, my lord," said Fell, self-exculpatory.

"I know, I know." Hornblower always felt testy when someone tried to excuse himself. "Well, we'll follow *Estrella* in if we don't catch her first."

"It will be an official visit, my lord?" asked Gerard quickly.

"It can hardly be anything else with my flag flying," said Hornblower. He took no pleasure in official visits. "We may as well kill two birds with one stone. It's time I called on the Spanish authorities, and we can fill up with water at the same time."

"Aye aye, my lord."

A visit of ceremony in a foreign port meant many calls on the activity of his staff—but not as many as on him, he told himself with irritation.

"I'll have my breakfast before anything else comes to postpone it," he said. The perfect good humour of the morning had quite evaporated now. He would be in a bad temper now if he allowed himself to indulge in the weakness of humanity.

When he came on deck again the failure to intercept *Estrella* was painfully obvious. The schooner was a full three miles ahead, and had weathered upon *Clorinda* until the latter lay almost in her wake. The coast of Puerto Rico was very well defined now. *Estrella* was entering into territorial waters and was perfectly safe. All hands were hard at work in every part of the ship bringing everything into that condition of perfection—really no more perfect than invariably prevailed—which a British ship must display when entering a foreign port and submitting herself to the jealous inspection of strangers. The deck had been brought to a whiteness quite dazzling in the tropical sun; the metalwork was equally dazzling—painful when the eye received a direct reflection; gleaming cutlasses and pikes were ranged in decorative patterns on the bulkhead aft; white cotton lines were being rove everywhere, with elaborate Turk's heads.

"Very good, Sir Thomas," said Hornblower approvingly.

"Authority in San Juan is represented by a captain-general, my lord," said Spendlove.

"Yes. I shall have to call upon him," agreed Hornblower. "Sir Thomas, I shall be obliged if you will accompany me."

"Aye aye, my lord."

"Ribbons and stars, I fear, Sir Thomas."

"Aye aye, my lord."

Fell had received his knighthood of the Bath after a desperate frigate action back in 1813. It had been a tribute to his courage if not to his professional abilities.

"Schooner's taking a pilot on board!" hailed the masthead lookout.

"Very well!"

"Our turn shortly," said Hornblower. "Time to array ourselves for our hosts. They will be grateful, I hope, that our arrival will take place after the hour of the siesta."

It was also the hour when the sea breeze was beginning to blow. The pilot they took on—a big handsome quadroon—took the ship in without a moment's difficulty, although, naturally, Fell stood beside him consumed with anxiety. Hornblower, free from any such responsibility, was able to go forward to the gangway and examine the approaches to the city; it was a time of peace, but Spain had been an enemy before and might perhaps be an enemy again, and at least nothing would be lost if he knew as much as possible about the defences firsthand. It did not take very long to perceive why San Juan had never been attacked, not to speak of captured, by the numerous enemies of Spain during the long life of the city. It was ringed by a lofty wall of stout masonry, with ditches and bastions, moats and drawbridges. On the lofty bluff overlooking the entrance Morro Castle covered the approaches with artillery; there was another fortress—which must be San Cristóbal—and battery succeeded battery along the water-front, with heavy guns visible in the embrasures. Nothing less than a formal siege, with a powerful army and a battering train, could make any impression on San Juan as long as it was defended by an adequate garrison.

The sea breeze brought them up the entrance passage; there was the usual momentary anxiety about whether the Spaniards were prepared to salute his flag, but the anxiety was speedily allayed as the guns in the Morro began to bang out their reply. Hornblower held himself stiffly to attention as the ship glided in, the forecastle saluting carronade firing at admirably regular intervals. The hands took in the canvas with a rapidity that did them credit—Hornblower was watching unobtrusively from under the brim of his cocked hat—and then *Clorinda* rounded-to and the anchor cable rumbled through the hawsehole. A deeply sunburned officer in a fine uniform came up the side and announced himself, in passable English, as the port medical officer, and received Fell's declaration that *Clorinda* had experienced no infectious disease during the past twenty-one days.

Now that they were in the harbour, where the sea breeze circulated with difficulty, and the ship was stationary, they were aware of the crushing heat; Hornblower felt instantly the sweat trickling down inside his shirt under his heavy uniform coat, and he turned his head uncomfortably from side to side, feeling the constriction of his starched neckcloth. A brief gesture from Gerard beside him pointed out what he had already observed—the *Estrella del Sur* in her gleaming white paint lying at the pier close beside them. It seemed as if the reek of her still reached his nostrils from her open hatchways. A file of soldiers, in blue coats with white crossbelts, was drawn up on the pier, standing somewhat negligently under command of a sergeant. From within the hold of the schooner came a most lamentable noise—prolonged and doleful wailings. As they watched they saw a string of naked Negroes come climbing with difficulty up through the hatchway. They could hardly walk—in fact some of them could not walk at all, but fell to their hands and knees and crawled in that fashion over the deck and onto the pier.

"They're landing their cargo," said Gerard.

"Some of it at least," replied Hornblower. In nearly a year of study he had learned much about the slave trade. The demand for slaves here in Puerto Rico was small compared with that at Havana. During the Middle Passage the slaves he saw had been confined on the slave decks, packed tight "spoon fashion," lying on their sides with their knees bent up into the bend of the knees of the next man. It was only to be expected that the captain of the *Estrella* would take this opportunity of giving his perishable cargo a thorough airing.

A hail from overside distracted them. A boat with the Spanish flag at the bow was approaching; sitting in the sternsheets was an officer in a brilliant gold-laced uniform that reflected back the setting sun.

"Here comes Authority," said Hornblower.

The side was manned and the officer came aboard to the trilling of the pipes of the bosun's mates, very correctly raising his hand in salute. Hornblower walked over to join Fell in receiving him. He spoke in Spanish, and Hornblower was aware that Fell had none of that language.

"Major Mendez-Castillo," the officer announced himself, "first and principal aide-de-camp to His Excellency the captain-general of Puerto Rico."

He was tall and slender, with a thin moustache that might have been put on with grease paint; he looked cautiously, without committing himself, at the two officers in their red ribbons and stars, and glittering epaulettes, who were receiving him.

"Welcome, Major," said Hornblower. "I am Rear Admiral Lord Hornblower, commander-in-chief of His Britannic Majesty's ships and vessels in West Indian waters. May I present Captain Sir Thomas Fell, commanding His Britannic Majesty's ship *Clorinda?*"

Mendez-Castillo bowed to each of them, his relief at knowing which was which faintly apparent.

"Welcome to Puerto Rico, Your Excellency," he said. "We had of course heard that the famous Lord Hornblower was now commander-in-chief here, and we had long hoped for the honour of a visit from him."

"Many thanks," said Hornblower.

"And welcome to you and to your ship, Captain," added Mendez-Castillo hastily, nervous in case it should be too apparent that he had been so engrossed in his meeting with the fabulous Hornblower that he had paid insufficient attention to a mere captain. Fell bowed awkwardly in reply—interpretation was unnecessary.

"I am instructed by His Excellency," went on Mendez-Castillo, "to inquire if there is any way in which His Excellency can be of service to Your Excellency on the notable occasion of this visit?"

In Spanish the phrasing of the pompous sentence was even more difficult than in English. And as Mendez-Castillo spoke, his glance wavered momentarily towards the *Estrella;* obviously all the details of the *Clorinda's* attempted interception were already known—much of the unavailing pursuit must have been visible from the Morro. Something in the major's attitude conveyed the impression that the subject of the *Estrella* was not open to discussion.

"We intend to make only a brief stay, Major. Captain Fell is anxious to renew the water supply of his ship," said Hornblower, and Mendez-Castillo's expression softened at once.

"Of course," he said hastily. "Nothing could be easier. I will give instructions to the captain of the port to afford Captain Fell every facility."

"You are too kind, Major," said Hornblower. Bows were exchanged again, Fell joining in, although unaware of what had been said.

"His Excellency has also instructed me," said Mendez-Castillo, "that he hopes for the honour of a visit from Your Excellency."

"I had hoped that His Excellency would be kind enough to invite me."

"His Excellency will be charmed to hear it. Perhaps Your Excellency would be kind enough to visit His Excellency this evening. His Excellency would be charmed to receive Your Excellency at eight o'clock, along with the members of Your Excellency's staff, at La Fortaleza, the Palace of Santa Catalina."

"His Excellency is too good. We shall be delighted, naturally."

"I shall inform His Excellency. Perhaps Your Excellency would find it convenient if I were to come on board at that time to escort Your Excellency and Your Excellency's party?"

"We shall be most grateful, Major."

The major took his leave after a final reference to the captain of the port and the watering of the ship. Hornblower explained briefly to Fell.

"Aye aye, my lord."

Here came another visitor, up the port side of the ship, a squat, heavily built man in dazzling white linen, wearing a broad-brimmed hat which he took off with scrupulous politeness as he reached the quarterdeck. Hornblower watched him address himself to the midshipman of the watch, and saw the latter hesitate and look round him while trying to make up his mind as to whether he should grant the request.

"Very well, midshipman," said Hornblower. "What does the gentleman want?"

He could guess very easily what the gentleman wanted. This might be an opportunity of making contact with the shore other than through official channels—something always desirable, and peculiarly so at this moment. The visitor came forward; a pair of bright quizzical blue eyes studied Hornblower closely as he did so.

"My lord?" he said. He at least could recognize an admiral's uniform when he saw it.

"Yes. I am Admiral Lord Hornblower."

"I fear to trouble you with my business, my lord." He spoke English like an Englishman, like a Tynesider, perhaps, but obviously as if he had not spoken it for years.

"What is it?"

"I came on board to address myself to your steward, my lord, and to the president of the wardroom mess, and to the purser. The principal ship chandler of the port. Beef cattle, my lord, chickens, eggs, fresh bread, fruits, vegetables."

"What is your name?"

"Eduardo Stuart—Edward Stuart, my lord. Second mate of the brig *Columbine*, out of London. Captured back in 1806, my lord, and brought in here as a prisoner. I made friends here, and when the Dons changed sides in 1808 I set up as ship chandler, and here I've been ever since."

Hornblower studied the speaker as keenly as the speaker was studying him. He could guess at much of what was left unsaid. He could guess at a fortunate marriage, and probably at a change of religion—unless Stuart had been born a Catholic, as was possible enough.

"And I am at your service, my lord," went on Stuart, meeting his gaze without flinching.

"In a moment I'll let you speak to the purser," said Hornblower. "But tell me first, what impression has our arrival made here?"

Stuart's face crinkled into a grin.

"The whole town was out watching your chase of the *Estrella del Sur*, my lord."

"I guessed as much."

"They all rejoiced when they saw her escape you. And then when they saw you coming in they manned the batteries."

"Indeed?"

The Royal Navy's reputation for prompt action, both daring and high-handed, must still be very much alive, if there could be even a momentary fear that a single frigate would attempt to snatch a prize from out of the shelter of a port as well guarded as San Juan.

"In ten minutes your name was being spoken in all the streets, my lord."

Hornblower's keen glance reassured him that he was not being paid an idle compliment.

"And what is the *Estrella* going to do now?"

"She has only come in to land a few sickly slaves and renew with water, my lord. It's a poor market for slaves here. She sails for Havana at once, as soon as she can be sure of your movements, my lord."

"At once?"

"She'll sail with the land breeze at dawn tomorrow, my lord, unless you are lying outside the port."

"I don't expect I shall be," said Hornblower.

"Then she'll sail without a doubt, my lord. She'll want to get her cargo landed and sold in Havana before Spain signs the Convention."

"I understand," said Hornblower.

Now what was this? Here were the old symptoms, as recognizable as ever, the quickened heart beat, the feeling of warmth under the skin, the general restlessness. There was something just below the horizon of his mind, some stirring of an idea. And within a second the idea was up over the horizon, vague at present, like a hazy landfall, but as certain and as reassuring as any landfall. And beyond, still over the horizon, were other ideas, only to be guessed at. He could not help glancing over at the *Estrella*, sizing up the tactical situation, seeking further inspiration there, testing what he already had in mind.

It was all he could do to thank Stuart politely for his information, without betraying the excitement he felt, and without terminating the interview with suspicious abruptness. A word to Fell made certain that Stuart would receive the business of supplying the *Clorinda*, and Hornblower waved away Stuart's thanks. Hornblower turned away with as great an appearance of nonchalance as he could manage.

There was plenty of bustle over there by the *Estrella*, just as there was round the *Clorinda,* with preparations being made for filling the water casks. It was hard to think in the heat and the noise. It was hard to face the cluttered deck. And darkness was approaching, and then would come eight o'clock, when he would be making his call upon the captain-general, and obviously everything must be thought out before that. And there were complications. Successive ideas were arising, one out of another, like Chinese boxes, and each one in turn had to be examined for flaws. The sun was down into the hills, leaving a flaming sky behind, when he came to his final resolution.

"Spendlove!" he snapped; excitement made him curt. "Come below with me."

Down in the big stern cabin it was oppressively hot. The red sky was reflected in the water of the harbour, shining up through the stern windows; the magnificent effect was dissipated with the lighting of the lamps. Hornblower threw himself into his chair; Spendlove stood looking at him keenly, as Hornblower was well aware. Spendlove could be in no doubt that his temperamental commander-in-chief had much on his mind. Yet even Spendlove was surprised at the scheme that was sketched out to him, and at the orders he received. He even ventured to protest.

"My lord—" he said.

"Carry out your orders, Mr. Spendlove. Not another word."

"Aye aye, my lord."

Spendlove left the cabin, with Hornblower sitting there alone, waiting. The minutes passed slowly—precious minutes; there were few to spare—before the knock that he expected came on the door. It was Fell, entering with every appearance of nervousness.

"My lord, have you a few minutes to spare?"

"Always a pleasure to receive you, Sir Thomas."

"But this is unusual, I fear, my lord. I have a suggestion to make —an unusual suggestion."

"Suggestions are always welcome too, Sir Thomas. Please sit down and tell me. We have an hour at least before we go ashore. I am most interested."

Fell sat bolt upright in his chair, his hands clutching the arms. He swallowed twice. It gave Hornblower no pleasure to see a man who had faced steel and lead and imminent death apprehensive before him; it made him uncomfortable.

"My lord—" began Fell, and swallowed again.

"You have all my attention, Sir Thomas," said Hornblower gently.

"It has occurred to me," said Fell, growing more fluent with each word until at last he spoke in a rush, "that we still might have a chance at the *Estrella*."

"Really, Sir Thomas? Nothing could give me greater pleasure, if it were possible. I would like to hear what you suggest."

"Well, my lord. She'll sail tomorrow. Most likely at dawn, with the land breeze. Tonight we might—we might fix some kind of drogue to her bottom. Perhaps to her rudder. She's no more than a knot or two faster than we are. We could follow her out and catch her at sea—"

"This is brilliant, Sir Thomas. Really ingenious—but nothing more than could be expected of a seaman of your reputation, let me add."

"You are too kind, my lord." There was a struggle only too perceptible in Fell's expression, and he hesitated before he went on at last—"It was your secretary, Spendlove, who put the idea in my mind, my lord."

"Spendlove? I can hardly believe it."

"He was too timid to make the suggestion to you, my lord, and so he came to me with it."

"I'm sure he did no more than set the wheels of your thought turning, Sir Thomas. In any case, since you have assumed the responsibility the credit must be yours, of course, if credit is to be awarded. Let us hope there will be a great deal."

"Thank you, my lord."

"Now about this drogue. What do you suggest, Sir Thomas?"

"It need be no more than a large sea anchor. A bolt of Number One canvas, sewn into a funnel, one end larger than the other."

"It would have to be reinforced even so. Not even Number One canvas could stand the strain with *Estrella* going at twelve knots."

"Yes, my lord, I was sure of that. Bolt-ropes sewn in in plenty. That would be easy enough, of course. We have a spare bob-stay chain on board. That could be sewn round the mouth of the drogue—"

"And could be attached to the *Estrella* to take the main strain."

"Yes, my lord. That was what I thought."

"It would serve to keep the drogue under water out of sight as well."

"Yes, my lord."

Fell found Hornblower's quickness in grasping the technical points vastly encouraging. His nervousness was now replaced by enthusiasm.

"And where would you propose to attach this drogue, Sir Thomas?"

"I was thinking—Spendlove suggested, my lord—that it might be passed over one of the lower pintles of the rudder."

"It would be likely to tear the rudder clean away when exerting its full force."

"That would serve our purpose equally well, my lord."

"Of course, I understand."

Fell walked across the cabin to where the great cabin window stood open wide.

"You can't see her from here as we lie now, my lord," he said. "But you can hear her."

"And smell her," said Hornblower, standing beside him.

"Yes, my lord. They're hosing her out at present. But you can hear her, as I said."

Over the water came very plainly to them, along with the miasma of her stench, the continued wailing of the wretched slaves; Hornblower fancied he could even hear the clanking of the leg irons.

"Sir Thomas," said Hornblower, "I think it would be very desirable if you would put a boat overside to row guard round the ship tonight."

"Row guard, my lord?" Fell was not very quick in the uptake. In the peacetime navy it was unnecessary to take elaborate precautions against desertion.

"Oh, yes, most certainly. Half these men would be overside swimming for the shore as soon as night falls. Surely you understand that, Sir Thomas. We must restrain their passion to desert from this brutal service. And in any case a guard boat will prevent the sale of liquor through the gunports."

"Er—yes, I suppose so, my lord." But Fell clearly had not grasped the implications of the suggestion, and Hornblower had to elaborate.

"Let us set a boat rowing guard now, before nightfall. I can explain to the authorities why it is necessary. Then when the time comes—"

"We'll have a boat ready in the water!" Enlightenment had broken in on Fell at last.

"Attracting no attention," supplemented Hornblower.

"Of course!"

The red sunset showed Fell's face lit up with animation.

"It would be best if you gave that order soon, Sir Thomas. But meanwhile there's little time to spare. We must have this drogue in the making before we go ashore."

"Shall I give the orders, my lord?"

"Spendlove has figures at his fingertips. He can work out the measurements. Would you be kind enough to send for him, Sir Thomas?"

The cabin was soon crowded with people as the work was put in hand. Spendlove came first; after him Gerard was sent for, and then Sefton, the first lieutenant. Next came the sail-maker, the armourer, the carpenter, and the boatswain. The sail-maker was an elderly Swede who had been forced into the British navy twenty years ago in some conscienceless action of the press gang, and who had remained in the service ever since. His wrinkled face broke into a grin, like a shattered window, as the beauties of the scheme dawned upon him when he was told about it. He just managed to restrain himself from slapping his thigh with glee when he remembered he was in the august presence of his admiral and his captain. Spendlove was busy sketching out with pencil and paper a drawing of the drogue, with Gerard looking over his shoulder.

"Perhaps even I might make a contribution to this scheme," said Hornblower, and everyone turned to look at him; he met Spendlove's eye with a glassy stare that forbade Spendlove to breathe a word to the effect that the whole scheme was his original idea.

"Yes, my lord?" said Fell.

"A length of spun yarn," said Hornblower, "made fast to the tail of the drogue and led for'rard and the other end secured to the chain. Just a single strand, to keep it tail end forward while *Estrella* gets under way. Then when she sets all sail and the strain comes—"

"The yarn will part!" said Spendlove. "You're right, my lord. Then the drogue will take the water—"

"And she'll be ours, let's hope," concluded Hornblower.

"Excellent, my lord," said Fell.

Was there perhaps a mild condescension, a tiny hint of patronage, in what he said? Hornblower felt that there was, and was momentarily nettled at it. Already Fell was quite convinced that the whole scheme was his own—despite his handsome earlier admission that Spendlove had contributed—and he was generously allowing Hornblower to add a trifling suggestion. Hornblower allayed his irritation with cynical amusement at the weaknesses of human nature.

"In this stimulating atmosphere of ideas," he said modestly, "one can hardly help but be infected."

"Y-yes, my lord," said Gerard, eyeing him curiously. Gerard was too sharp altogether, and knew him too well. He had caught the echo of mock modesty in Hornblower's tone, and was on the verge of guessing the truth.

"No need for you to put your oar in, Mr. Gerard," snapped Hornblower. "Do I have to recall you to your duty? Where's my dinner, Mr. Gerard? Do I always have to starve while I'm under your care? What will Lady Barbara say when she hears you allow me to go hungry?"

"I beg pardon, my lord," spluttered Gerard, entirely taken aback. "I'd quite forgotten—you've been so busy, my lord—"

His embarrassment was intense; he turned this way and that in the crowded cabin as if looking about him for the missing dinner.

"No time now, Mr. Gerard," said Hornblower. Until the need for distracting Gerard's attention had arisen he had been equally forgetful of the need for dinner. "Let's hope His Excellency will offer us some small collation."

"I really must beg your pardon, my lord," said Fell, equally embarrassed.

"Oh, no matter, Sir Thomas," said Hornblower, waving the apologies aside testily. "You and I are in the same condition. Let me see that drawing, Mr. Spendlove."

He was continually being led into playing the part of a peppery old gentleman, when he knew himself to be nothing of the sort. He was able to mellow again as they went once more through the details of the construction of the drogue, and he gave his approval.

"I believe, Sir Thomas," he said, "that you have decided to entrust the work to Mr. Sefton during our absence ashore?"

Fell bowed his agreement.

"Mr. Spendlove will remain under your orders, Mr. Sefton. Mr. Gerard will accompany Sir Thomas and me. I don't know what you have decided, Sir Thomas, but I would suggest that you bring a lieutenant and a midshipman with you to His Excellency's reception."

"Aye aye, my lord."

"Mr. Sefton, I am sure I can trust you to have this work completed by the time of our return, early in the middle watch, I fancy?"

"Yes, my lord."

So there it was all settled, except for the dreary interval of waiting. This was just like wartime, standing by with a crisis looming in the near future.

"Dinner, my lord?" suggested Gerard eagerly.

He wanted no dinner. He was weary now that all was settled and the tension easing.

"I'll call for Giles if I want some," he said, looking round the crowded cabin. He wanted to dismiss this horde of people, and sought words to do so politely.

"Then I'll attend to my other duties, my lord," said Fell, suddenly and surprisingly tactful.

"Very well, Sir Thomas, thank you."

The cabin emptied itself rapidly; Hornblower was able by a mere look to put an end to Gerard's tendency to linger. Then he could sink back into his chair and relax, sturdily ignoring Giles when he came in with another lighted lamp for the darkening cabin. The ship was full of the sound of the business of watering, sheaves squealing in blocks, pumps clanking, hoarse orders; the noise was sufficiently distracting to prevent his thoughts maintaining any regular course. He was in half a doze when a knock on the door preceded the arrival of a midshipman.

"Cap'n's respects, my lord, and the shore boat is approaching."

"My compliments to the captain, and I'll be on deck at once."

The shore boat was bright with a lantern hanging over the sternsheets in the midst of the darkness of the harbour. It lit up Mendez-Castillo's resplendent uniform. Down the side they went, midshipman, lieutenants, captain, admiral, in the reversed order of naval precedence, and powerful strokes of the oars carried them over the black water towards the city, where a few lights gleamed. They passed close by the *Estrella*; there was a light hanging in her rigging, but apparently she had completed her watering, for there was no activity about her.

Nevertheless there came a continuous faint wailing from up her open hatchways. Perhaps the slaves there were mourning the departure of those of them who had been taken from them; perhaps they were voicing their apprehension at what the future held in store for them. It occurred to Hornblower that these unfortunate people, snatched from their homes, packed into a ship whose like they had never seen before, guarded by white men (and white faces must be as extraordinary to them as emerald green ones would be to a European), could have no idea at all of what lay in store for them, any more than he himself would have if he were to be abducted to another planet.

"His Excellency," said Mendez-Castillo beside him, "has had pleasure in deciding to receive Your Excellency with full ceremonial."

"That is most kind of His Excellency," replied Hornblower, recalling himself to his present duties with an effort, and expressing himself in Spanish with even more effort.

The tiller was put over and the boat turned abruptly round a corner, revealing a brightly lit jetty, with a massive gateway beyond. The boat ran alongside and half a dozen uniformed figures stood to attention as the party climbed on shore.

"This way, Your Excellency," murmured Mendez-Castillo.

They passed through the gateway into a courtyard lit by scores of lanterns, which shone on ranks of soldiers drawn up in two treble lines. As Hornblower emerged into the courtyard a shouted order brought the muskets to the present, and at the same moment a band burst into music. Hornblower's tone-deaf ear heard the jerky braying, and he halted at attention with his hand to the brim of his cocked hat, his fellow officers beside him, until the deafening noise—echoed and multiplied by the surrounding walls—came to an end.

"A fine military appearance, Major," said Hornblower, looking down the rigid lines of white crossbelts.

"Your Excellency is too kind. Would Your Excellency please proceed to the door in front?"

An imposing flight of steps, lined on either side with more uniforms; beyond that an open doorway and a vast room. A prolonged whispered conference between Mendez-Castillo and an official beside the door, and then their names blared out in resounding Spanish—Hornblower had long given up hope of ever hearing his name pronounced intelligibly by a foreign tongue.

The central figure in the room rose from his chair—which was almost a throne—to receive the British commander-in-chief standing. He was a much younger man than Hornblower had expected, in his thirties, dark complexioned, with a thin mobile face and a humorous expression at odds with his arrogant hooked nose. His uniform gleamed with gold lace, with the Order of the Golden Fleece on his breast.

Mendez-Castillo made the presentations; the Englishmen bowed deeply to the representative of His Most Catholic Majesty and each received a polite inclination in return. Mendez-Castillo ventured so far as to murmur their host's titles—probably a breach of etiquette, thought Hornblower, for it should be assumed that visitors were fully aware of them.

"His Excellency the Marqués de Ayora, Captain-General of His Most Catholic Majesty's dominion of Puerto Rico."

Ayora smiled in welcome.

"I know you speak Spanish, Your Excellency," he said. "I have already had the pleasure of hearing you do so."

"Indeed, Your Excellency?"

"I was a major of migueletes under Claros at the time of the attack on Rosas. I had the honour of serving beside Your Excellency —I remember Your Excellency well. Your Excellency would naturally not remember me."

It would have been too flagrant to pretend he did, and Hornblower was for once at a loss for a word, and could only bow again.

"Your Excellency," went on Ayora, "has changed very little since that day, if I may venture to say so. It is eleven years ago."

"Your Excellency is too kind." That was one of the most useful phrases in polite language.

Ayora had a word for Fell—a compliment on the appearance of his ship—and a supplementary smile for the junior officers. Then as if it were a moment for which he had been waiting, Mendez-Castillo turned to them.

"Perhaps you gentlemen would care to be presented to the ladies of the company?" he said; his glance passed over Hornblower and Fell and took in only the lieutenants and the midshipman. Hornblower translated, and saw them depart a little nervously under Mendez-Castillo's escort.

Ayora, etiquette and Spanish training notwithstanding, wasted no time in coming to the point the moment he found himself alone with Hornblower and Fell.

"I watched your pursuit of the *Estrella del Sur* today through my telescope," he said, and Hornblower once more found himself at a loss for a word; a bow and a smile also seemed out of place in this connection. He could only look blank.

"It is an anomalous situation," said Ayora. "Under the preliminary convention between our governments the British navy has the right to capture on the high seas Spanish ships laden with slaves. But once within Spanish territorial waters those ships are safe. When the new convention for the suppression of the slave trade is signed, then those ships will be forfeit to His Most Catholic Majesty's government, but until that time it is my duty to give them every protection in my power."

"Your Excellency is perfectly correct, of course," said Hornblower. Fell was looking perfectly blank, not understanding a word of what was said, but Hornblower felt that the effort of translating was beyond him.

"And I fully intend to carry out my duty," said Ayora firmly.

"Naturally," said Hornblower.

"So perhaps it would be best to come to a clear understanding regarding future events."

"There is nothing I would like better, Your Excellency."

"It is clearly understood, then, that I will tolerate no interference with the *Estrella del Sur* while she is in waters under my jurisdiction?"

"Of course I understand that, Your Excellency," said Hornblower.

"The *Estrella* wishes to sail at the first light of morning tomorrow."

"That is what I expected, Your Excellency."

"And for the sake of the amity between our governments it would be best if your ship were to remain in this harbour until after she sails."

Ayora's eyes met Hornblower's in a steady stare. His face was perfectly expressionless; there was no hint of a threat in that glance. But a threat was implied, the ultimate hint of superior strength was there. At Ayora's command a hundred thirty-two-pounders could sweep the waters of the harbour. Hornblower was reminded of the Roman who agreed with his Emperor because it was ill arguing with the master of thirty legions. He adopted the same pose as far as his acting ability allowed. He smiled the smile of a good loser.

"We have had our chance and lost it, Your Excellency," he said. "We can hardly complain."

If Ayora felt any relief at his acquiescence it showed no more plainly than his previous hint of force.

"Your Excellency is most understanding," he said.

"Naturally we are desirous of taking advantage of the land breeze to leave tomorrow morning," said Hornblower deferentially. "Now that we have refilled with water—for the opportunity of doing so I have to thank Your Excellency—we would not like to trespass too far upon Your Excellency's hospitality."

Hornblower did his best to maintain an appearance of innocence under Ayora's searching stare.

"Perhaps we might hear what Captain Gomez has to say," said Ayora, turning aside to summon someone close at hand. He was a young man, strikingly handsome, dressed in plain but elegant blue clothes with a silver-hilted sword at his side.

"May I present," said Ayora, "Don Miguel Gomez y Gonzalez, captain of the *Estrella del Sur?*"

Bows were exchanged.

"May I felicitate you on the sailing qualities of your ship, Captain?" said Hornblower.

"Many thanks, *señor.*"

"*Clorinda* is a fast frigate, but your ship is superior at all points of sailing." Hornblower was not too sure about how to render that technical expression into Spanish, but apparently he contrived to make himself understood.

"Many thanks again, *señor.*"

"And I could even venture"—Hornblower spread his hands deprecatingly—"to congratulate her captain on the brilliance with which he managed her."

Captain Gomez bowed, and Hornblower suddenly checked himself. These highflown Spanish compliments were all very well, but they could be overdone. He did not want to give the impression of a man too anxious to please. But he was reassured by a glance at the expression on Gomez' face. He was actually simpering; that was the only word for it. Hornblower mentally classified him as a young man of great ability and well pleased with himself. Another compliment would not be one too many.

"I shall suggest to my government," he went on, "that they request permission to take off the lines of the *Star of the South*, and study the plan of her sails, in order to build a similar vessel. She would be ideal for the work of the navy in these waters. But of course it would be hard to find a suitable captain."

Gomez bowed once more. It was hard not to be self-satisfied when complimented by a seaman with the legendary reputation of Hornblower.

"His Excellency," put in Ayora, "is desirous of leaving the harbour tomorrow morning."

"So we understood," said Gomez.

Even Ayora looked a trifle disconcerted at the admission. Hornblower could see it plainly. Stuart, so helpful with his information, had not hesitated to help both sides, as Hornblower had expected he would. He had gone straight to the Spanish authorities with the intelligence Hornblower had supplied him with. But Hornblower had no desire to allow a jarring note to creep into the present conversation.

"You can understand, Captain," he said, "that I would be glad to leave on the same tide and with the same land breeze that takes you out. After our experience today I fear you need be under no apprehension."

"None at all," said Gomez. There was something of condescension in his smile. That agreement was all that Hornblower wanted. He was at pains to conceal his relief.

"It will be my duty to pursue you if you are still in sight when I leave," he said apologetically; by his glance he made it clear that the remark was addressed to the captain-general as well as to Gomez, but it was Gomez who answered.

"I have no fear," he said.

"In that case, Your Excellency," said Hornblower, clinching the matter, "I can inform Your Excellency officially that His Majesty's ship in which my flag is being flown will leave harbour tomorrow morning as early as suits Captain Gomez' convenience."

"That is understood," agreed Ayora. "I regret greatly that Your Excellency's visit should be so brief."

"In the life of a sailor," said Hornblower, "duty seems invariably to interfere with inclination. But at least during this brief visit I have had the pleasure of making the acquaintance of Your Excellency, and of Captain Gomez."

"There are numerous other gentlemen here also desirous of making Your Excellency's acquaintance," said Ayora. "May I be permitted to present them to Your Excellency?"

The real business of the evening had been transacted, and now it was only necessary to go through the other formalities. The rest of the reception was as dreary as Hornblower had expected and feared; the Puerto Rican magnates who were led up in turn to meet him were as dull. At midnight Hornblower caught the eyes of Gerard and gathered his flock together. Ayora noted the gesture and gave, in courteous terms, the leave to depart which as His Catholic Majesty's representative he had to give unless his guests were to be guilty of discourtesy.

"Your Excellency has doubtless need to rest in readiness for your early start tomorrow," he said. "I will not attempt to detain Your

Excellency in consequence, much as Your Excellency's presence here has been appreciated."

The good-byes were said, and Mendez-Castillo undertook to escort the party back to the *Clorinda*. It was something of a shock to Hornblower to find that the band and the guard of honour were still in the courtyard to offer the official compliments on his departure. He stood at the salute while the band played some jerky tune or other; then they went down into the waiting boat.

The harbour was pitch dark as they rowed out into it, the few lights visible doing almost nothing to alleviate the blackness. They rounded the corner and passed astern of the *Estrella* again. There was a single lantern hanging in her main rigging, and she was quiet by now—no; in the still night, at one moment, Hornblower heard the faint rattle of leg irons as some one of the slaves in her hold indicated that he was still awake and restless. That was good. Farther along a quiet challenge came over the inky water, issuing from a nucleus of darkness even more solid than the darkness surrounding it.

"Flag," answered the midshipman, "*Clorinda*."

The two brief words were all that were needed to inform the guard boat that an admiral and a captain were approaching.

"You see, Major," said Hornblower, "that Captain Fell deemed it necessary to row guard round the ship during the night."

"I understood that to be the case, Your Excellency," answered Mendez-Castillo.

"Our seamen will go to great lengths to indulge themselves in the pleasures of the shore."

"Naturally, Your Excellency," said Mendez-Castillo.

The boat ran alongside the *Clorinda;* standing awkwardly in the sternsheets, Hornblower said his last good-byes and uttered his last words of thanks to the representative of his host before going up the side. From the entry port he watched the boat shove off again and disappear into the darkness.

"Now," he said, "we can make better use of our time."

On the maindeck, just visible in the light from the lantern hanging from the mainstay, was a Thing; that was the only way to describe it, something of canvas and cordage, with a length of chain attached to it. Sefton was standing beside it.

"I see you've finished it, Mr. Sefton."

"Yes, my lord. A full hour ago. The sail-maker and his mates worked admirably."

Hornblower turned to Fell.

"I fancy, Sir Thomas," he said, "that you have in mind the necessary orders to give. Perhaps you would be kind enough to tell me about them before you issue them?"

"Aye aye, my lord."

That eternal navy answer was the only one Fell could make in the circumstances, even if Fell had not yet given full thought to the next problems. Down in the cabin alone with his admiral Fell's unreadiness was a little apparent.

"I suppose," prompted Hornblower, "that you will tell off the necessary personnel for the expedition. Which officer can you trust fully to exercise discretion?"

Little by little the details were settled. Powerful swimmers who could work under water; an armourer's mate who could be relied upon to put the final shackle in the chain in the darkness; the boat's crew was decided upon, summoned, and instructed in all the details of the plan. When the guard boat came in for the relief of its crew, there was another crew standing by all ready, who went down overside rapidly and quietly although encumbered with the Thing and the necessary gear.

It pushed off again into the darkness, and Hornblower stood on the quarterdeck to watch it go. There might be an international incident arising out of this, or he might be made to appear a fool in the eyes of the world, which would be just as bad. He strained his ears for any sounds in the darkness which would tell him how the work was progressing, but he could hear nothing. The land breeze had just begun to blow, gently, but strongly enough to swing *Clorinda* to her anchor; it would carry any sounds away from him, he realized—but it would also serve to obscure any suspicious noises if anyone in the *Estrella* was awake enough to hear them. She had a full counter, with, as was only to be expected, plenty of rake. A swimmer who reached her stern unobserved would be able to work at her rudder unobserved, certainly.

"My lord," said Gerard's voice quietly beside him, "would not this be a suitable time to rest?"

"You are quite right, Mr. Gerard. A most suitable time," answered Hornblower, continuing to lean against the rail.

"Well, then, my lord—?"

"I have agreed with you, Mr. Gerard. Surely you can be content with that?"

But Gerard's voice went on, remorseless as the voice of conscience. "There is cold beef laid out in the cabin, my lord. Fresh bread and a bottle of Bordeaux."

That was a different story. Hornblower suddenly realized how hungry he was; during the past thirty hours he had eaten one meagre meal, because the cold collation he had expected at the reception had failed to materialize. And he could still pretend to be superior to the weaknesses of the flesh.

"You would have made an excellent wet nurse, Mr. Gerard," he said, "if nature had treated you more generously. But I suppose my life will be unbearable until I yield to your importunity."

On the way to the companion they passed Fell; he was striding up and down the quarterdeck in the darkness, and they could hear his hard breathing. It pleased Hornblower to know that even these muscular heroes could feel anxiety. It might be polite, even kind, to invite Fell to join them at this cold supper, but Hornblower dismissed the idea. He had had as much of Fell's company already as he could bear.

Down below Spendlove was waiting in the lighted cabin.

"The vultures are gathered together," said Hornblower. It was amusing to see Spendlove was pale and tense too. "I hope you gentlemen will join me."

The younger men were silent as they ate. Hornblower put his nose to his glass of wine and sipped thoughtfully.

"Six months in the tropics has done this Bordeaux no good," he commented; it was inevitable that as host, and admiral, and older man, his opinion should be received with deference. Spendlove broke the next silence.

"That length of spun yarn, my lord," he said. "The breaking strain—"

"Mr. Spendlove," said Hornblower, "all the discussion in the world won't change it now. We shall know in good time. Meanwhile let's not spoil our dinner with technical discussions."

"Your pardon, my lord," said Spendlove, abashed. Was it by mere coincidence or through telepathy that Hornblower had been thinking at that very moment about the breaking strain of that length of spun yarn in the drogue; but he would not dream of admitting that he had been thinking about it. The dinner continued.

"Well," said Hornblower, raising his glass, "we can admit the existence of mundane affairs long enough to allow of a toast. Here's to head money."

As they drank they heard unmistakable sounds on deck and overside. The guard boat had returned from its mission. Spendlove and Gerard exchanged glances, and poised themselves ready to stand up. Hornblower forced himself to lean back and shake his head sadly, his glass still in his hand.

"Too bad about this Bordeaux, gentlemen," he said.

Then came the knock on the door and the expected message.

"Cap'n's respects, my lord, and the boat has returned."

"My compliments to the captain, and I'll be glad to see him and the lieutenant here as soon as is convenient."

One glance at Fell as he entered the cabin was sufficient to indicate that the expedition had been successful, so far, at least.

"All well, my lord," he said, his florid face suffused with excitement.

"Excellent." The lieutenant was a grizzled veteran older than Hornblower; and Hornblower could not help but think to himself that had he not enjoyed great good fortune on several occasions he would be only a lieutenant too. "Will you sit down, gentlemen? A glass of wine? Mr. Gerard, order fresh glasses, if you please. Sir Thomas, would you mind if I hear Mr. Field's story from his own lips?"

Field had no fluency of speech. His story had to be drawn from him by questions. Everything had gone well. Two strong swimmers, their faces blackened, had slipped overside from the guard boat and had swum unseen to the *Estrella*. Working with their knives, they had been able to prise off the copper from the second rudder-brace below the waterline. With an auger they had made a space large enough to pass a line through. The most ticklish part of the work had been approaching near enough in the guard boat and putting the drogue overside after it had been attached to the line, but Field reported that no hail had come from the *Estrella*. The chain had followed the line and had been securely shackled. Now the drogue hung at *Estrella*'s stern, safely out of sight below the surface, ready to exert its full force on her rudder when—and if—the spun yarn which held the drogue reversed should part.

"Excellent," said Hornblower again, when Field's last halting sentence was uttered. "You've done very well, Mr. Field, thank you."

"Thank you, my lord."

When Field had left, Hornblower could address himself to Fell. "Your plan has worked out admirably, Sir Thomas. Now it only remains to catch the *Estrella*. I would strongly recommend you to make all preparations for getting under way at daylight. The sooner we leave after the *Estrella* has sailed, the better, don't you think?"

"Aye aye, my lord."

The ship's bell overhead anticipated the next question Hornblower was about to ask.

"Three hours to daylight," he said. "I'll say good night to you gentlemen, then."

It had been a busy day, of ceaseless activity, mental if not physical, since dawn. After a long hot evening it seemed to Hornblower that his feet had swollen to twice their ordinary size and that his gold-buckled shoes had made no allowance for this expansion—he could hardly pry them off. He took off ribbon and star and gold-laced coat, and reluctantly reminded himself that he would have to put them on again for his ceremonial departure in three hours' time. He sponged himself down with water from his washbasin, and sank down, sighing with relief, on his cot in the night cabin.

He woke automatically when the watch was called; the cabin was still quite dark and he was at a loss, for a couple of seconds, about why there should be this feeling of urgency within him. Then he remembered, and was wide awake at once, shouting to the sentry at the door to pass the word for Giles. He shaved by lamplight in feverish haste, and then, once more in the hated full-dress uniform, he sped up the ladder to the quarterdeck. It was still pitch dark; no, perhaps there was the slightest glimmering of daylight. Perhaps the sky was the smallest trifle brighter over the Morro. Perhaps. The quarterdeck was crowded with shadowy figures, more even than would be found there with the ship's company at stations for getting under way. At sight of them he nearly turned back, having no wish to reveal that he shared the same weaknesses as the rest of them, but Fell had caught sight of him.

"Good morning, my lord."

"Morning, Sir Thomas."

"Land breeze blowing full, my lord."

No doubt about that; Hornblower could feel it breathing round him, delightful after the sweltering stuffiness of the cabin. In these midsummer tropics it would be of short duration; it would be cut off short as soon as the sun, lifting over the horizon, should get to work in its brassy strength upon the land.

"*Estrella*'s making ready for sea, my lord."

There was no doubt about that either; the sounds of it made their way over the water through the twilight.

"I don't have to ask if you are ready, Sir Thomas."

"All ready, my lord. Hands standing by at the capstan."

"Very well."

Undoubtedly it was lighter already; the figures on the quarter-deck—now much more clearly defined—had all moved over to the starboard side, lining the rail. Half a dozen telescopes were being extended and pointed towards the *Estrella*.

"Sir Thomas, put an end to that, if you please. Send that crowd below."

"They're anxious to see—"

"I know what they want to see. Send them below immediately."

"Aye aye, my lord."

Everyone, of course, was desperately anxious to see if anything was visible at the *Estrella*'s waterline aft, which might reveal what had been done at night. But there could be no surer way of calling the attention of the *Estrella*'s captain to something suspicious under his stern than by pointing telescopes at it.

"Officer of the watch!"

"My lord?"

"See to it that no one points a telescope for one moment towards the *Estrella*."

"Aye aye, my lord."

"When there's enough light to see clearly, you can sweep round the harbour as you might be expected to do. Not more than five seconds for the *Estrella*, but make sure you see all there is to see."

"Aye aye, my lord."

The eastern sky was now displaying faint greens and yellows, against which the Morro silhouetted itself magnificently though faintly, but in its shadow all was still dark. Even before breakfast it was a romantic moment. It occurred to Hornblower that the presence of an admiral in full dress on the quarterdeck so early might itself be a suspicious circumstance.

"I'm going below, Sir Thomas. Please keep me informed."

"Aye aye, my lord."

In the day cabin Gerard and Spendlove sprang to their feet as he entered; presumably they had been among those driven below by Fell's order.

"Mr. Spendlove, I am profiting by your admirable example of yesterday. I shall make sure of my breakfast while I may. Would you please order breakfast, Mr. Gerard? I presume you gentlemen will favour me with your company."

He threw himself negligently into a chair and watched the preparations. Half-way through them a knock at the door brought in Fell himself.

"*Estrella*'s clearly in sight now, my lord. And there's nothing visible under her stern."

"Thank you, Sir Thomas."

A cup of coffee was welcome at this time in the morning. Hornblower did not have to pretend eagerness to drink it. Daylight was creeping in through the cabin windows, making the lamplight garish and unnecessary. Another knock brought in a midshipman.

"Cap'n's respects, my lord, and *Estrella*'s casting off."

"Very well."

Soon she would be under way, and their device would be put to the test. Hornblower made himself bite and masticate another mouthful of toast.

"Can't you young men sit still for even a moment?" he snapped. "Pour me some more coffee, Gerard."

"*Estrella*'s warping out into the channel, my lord," reported the midshipman again.

"Very well," said Hornblower, sipping fastidiously at his coffee, and hoping that no one could guess how much his pulse rate had accelerated. The minutes dragged by.

"*Estrella*'s preparing to make sail, my lord."

"Very well." Hornblower put down his coffee cup, slowly, and as slowly as he could manage it, rose from his chair, the eyes of the two young men never leaving him.

"I think," he said, dragging out his words, "we might now go on deck."

Pacing as slowly as when he had been a mourner at Nelson's funeral he walked out past the sentry and up the ladder; behind him the young men had to curb their impatience. It was dazzling bright on deck; the sun was just over the Morro. In the centre of the fairway at less than a cable's length distance lay the *Estrella*, gleaming in her white paint. As Hornblower's eyes rested on her, her jib extended itself upwards, to catch the wind and swing her round. Next moment her mainsail took the wind, and she steadied herself, gathering way; in a few seconds she was moving forward past the *Clorinda*. This was the moment. Fell was standing staring at her and muttering to himself; he was blaspheming in his excitement. *Estrella* dipped her colours; on her deck Hornblower was able to recognize the figure of Gomez, standing directing the handling of the schooner. Gomez caught sight of him at the same moment, and bowed, holding his hat across his chest, and Hornblower returned the compliment.

"She's not making two knots through the water," said Hornblower.

"Thank God for that," said Fell.

Estrella glided on towards the entrance, preparatory to making the dog-legged turn out to sea; Gomez was handling her beautifully under her very easy sail.

"Shall I follow her now, my lord?"

"I think it's time, Sir Thomas."

"Hands to the capstan, there! Headsail sheets, Mr. Field!"

Even at two knots there would be some strain on that length of spun yarn. It must not part—it must not—before *Estrella* was well out to sea. Lusty arms and sturdy backs were heaving *Clorinda's* cable short.

"Clear away the saluting carronade, there!"

Estrella had made the turn; the last of her mainsail was vanishing round the corner. Fell was giving his orders to get *Clorinda* under way steadily and clearly, despite his excitement. Hornblower was watching him narrowly; this was not a bad test of how he would behave in action, of how he would take his ship down into the smoke and fury of a battle.

"Main tops'l braces!"

Fell was bringing the big frigate round in as neat a fashion as Gomez had handled *Estrella*. *Clorinda* steadied herself and gathered way, moving down the channel.

"Man the rail!"

Whatever was going on round the corner, whatever was happening to the *Estrella* out of sight, the compliments must be paid. Nine-tenths of *Clorinda's* crew on deck could be spared for the purpose; with the ship creeping forward before the land breeze the other one-tenth sufficed to keep her under control. Hornblower drew himself up and faced the Spanish flag flying over the Morro, his hand to his hat brim, Fell beside him, the other officers in rank behind, while the salute banged out and was returned, the flags dipping respectfully.

"Carry on!"

They were approaching the turn. It was possible that at any moment one of those grinning cannons up there would pitch a warning shot at them—a shot warning them that a hundred other guns were ready to pound them into a wreck; that would be if the drogue had begun to take obvious effect on the *Estrella.*

"Main tops'l braces!" came Fell's order again.

Already the big Atlantic rollers were making their effect felt; Hornblower could feel *Clorinda's* bows lift momentarily to a dying surge.

"Hard a-starboard!" *Clorinda* turned steadily. "Meet her! Steady as you go."

She had hardly settled on her new course when *Estrella* came in sight again a mile farther out to sea, her bows pointed in almost the opposite direction; she was still under very easy canvas, thank God, steadying herself for the final turn from the channel out into the ocean. *Clorinda's* main topsail shivered briefly as the Morro height intercepted the land breeze, but drew again instantly. *Estrella* was turning again now. She was hardly within cannon shot of the Morro.

"Port!" came Fell's order. "Steady!"

The land breeze was right aft now, but dying away, partly with their increased distance from land and partly with the growing heat of the sun.

"Set the mains'l."

Fell was quite right; there was need to hasten, lest the ship be delayed in the belt of doldrums between the land breeze and the trade wind. The enormous sail area of the main course carried *Clorinda* forward boldly, and once more the sound of the ship's way through the water became audible. *Estrella* was clear of the channel now; Hornblower, watching anxiously, saw her set foresail and staysails and jibs, all her fore-and-aft canvas in fact. She was holding her course northward, close-hauled, directly away from the land; she must have caught the trade wind and was making northing, very sensibly, because she would have to weather Haiti before next morning on her course to the Old Bahama Channel and Havana. They were far enough from the Morro now, and from *Estrella,* to incur no suspicion by staring through telescopes at her. Hornblower looked long and carefully. He could detect nothing unusual about her appearance. It suddenly occurred to him that perhaps Gomez had detected the drogue under his stern and had removed it. He might even now be exploding with laughter, along with his officers, looking back at the British frigate hopefully following them.

"Port!" came Fell's order again, and *Clorinda* took the final turn.

"Leading marks in line, sir!" reported the master, looking aft at the land with his telescope to his eye.

"Very well. Steady as you go."

Now the waves they were encountering were true Atlantic rollers, heaving up *Clorinda's* starboard bow, and passing aft as the bows dipped to heave up the port quarter. *Estrella* right ahead was still close-hauled on a northerly course under fore-and-aft canvas.

"She'll be making six knots," estimated Gerard, standing with Spendlove a yard from Hornblower.

"That spun yarn should hold at six knots," said Spendlove meditatively.

"No bottom with this line!" reported the leadsman in the chains.

"All hands make sail!"

The order was being piped through the ship. Topgallants and royals were being spread; it was not long before *Clorinda* had every stitch of canvas set.

Yet the land breeze was dying fast. *Clorinda* was hardly making steerage way. Once, twice, the sails flapped like thunder, but she still held her course, creeping forward over the blue and white sea, with the sun blazing down upon her from a blue sky with hardly a fleck of cloud.

"Can't keep her on her course, sir," reported the quartermaster.

Clorinda was yawing sluggishly as the rollers came at her. Far ahead the *Estrella* was almost hull down. Now came a breath of a different air, the tiniest breath; Hornblower felt it, nearly imperceptible, on his sweating face long before *Clorinda* made response. It was a different air indeed, not the heated air of the land breeze, but the fresher air of the trade wind, clean with its passage over three thousand miles of ocean. The sails flapped and shivered; *Clorinda* swung more meaningly.

"Here it comes!" exclaimed Fell. "Full and by!"

A stronger puff came, so that the rudder could bite. A lull, another puff, another lull, another puff, yet each puff was stronger yet. The next puff did not die away. It endured, heeling *Clorinda* over. A roller burst against her starboard bow in a dazzling rainbow. Now they had caught the trade wind; now they could thrust their way northwards close-hauled in the trail of the *Estrella*. With the clean fresh wind blowing, and the sensation of successful striving with it, a new animation came over the ship. There were smiles to be seen.

"She hasn't set her tops'ls yet, my lord," said Gerard, his telescope still to his eye.

"I doubt if she will while she makes her northing," replied Hornblower.

"On a wind she can weather and headreach on us," said Spend-love. "Just as she did yesterday."

Yesterday? Was it only yesterday? It could have been a month ago, so much had happened since yesterday's chase.

"Do you think that drogue ought to have any effect?" asked Fell, approaching them.

"None, sir, practically speaking," answered Spendlove. "Not while that spun yarn keeps it tail forward."

Fell had one huge hand clasped in the other, grinding his knuckles into his palm.

"For me," said Hornblower, and every eye turned to him, "I am going to say farewell to gold lace. A cooler coat and a looser neckcloth."

Let Fell display worry and nervousness; he himself was going below as if he had no interest whatever in the outcome of the affair. Down in the hot cabin it was a relief to throw off his full-dress uniform—ten pounds of broadcloth and gold—and to have Giles get out a clean shirt and white duck trousers.

"I'll take my bath," said Hornblower meditatively.

He knew perfectly well that Fell thought it undignified and dangerous to discipline that an admiral should disport himself under the wash-deck pump, hosed down by grinning seamen, and he neither agreed nor cared. No miserable sponging down could take the place of his bath. The seamen pumped vigorously, and Hornblower pranced with middle-aged abandon under the stinging impact of the water. Now the clean shirt and trousers were doubly delightful; he felt a new man as he came on deck again, and his unconcern was not all pretence when Fell nervously approached him.

"She's running clean away from us again, my lord," he said.

"We know she can, Sir Thomas. We can only wait until she puts her helm up and sets her tops'ls."

"As long as we can keep her in sight—" said Fell.

Clorinda was lying right over, fighting her way to the northward.

"I can see that we're doing all we can, Sir Thomas," said Hornblower soothingly.

The morning was wearing on. "Up spirits!" was piped, and Fell agreed with the sailing master that it was noon, and the hands were sent to dinner. Now it was only when *Clorinda* lifted to a wave that a telescope, trained over the starboard bow from the quarterdeck, could detect the gleam of *Estrella's* sails over the horizon. She still had no topsails set; Gomez was acting on the knowledge that close-hauled his schooner behaved better without her square sails—unless he was merely playing with his pursuers. The hills of Puerto Rico had sunk out of sight below the horizon far, far astern. And the roast beef at dinner, roast fresh beef, had been most disappointing, tough and stringy and without any taste whatever.

"Stuart said he'd send me the best sirloin the island could produce, my lord," said Gerard, in answer to Hornblower's expostulations.

"I wish I had him here," said Hornblower. "I'd make him eat it, every bit, without salt. Sir Thomas, please accept my apologies."

"Er—yes, my lord," said Fell, who had been invited to his admiral's table and who had been recalled from his own private thoughts by Hornblower's apologies. "That drogue—"

Having said those words—that special word, rather—he was unable to say more. He looked across the table at Hornblower. His lantern-jawed face—the brick-red cheeks always looked odd in that conformation—showed his anxiety, which was accentuated by the look in his eyes.

"If we don't know all about it today," said Hornblower, "we'll hear all about it at some later date."

It was the truth, even though it was not the kindest thing to say.

"We'll be the laughingstock of the islands," said Fell.

No one in the world could look more miserable than he did at that moment. Hornblower himself was inclined to give up hope, but the sight of that despair roused his contrary nature.

"There's all the difference in the world between six knots, which she's making now close-hauled, and twelve knots, which she'll make when she puts up her helm," he said. "Mr. Spendlove here will tell you that the water resistance is a function of the square of the speed. Isn't that so, Mr. Spendlove?"

"Perhaps a function of the cube or even one of the higher powers, my lord."

"So we can still hope, Sir Thomas. That spun yarn will have eight times the pull upon it when she alters course."

"It'll be chafing now, as well, my lord," added Spendlove.

"If they didn't see the thing last night and cast it off," said Fell, still gloomy.

When they reached the deck again the sun was inclining towards the west.

"Masthead, there!" hailed Fell. "Is the chase still in sight?"

"Yes, sir. Hull down from here, sir, but plain in sight. Two points or thereabouts on the weather-bow."

"She's made all the northing she needs," grumbled Fell. "Why doesn't she alter course?"

There was nothing to do except wait, to try to extract some pleasure from the clean wind and the blue and white sea; but the pleasure was only faint now, the sea did not seem so blue. Nothing to do except wait, with the minutes dragging like hours. Then it happened.

"Deck, there! Chase is altering course to port. She's running right before the wind."

"Very well."

Fell looked round at all the faces of the crowd on the quarterdeck. His own was as tense as anyone else's.

"Mr. Sefton, alter course four points to port."

He was going to play the game out to the bitter end, even though yesterday's experience, closely parallel to the present, had shown that *Clorinda* stood no chance in normal circumstances of intercepting.

"Deck, there! She's settin' her tops'ls. T'garns'ls, too, sir!"

"Very well."

"We'll soon know now," said Spendlove. "With the drogue in action she *must* lose speed. She *must*."

"Deck, there! Cap'n, sir!" The lookout's voice had risen to a scream of excitement. "She's flown up into the wind! She's all aback! Fore topmast's gone, sir!"

"So have her rudder pintles," said Hornblower, grimly.

Fell was leaping on the deck, actually dancing with joy, his face radiant. But he recollected himself with all speed.

"Come two points to starboard," he ordered. "Mr. James, get aloft with you and tell me how she bears."

"She's taking in her mains'l!" shouted the lookout.

"Trying to get before the wind again," commented Gerard.

"Cap'n, sir!" This was James's voice from the masthead. "You're heading a point to loo'ard of her."

"Very well."

"She's coming before the wind—no, she's all aback again, sir!"

The Thing still had her by the tail, then; her struggles would be as unavailing as those of a deer in the claws of a lion.

"Steer small, you ——," said Fell, using a horrible word to the helmsman.

Everyone was excited; everyone seemed to be obsessed with the fear that *Estrella* would clear away the wreck and make her escape after all.

"With her rudder gone she'll never be able to hold a course," said Hornblower. "And she's lost her fore topmast, too."

Another wait, but of a very different nature now. *Clorinda*, thrashing along, seemed to have caught the excitement and to have put on a spurt as she hurled herself at her quarry, racing forward to triumph.

"There she is!" said Gerard, telescope trained forward. "All aback still."

As the next wave lifted *Clorinda*, they all caught sight of her; they were approaching her fast. A sorry, pitiful sight she looked, her fore topmast broken off clean at the cap, her sails shivering in the wind.

"Clear away the bow chaser," ordered Fell. "Fire a shot across her bow."

The shot was fired. Something rose to the schooner's main peak, and broke out into the red and gold of Spain. It hung there for a moment and then came slowly down again.

"Congratulations on the success of your plans, Sir Thomas," said Hornblower.

"Thank you, my lord," answered Fell. He was beaming with pleasure. "I could have done nothing without your lordship's acceptance of my suggestions."

"That is very good of you, Sir Thomas," said Hornblower, turning back to look at the prize.

The *Estrella* was a pitiful sight, the more pitiful as they approached her and could see more clearly the raffle of wreckage dangling forward, and the rudder torn loose aft. The sudden tug of the drogue when it took effect, using enormous force and leverage, had broken or pulled straight the stout bronze pintles on which the rudder had hung suspended. The drogue itself, weighted by its chain, still hung out of sight below the dangling rudder. Gomez, brought triumphantly aboard, had still no idea of the cause of the disaster, and had not guessed at the reason for the loss of his rudder. He had been young and handsome and dignified in the face of undeserved misfortune when he arrived on *Clorinda's* deck. There was no pleasure in observing the change in him when he was told the truth. No pleasure at all. The sight even took away the feeling of pleasure over a professional triumph, to see him wilting under the eyes of his captors. But still, more than three hundred slaves had been set free.

* * *

Hornblower was dictating his despatch to Their Lordships, and Spendlove, who numbered this newfangled shorthand among his surprising accomplishments, was slashing down the sentences at a speed that made light of Hornblower's stumbling sentences—Hornblower had not yet acquired the art of dictation.

"In conclusion," said Hornblower, "it gives me particular pleasure to call Their Lordships' attention to the ingenuity and activity of Captain Sir Thomas Fell, which made this exemplary capture possible."

Spendlove looked up from his pad and stared at him. Spendlove knew the truth; but the unblinking stare which answered him defied him to utter a word.

"Add the usual official ending," said Hornblower.

It was not for him to explain his motives to his secretary. Nor could he have explained them if he had tried. He liked Fell no better now than before.

"Now a letter to my agent," said Hornblower.

"Aye aye, my lord," said Spendlove, turning a page.

Hornblower began to assemble in his mind the sentences composing this next letter. He wanted to say that because the capture was due to Sir Thomas's suggestions he did not wish to apply for his share of head money for himself. It was his desire that the share of the Flag should be allocated to Sir Thomas.

"No," said Hornblower. "Belay that. I won't write after all."

"Aye aye, my lord," said Spendlove.

It was possible to pass on to another man distinction and honour, but one could not pass on money. There was something obvious, something suspicious, about that. Sir Thomas might guess, and Sir Thomas's feelings might be hurt, and he would not risk it. But he wished he liked Sir Thomas better, all the same.

3

Oh, the dames of France are fo-ond a-and free
And Flemish li-ips a-are willing.

That was young Spendlove singing lustily only two rooms away from Hornblower's at Admiralty House and he might as well be in the same room, as all the windows were open to let in the Jamaican sea breeze.

And sweet the maids of I-Ita-aly—

That was Gerard joining in.

"My compliments to Mr. Gerard and Mr. Spendlove," growled Hornblower to Giles, who was helping him dress, "and that caterwauling is to stop. Repeat that to make sure you have the words right."

"His lordship's compliments, gentlemen, and that caterwauling is to stop," repeated Giles dutifully.

"Very well, run and say it."

Giles ran, and Hornblower was gratified to hear the noise cease abruptly. The fact that those two young men were singing—and still more the fact that they had forgotten he was within earshot—was proof that they were feeling lighthearted, as might be expected, seeing they were dressing for a ball. Yet it was no excuse, for they knew well enough that their tone-deaf commander-in-chief detested music, and they should also have realized that he would be more testy than usual, on account of that very ball, because it meant that he would be forced to spend a long evening listening to those dreary sounds, cloying and irritating at the same moment. There would certainly be a table or two of whist—Mr. Hough would be aware of his principal guest's tastes—but it was too much to hope for that all sound of music would be excluded from the card room. The prospect of a ball was by no means as exhilarating to Hornblower as to his flag lieutenant and to his secretary.

Hornblower tied his white neckcloth and painfully adjusted it to geometrical symmetry, and Giles helped him into his black dress coat. Hornblower regarded the result in the mirror, by the light of the candles round its frame. At least tolerable, he said to himself. The growing peacetime convention whereby naval and military men appeared in civilian clothes had a good deal to recommend it; so had the other increasing fad for men to wear black dress coats. Barbara had helped him select this one, and had supervised its fitting by the tailor. The cut was excellent, Hornblower decided, turning back and forth before the mirror, and black and white suited him. "Only gentlemen can wear black and white," Barbara had said, and that was very gratifying.

Giles handed him his tall hat and he studied the additional effect. Then he took up his white gloves, remembered to remove his hat again, and stepped out through the door, which Giles opened for him, and entered the corridor, where Gerard and Spendlove, in their best uniforms, were waiting for him.

"I must apologize on behalf of Spendlove and myself for the singing, my lord," said Gerard.

The softening effect of the black dress coat was evident when Hornblower refrained from a rasping reprimand.

"What would Miss Lucy say, Spendlove, if she heard you singing about the dames of France?" he asked.

Spendlove's answering grin was very attractive.

"I must ask your lordship's further indulgence not to tell her about it," he said.

"I'll make that conditional upon your further good behaviour," said Hornblower.

The open carriage was waiting outside the front door of Admiralty House; four seamen stood by with lanterns to add to the light thrown by the lamps on the porch. Hornblower climbed in and seated himself. Etiquette was different here on land; Hornblower missed the shrilling of the pipes that he felt should accompany this ceremonial, as it would if it were a boat he was entering, and in a carriage the senior officer entered first, so that after he was seated, Spendlove and Gerard had to run round and enter by the other door. Gerard sat beside him and Spendlove sat opposite, his back to the horses. As the door shut, the carriage moved forward, between the lanterns at the gate, and out to the pitch-dark Jamaican night. Hornblower breathed the warm tropical air and grudgingly admitted to himself that after all it was no great hardship to attend a ball.

"Perhaps you have a rich marriage in mind, Spendlove?" he asked. "I understand Miss Lucy will inherit it all. But I advise you to make certain before committing yourself that there are no nephews on the father's side."

"A rich marriage might be desirable, my lord," replied Spendlove's voice out of the darkness. "But I must remind you that in affairs of the heart I have been handicapped from birth—or at least from my baptism."

"From your baptism?" repeated Hornblower, puzzled.

"Yes, my lord. You remember my name, perhaps?"

"Erasmus," said Hornblower.

"Exactly, my lord. It is not adapted to endearments. Could any woman fall in love with an Erasmus? Could any woman bring herself to breathe the words 'Razzy, darling'?"

"I fancy it could happen," said Hornblower.

"May I live long enough to hear it," said Spendlove.

It was remarkably agreeable to be driving thus through the Jamaican night behind two good horses and with two pleasant young men; especially, as he told himself smugly, because he had done work satisfactory enough to justify relaxation. His command was in good order, the policing of the Caribbean was proceeding satisfactorily, and smuggling and piracy were being reduced to small proportions. Tonight he had no responsibilities. He was in no danger at all, not any. Danger was far away, over the horizons both of time and space. He could lean back, relaxed, against the leather cushions of the carriage, taking only moderate care not to crease his black dress coat or crumple the careful pleats of his shirt.

Naturally his reception at the Houghs' house was somewhat overpowering. There was a good deal of "my lord" and "his lordship." Hough was a substantial planter, a man of considerable wealth, with enough of dislike for English winters not to be the usual West Indian absentee landlord. Yet for all his wealth he was greatly impressed by the fact that he was entertaining, in one and the same person, a peer and an admiral and a commander-in-chief—and someone whose influence might at any moment be of great importance to him. The warmth of his greeting, and of Mrs. Hough's, was so great that it even overflowed round Gerard and Spendlove as well. Perhaps the Houghs felt that if they wished to be sure of standing well with the commander-in-chief it might be as well to cultivate good relations with his flag lieutenant and secretary too.

Lucy Hough was a pretty enough girl of some seventeen or eighteen years of age whom Hornblower had already met on a few occasions. Hornblower told himself he could feel no interest in a child straight from the schoolroom—almost straight from the nursery—however pretty. He smiled at her and she dropped her eyes, looked up at him again, and once more looked away. It was interesting that she was not nearly so timid when she met the glances and acknowledged the bows of the young men who were far more likely to be of interest to her.

"Your lordship does not dance, I understand?" said Hough.

"It is painful to be reminded of what I am missing in the presence of so much beauty," replied Hornblower with another smile at Mrs. Hough and at Lucy.

"Perhaps a rubber of whist, then, my lord?" suggested Hough.

"The Goddess of Chance instead of the Muse of Music," said Hornblower—he always tried to talk about music as if it meant something to him—"I will woo the one instead of the other."

"From what I know about your lordship's skill at whist," said Hough, "I would say that as regards your lordship, the Goddess of Chance has but small need for wooing."

The ball had been in progress, apparently, for some time before Hornblower's arrival. There were two score young people on the floor of the great room, a dozen dowagers on chairs round the wall, an orchestra in the corner. Hough led the way to another room; Hornblower dismissed his two young men with a nod, and settled down to whist with Hough and a couple of formidable old ladies. The closing of the heavy door shut out, luckily, nearly all the exasperating din of the orchestra; the old ladies played a sound game, and a pleasant enough hour went by. It was terminated by the entrance of Mrs. Hough.

"It is time for the polonaise before supper," she announced. "I really must beg you to leave your cards and come and witness it."

"Would your lordship—?" asked Hough apologetically.

"Mrs. Hough's wish is my command," said Hornblower.

The ballroom was of course stifling hot. Faces were flushed and shiny, but there was no lack of energy apparent as the double line formed up for the polonaise while the orchestra grated out its mysterious noises to encourage the young people. Spendlove was leading Lucy by the hand and they were exchanging happy glances. Hornblower, from the weary age of forty-six, could look with condescension at these young men and women in their immature teens and twenties, tolerant of their youth and enthusiasm. The noises the orchestra made became more jerky and confusing, but the young people could find some sense in them. They capered round the room, skirts swaying and coattails flapping, every one smiling and light-hearted; the double lines became rings, melted into lines again, turned and reformed, until in the end with a final hideous crash from the orchestra the women sank low in curtseys and the men bent themselves double before them—a pretty sight once the music had ceased. There was a burst of laughter and applause before the lines broke up. The women, with sidelong looks at each other, gathered into groups which edged out of the room. They were retiring to repair the damages sustained in the heat of action.

Hornblower met Lucy's eyes again, and once more she looked away and then back at him. Shy? Eager? It was hard to tell with these mere children; but it was not the sort of glance she had bestowed on Spendlove.

"Ten minutes at least before the supper march, my lord," said Hough. "Your lordship will be kind enough to take in Mrs. Hough?"

"Delighted, of course," replied Hornblower.

Spendlove approached. He was mopping his face with his handkerchief.

"I would enjoy a breath of cooler air, my lord," he said. "Perhaps—"

"I'll come with you," said Hornblower, not sorry to have an excuse to be rid of Hough's ponderous company.

They stepped out into the dark garden; so bright had been the candles in the ballroom that they had to tread cautiously at first.

"I trust you are enjoying yourself," said Hornblower.

"Very much indeed, thank you, my lord."

"And your suit is making progress?"

"Of that I am not so sure, my lord."

"You have my best wishes in any case."

"Thank you, my lord."

Hornblower's eyes were more accustomed now to the darkness. He could see the stars now when he looked up. Sirius was visible, resuming once more his eternal chase of Orion across the night sky. The air was warm and still with the cessation of the sea breeze.

Then it happened. Hornblower heard a movement behind him, a rustling of foliage, but before he could pay attention to it hands gripped his arms, a hand came over his mouth. He began to struggle. A sharp burning pain under his right shoulder made him jump.

"Quiet," said a voice, a thick heavy voice. "Or this."

He felt the pain again. It was a knife point in his back, and he held himself still. The unseen hands began to hustle him away; there were at least three men round him. His nose told him they were sweating—with excitement, perhaps.

"Spendlove?" he said.

"Quiet," said the voice again.

He was being hustled down the long garden. A momentary sharp cry, instantly stifled, presumably came from Spendlove behind him. Hornblower had difficulty in preserving his balance as he was hurried along, but the arms that held him sustained him; when he stumbled he could feel the pressure of the knife point against his back sharpen into pain as it pierced his clothes. At the far end of the garden they emerged into a narrow path where a darkness loomed up in the night. Hornblower bumped into something that snorted and moved—a mule, apparently.

"Get on," said the voice beside him.

Hornblower hesitated, and felt the knife against his ribs.

"Get on," said the voice; someone else was wheeling the mule round again for him to mount.

There were neither stirrups nor saddle. Hornblower put his hands on the withers and hauled himself up astride the mule. He could find no reins, although he heard the chink of a bit. He buried his fingers in the scanty mane. All round him he could hear a bustle as the other mules were mounted. His own mule started with something of a jerk that made him cling wildly to the mane. Someone had mounted the mule ahead and was riding forward with a leading rein attached to his mule. There seemed to be four mules altogether, and some eight men. The mules began to trot, and Hornblower felt himself tossed about precariously on the slippery back of the mule, but there was a man running on each side of him helping to keep him on his perch. A second or two later they slowed down again as the leading mule turned a difficult corner.

"Who are you?" demanded Hornblower, with the first breath that the motion had not shaken out of his body.

The man by his right knee waved something at him, something

bright enough to shine in the starlight. It was a cutlass—the machete of the West Indies.

"Quiet," he said. "Or I cut off your leg."

The next moment the mule broke into a trot again, and Hornblower could have said no more even if he were inclined to do so. Mules and men hurried along a path between great fields of cane, with Hornblower bouncing about on the mule's back. He tried to look up at the stars to see which way they were going, but it was difficult, and they altered course repeatedly, winding about over the countryside. They left the cane behind, and seemed to emerge into open savannah. Then there were trees; then they slowed down for a sharp ascent, broke into a trot again down the other side—the men on foot running tirelessly beside the mules—and climbed again, the mules slipping and plunging on what appeared to be an insecure surface. Twice Hornblower nearly fell off, to be heaved back again by the man beside him. Soon he was atrociously saddlesore—if the word could be considered appropriate when he was riding bareback —and the ridge of the mule's spine caused him agony. He was drenched with sweat, his mouth was parched, and he was desperately weary. He grew stupefied with misery, despite the pain he suffered. More than once they splashed across small streams roaring down from the mountains; again they made their way through a belt of trees. Several times they seemed to be threading narrow passes.

Hornblower had no idea how long they had been travelling when they found themselves beside a small river, seemingly placid as it reflected the stars. On the far side, faint in the darkness, towered a lofty cliff. Here the party halted, and the man beside him tugged at his knee in an obvious invitation to dismount. Hornblower slid down the mule's side—he had to lean against the animal for a moment when his legs refused to hold him up. When he was able to stand upright and look about him, he saw a white face among the dark ones that surrounded him. He could just make out Spendlove, his knees sagging and his head lolling as he stood supported on either side.

"Spendlove!" he said.

There was an agonizing moment of waiting before the drooping figure said, "My lord?" The voice was thick and unnatural.

"Spendlove! Are you wounded?"

"I'm—well—my lord."

Someone pushed Hornblower in the back.

"Come. Swim," said a voice.

"Spendlove!"

Several hands turned Hornblower away and thrust him stumbling down to the water's edge. It was hopeless to resist; Hornblower could only guess that Spendlove had been stunned by a blow and was only now recovering, his unconscious body having been carried so far by mule.

"Swim," said the voice, and a hand pressed him forward to the water.

"No!" croaked Hornblower.

The water seemed immeasurably wide and dark. Even while Hornblower struggled at the water's edge he had a horrible realization of the indignity he was undergoing, as a commander-in-chief, acting like a child in the hands of these people. Somebody led a mule slowly down into the water beside him.

"Hold his tail," said the voice, and there was the knife in his back again.

He took hold of the mule's tail and despairingly let himself flop into the water, spread-eagled. For a moment the mule floundered and then struck out; the water, as it closed round Hornblower, seemed hardly colder than the warm air. It was no more than a moment, it seemed, before the mule was plunging up the other bank, and Hornblower found the bottom under his feet and waded out after him, the water streaming from his clothes, the rest of the gang and the animals splashing after him. The hand was back on his shoulder, turning him to one side and urging him along. He heard an odd creaking in front of him and a swaying object struck him on the chest. His hands felt smooth bamboo and some sort of creeper, liana, knotted to it—it was a makeshift rope ladder dangling in front of him.

"Up!" said the voice. "Up!"

He could not—he would not—and there was the knife point at his back again. He stretched his arms up and grasped a rung, feeling desperately with his feet for another.

"Up!"

He began the climb, with the ladder writhing under his feet in the animal fashion rope ladders always display. It was horrible in the darkness, feeling with his feet for each elusive rung in turn, clutching desperately with his hands. His sodden shoes tended to slip on the smooth bamboo. Nor did his hands feel secure on the creeper. Someone else was climbing close after him, and the ladder

twined about unpredictably. He knew himself to be swaying pendu-
lum-fashion in the darkness. Up he went, one rung at a time, his
hands gripping so convulsively that it was only by a conscious effort
that he was able to make each one unclasp in turn and seek a fresh
hold. Then the gyrations and swinging grew less. His upward-
stretching hand touched earth, or rock. The next moment was not
easy; he was unsure of his handhold and he hesitated. He knew
himself to be a prodigious height up in the air. Just below him on
the ladder he heard a sharp command issued by the man following
him, and then a hand above him grasped his wrist and pulled. His
feet found the next rung, and there he was, lying on his belly on
solid earth, gasping. The hand dragged at him again and he crawled
on all fours forward to make room for the man behind him. He was
almost sobbing; there was no trace left now of the haughty and self-
satisfied human who had admired himself in the mirror not so many
hours ago.

Other people trod past him.

"My lord! My lord!"

That was Spendlove asking for him.

"Spendlove!" he answered, sitting up.

"Are you all right, my lord?" asked Spendlove, stooping over him.

Was it sense of humour or sense of the ridiculous, was it natural
pride or force of habit which made him take a grip on himself?

"As right as I might expect to be, thank you, after these rather remarkable experiences," he said. "But you—what happened to you?"

"They hit me on the head," replied Spendlove simply.

"Don't stand there. Sit down," said Hornblower, and Spendlove
collapsed beside him.

"Do you know where we are, my lord?" he asked.

"Somewhere at the top of a cliff, as far as I can estimate," said
Hornblower.

"But where, my lord?"

"Somewhere in His Majesty's loyal colony of Jamaica. More than
that I can't say."

"It will be dawn soon, I suppose," said Spendlove weakly.

"Soon enough."

Nobody about them was paying them any attention. There was
a great deal of chatter going on, in marked contrast with the silence
—the almost disciplined silence—which had been preserved during
their dash across-country. The chatter mingled with the sound of a

small waterfall, which he realized he had been hearing ever since his climb. The conversations were in a thick English which Hornblower could hardly understand, but he could be sure that their captors were expressing exultation. He could hear women's voices, too, while figures paced about, too excited to sit down despite the fatigues of the night.

"I doubt if we're at the top of the cliff, my lord, if you'll pardon me," said Spendlove.

He pointed upwards. The sky was growing pale, and the stars were fading; vertically over their heads they could see the cliff above them, overhanging them. Looking up, Hornblower could see foliage silhouetted against the sky.

"Strange," he said. "We must be on some sort of shelf."

On his right hand the sky was showing a hint of light, of the palest pink, even while on his left it was still dark.

"Facing north—nor'west," said Spendlove.

The light increased perceptibly; when Hornblower looked to the east again the pink had turned to orange, and there was a hint of green. They seemed immeasurably high up; almost at their feet, it seemed, as they sat, the shelf ended abruptly, and far down below them the shadowy world was taking form, concealed at the moment by a light mist. Hornblower was suddenly conscious of his wet clothes, and shivered.

"That might be the sea," said Spendlove, pointing.

The sea it was, blue and lovely in the far distance; a broad belt of land, some miles across, extended between the cliff on which they were perched and the edge of the sea; the mist still obscured it. Hornblower rose to his feet, took a step forward, leaning over a low crude parapet of piled rock; he shrank back before nerving himself to look again. Under his feet there was nothing. They were indeed on a shelf in the face of the cliff—about the height of a frigate's main yard, sixty feet or so. Vertically below them he could see the small stream he had crossed holding the mule's tail; the rope ladder still hung down from where he stood to the water's edge; when, with an effort of will, he forced himself to lean out and look over he could see the mules standing dispiritedly below him in the narrow area between the river and the foot of the cliff; the overhang must be considerable. They were on a shelf in a cliff, undercut through the ages by the river below when in spate. Nothing could reach them from above, and nothing from below if the ladder were to be drawn up. The shelf was perhaps ten yards wide at its widest, and perhaps a hundred yards long. At one end the waterfall he had heard tumbled down the cliff face in a groove it had cut for itself; it splashed against a cluster of gleaming rocks and then leaped out again. The sight of it told him how thirsty he was, and he walked along to it. It was a giddy thing to do, to stand there with the cliff face at one elbow and a vertical drop under the other, with the spray bursting round him, but he could fill his cupped hands with water and drink, and drink again, before splashing his face and head refreshingly. He drew back to find Spendlove waiting for him to finish. Matted in Spendlove's thick hair and behind his left ear and down his neck was a black clot of blood. Spendlove knelt to drink and to wash, and rose again touching his scalp cautiously.

"They spared me nothing," he said.

His uniform was spattered with blood too. At his waist dangled an empty scabbard; his sword was missing, and as they turned back from the waterfall they could see it—it was in the hand of one of their captors, who was standing waiting for them. He was short and square and heavily built, not entirely Negro, possibly as much as half white. He wore a dirty white shirt and loose ragged blue trousers, with dilapidated buckled shoes on his splay feet.

"Now, lord," he said.

He spoke with the Island intonation, with a thickening of the vowels and a slurring of the consonants.

"What do you want?" demanded Hornblower, putting all the rasp into his voice that he could manage.

"Write us a letter," said the man with the sword.

"A letter? To whom?"

"To the governor."

"Asking him to come and hang you?" asked Hornblower.

The man shook his big head.

"No. I want a paper, a paper with a seal on it. A pardon. For us all. With a seal on it."

"Who are you?"

"Ned Johnson." The name meant nothing to Hornblower, nor, as a glance showed, did it mean anything to the omniscient Spendlove.

"I sailed with Harkness," said Johnson.

"Ah!"

That meant something to both the British officers. Harkness was one of the last of the petty pirates. Hardly more than a week ago his sloop *Blossom* had been cut off by the *Clorinda* off Savanna-la-Mar, and her escape to leeward intercepted. Under long-range fire from the frigate she had despairingly run herself aground at the mouth of the Sweet River, and her crew had escaped into the marshes and mangrove swamps of that section of coast, all except her captain, whose body had been found on her deck almost cut in two by a round shot from *Clorinda*. This was her crew, left leaderless—unless Johnson could be called their leader—and to hunt them down the governor had called out two battalions of troops as soon as *Clorinda* beat back to Kingston with the news. It was to cut off their escape by sea that the governor, at Hornblower's suggestion, had posted guards at every fishing beach in the whole big island—otherwise the cycle they had already probably followed would be removed, with the theft of a fishing boat, the capture of a large craft, and so on until they were a pest again.

"There's no pardon for pirates," said Hornblower.

"Yes," said Johnson. "Write us a letter, and the governor will give us one."

He turned aside and from the foot of the cliff at the back of the shelf he picked up something. It was a leather-bound book—the second volume of *Waverley*, Hornblower saw when it was put in his hands—and Johnson produced a stub of pencil and gave him that as well.

"Write to the governor," he said; he opened the book at the beginning and indicated the flyleaf as the place to write on.

"What do you think I would write?" asked Hornblower.

"Ask him for a pardon for us. With his seal on it."

Apparently Johnson must have heard somewhere, in talk with fellow pirates, of "a pardon under the Great Seal," and the memory had lingered.

"The governor would never do that."

"Then I send him your ears. Then I send him your nose," said Johnson.

That was a horrible thing to hear. Hornblower glanced at Spendlove, who had turned white at the words.

"You the admiral," continued Johnson. "You the lord. The governor will do that."

"I doubt if he would," said Hornblower.

He conjured up in his mind the picture of fussy old General Sir Augustus Hooper, and tried to imagine the reaction produced by

Johnson's demand. His Excellency would come near to bursting a blood vessel at the thought of granting pardons to two dozen pirates. The home government, when it heard the news, would be intensely annoyed, and without doubt most of the annoyance would be directed at the man whose idiocy in allowing himself to be kidnapped had put everyone in this absurd position. That suggested a question.

"How did you come to be in the garden?" he asked.

"We was waiting for you to go home, but you came out first."

If they had been intending—

"Stand back!" yelled Johnson.

He leaped backwards with astonishing agility for his bulk, bracing himself, knees bent, body tense, on guard with the sword. Hornblower looked round in astonishment, in time to see Spendlove relax; he had been poising himself for a spring. With that sword in his hand and its point against Johnson's throat, the position would have been reversed. Some of the others came running up at the cry; one of them had a staff in his hand—a headless pike stave apparently —and thrust it cruelly into Spendlove's face. Spendlove staggered back, and the staff was whirled up to strike him down. Hornblower leaped in front of him.

"No!" he yelled, and they all stood looking at each other, the drama of the situation ebbing away. Then one of the men came sidling towards Hornblower, cutlass in hand.

"Cut off his ear?" he asked over his shoulder to Johnson.

"No. Not yet. Sit down, you two." When they hesitated Johnson's voice rose to a roar. "Sit down!"

Under the menace of the cutlass there was nothing to do but sit down, and they were helpless.

"You write that letter?" asked Johnson.

"Wait a little," said Hornblower wearily; he could think of nothing else to say in that situation. He was playing for time, hopelessly, like a child at bedtime confronted by stern guardians.

"Let's have some breakfast," said Spendlove.

At the far end of the shelf a small fire had been lighted, its smoke clinging in the still dawn in a thin thread to the sloping overhang of the cliff. An iron pot hung from a chain attached to a tripod over the fire, and two women were crouching over it attending to it. Packed against the back wall of the shelf were chests and kegs and barrels. Muskets were ranged in a rack. It occurred to Hornblower that he was in the situation common in popular romances; he was in the pirates' lair. Perhaps those chests contained untold treasures of pearls and gold. Pirates, like any other seafarers, needed a land base, and these pirates had established one here instead of on some lonely cay. His brig *Clement* had cleaned out one of those last year.

"You write that letter, lord," said Johnson. He poked at Hornblower's breast with the sword, and the point pierced the thin shirt front to prick him over the breastbone.

"What is it you want?" asked Hornblower.

"A pardon. With a seal."

Hornblower studied the swarthy features in front of him. The jig was up for piracy in the Caribbean, he knew. American ships of war in the north, French ships of war working from the Lesser Antilles, and his own busy squadron based on Jamaica had made the business both unprofitable and dangerous. And this particular band of pirates, the remains of the Harkness gang, were in a more precarious position than any, with the loss of their ship, and with their escape to sea cut off by his precautions. It had been a bold plan, and well executed, to save their necks by kidnapping him. Presumably the plan had been made and executed by this rather stupid-seeming fellow, almost bewildered in appearance, before him. Appearances might be deceitful, or else the desperate need of the situation had stimulated that dull mind into unusual activity.

"You hear me?" said Johnson, offering another prick with the sword, and breaking in upon Hornblower's train of thought.

"Say you will, my lord," muttered Spendlove close to Hornblower's ear. "Gain time."

Johnson turned on him, sword pointed at his face.

"Shut that mouth," he said. Another idea occurred to him, and he glanced round at Hornblower. "You write. Or I prick his eye."

"I'll write," said Hornblower.

Now he sat with the volume of *Waverley* open at the flyleaf, and the stub of pencil in his hand, while Johnson withdrew for a couple of paces, presumably to allow free play for inspiration. What was he to write? "Dear Sir Augustus"? "Your Excellency"? That was better. "I am held to ransom here along with Spendlove by the survivors of the Harkness gang. Perhaps the bearer of this will explain the conditions. They demand a free pardon in exchange for—" Hornblower held the pencil poised over the paper debating the next words. "Our lives"? He shook his head to himself and wrote "our freedom." He wanted no melodrama. "Your Excellency will of course be a better judge of the situation than I am. Your ob'd't servant." Hornblower hesitated again, and then he dashed off the "Hornblower" of his signature.

"There you are," he said, holding out the volume to Johnson, who took it and looked at it curiously, and turned back to the group of a dozen or so of his followers who had been squatting on the ground behind him silently watching the proceedings.

They peered at the writing over Johnson's shoulder; others came to look as well, and they fell into a chattering debate.

"Not one of them can read, my lord," commented Spendlove.

"So it appears."

The pirates were looking from the writing over to their prisoners and back again; the argument grew more intense. Johnson seemed to be expostulating, or exhorting, and some of the men he addressed drew back shaking their heads.

"It's a question of who shall carry that note to Kingston," said Hornblower. "Who shall beard the lion."

"That fellow has no command over his men," commented Spendlove. "Harkness would have shot a couple of them by now."

Johnson returned to them, pointing a dark stubby finger at the writing.

"What you say here?" he asked.

Hornblower read the note aloud; it did not matter whether he spoke the truth or not, seeing they had no way of knowing. Johnson stared at him, studying his face; Johnson's own face betrayed more of the bewilderment Hornblower had noticed before. The pirate was facing a situation too complex for him; he was trying to carry out a plan which he had not thought out in all its details beforehand. No one of the pirates was willing to venture into the grip of justice bearing a message of unknown content. Nor, for that matter, would the pirates trust one of their number to go off on such a mission; he might well desert, throwing away the precious message, to try to make his escape on his own. The poor, ragged, shiftless devils and their slatternly women were in a quandary, with no master mind to find a way out for them. Hornblower could have laughed at their predicament, and almost did, until he thought of what this unstable mob could do in a fit of passion to the prisoners in their power. The debate went on furiously, with a solution apparently no nearer.

"Do you think we could get to the ladder, my lord?" asked Spendlove, and then answered his own question. "No. They'd catch us before we could get away. A pity."

"We can bear the possibility in mind," said Hornblower.

One of the women cooking over the fire called out at this moment in a loud raucous voice, interrupting the debate. Food was being ladled out into wooden bowls. A young mulatto woman, hardly more than a child, in a ragged gown that had once been magnificent, brought a bowl over to them—one bowl, no spoon or fork. They stared at each other, unable to keep from smiling. Then Spendlove produced a penknife from his breeches pocket, and tendered it to his superior after opening it.

"Perhaps it may serve, my lord," he said apologetically, adding, after a glance at the contents of the bowl, "Not such a good meal as the supper we missed at the Houghs', my lord."

Boiled yams and a trifle of boiled salt pork, the former presumably stolen from some slave garden and the latter from one of the hogsheads stored here on the cliff. They ate with difficulty, Hornblower insisting on their using the penknife turn about, juggling with the hot food for which both of them discovered a raging appetite. The pirates and the women were mostly squatting on their heels as they ate. After their first mouthfuls they were beginning to argue again over the use to be made of their prisoners.

Hornblower looked out again from the shelf at the view extended before them.

"That must be the Cockpit Country," he said.

"No doubt of it, my lord."

The Cockpit Country was territory unknown to any white man, an independent republic in the northwest of Jamaica. At the conquest of the island from the Spaniards, a century and a half earlier, the British had found this area already populated by runaway slaves and the survivors of the Indian population. Several attempts to subdue the area had failed disastrously—yellow fever and the appalling difficulty of the country allying themselves with the desperate valour of the defenders—and a treaty had finally been concluded granting independence to the Cockpit Country on the sole condition that the inhabitants should not harbour runaway slaves in future. That treaty had already endured fifty years and seemed likely to endure far longer. The pirates' lair was on the edge of this area, with the mountains at the back of it.

"And that's Montego Bay, my lord," said Spendlove, pointing.

Hornblower had visited the place in *Clorinda* last year—a lonely roadstead providing fair anchorage, and shelter for a few fishing boats. He gazed over to the distant blue water with longing. He tried to think of ways of escape, of some method of coming to honourable terms with the pirates, but a night entirely without sleep made his brain sluggish, and now that he had eaten, it was more sluggish still. He caught himself nodding and pulled himself up with a jerk. Now that he was in his middle forties the loss of a night's sleep was a serious matter, especially when the night had been filled with violent and unaccustomed exertion.

Spendlove had seen him nod.

"I think you could sleep, my lord," he said gently.

"Perhaps I could."

He let his body sink to the hard ground. He was pillowless and uncomfortable.

"Here, my lord," said Spendlove.

Two hands on his shoulders eased him round, and now he was pillowed on Spendlove's thigh. The world whirled round him for a moment. There was the whisper of a breeze; the loud debate of the pirates and their women was monotonous in pitch; the waterfall was splashing and gurgling; then he was asleep.

He awoke some time later, with Spendlove touching his shoulder.

"My lord, my lord."

He lifted his head, a little surprised to find where it had been resting; it took him several seconds to recall where he was and how he had come there. Johnson and one or two other pirates were standing before him; in the background one of the women was looking on, in an attitude that conveyed the impression that she had contributed to the conclusion that had evidently been reached.

"We send you to the governor, lord," said Johnson.

Hornblower blinked up at him; although the sun had moved round behind the cliff the sky above was dazzling.

"*You*," said Johnson. "*You* go. We keep *him*."

Johnson indicated Spendlove by a gesture.

"What do you mean?" asked Hornblower.

"*You* go to the governor and get our pardon," said Johnson. "You can ask him, and he will give it. *He* stays here. We can cut off his nose, we can dig out his eyes."

"Good God Almighty," said Hornblower.

Johnson or his advisers—perhaps that woman over there—were

people of considerable insight after all. They had some conception of honour, of gentlemanly obligations. They had perceived something of the relationship between Hornblower and Spendlove—they may have been guided by the sight of Hornblower sleeping with his head pillowed on Spendlove's thigh. They knew that Hornblower could never abandon Spendlove to the mercy of his captors, that he would do everything possible to obtain his freedom. Even perhaps —Hornblower's imagination surged in a great wave over the barrier of his sleepiness—even perhaps to the extent of coming back to share Spendlove's captivity and fate in the event of not being able to obtain the necessary pardons.

"We send you, lord," said Johnson.

The woman in the background said something in a loud voice.

"We send you now," said Johnson. "Get up."

Hornblower rose slowly; he would have taken his time in any case in an effort to preserve what dignity was left to him, but he could not have risen swiftly if he had wanted to. His joints were stiff—he could almost hear them crack as he moved. His body ached horribly.

"These two men take you," said Johnson.

Spendlove had risen to his feet too.

"Are you all right, my lord?" he asked anxiously.

"Only stiff and rheumaticky," replied Hornblower. "But what about you?"

"Oh, I'm all right, my lord. Please don't give another thought to me, my lord."

That was a very straight glance that Spendlove gave him, a glance that tried to convey a message.

"Not another thought, my lord," repeated Spendlove.

He was trying to tell his chief that he should be abandoned, that nothing should be done to ransom him, that he was willing to suffer whatever tortures might be inflicted on him so long as his chief came well out of the business.

"I'll be thinking about you all the time," said Hornblower, giving back glance for glance.

"Hurry," said Johnson.

The rope ladder still dangled down from the lip of the shelf. It was a tricky business to lower himself with his creaking joints over the edge and to find foothold on the slippery bamboo rungs. The ladder swung away under the thrust of his feet as if it were a live thing determined to cast him down; he clung with frantic hands,

back downward, forcing himself, against his instincts, to straighten
up and allow the ladder to swing back again. Gingerly his feet found
foothold again, and he continued his descent. Just as he grew accustomed to the motion of the ladder his rhythm was disturbed by
the first of his escorts lowering himself upon the ladder above him;
he had to cling and wait again before he resumed his downward
progress. His feet had hardly gratefully touched ground than first
one and then the other of his escorts dropped beside him.

"Good-bye, my lord. Good luck!"

That was Spendlove calling from above. Hornblower, standing on
the very edge of the river, his face towards the cliff, had to bend
far backwards to see Spendlove's head over the parapet and his waving hand, sixty feet above. He waved back as his escorts led the
mules to the water's edge.

Once more it was necessary to swim the river. It was no more than
thirty feet across; he could have swum it last night without assistance
had he been sure about that in the darkness. Now he let himself
flop into the water, clothes and all—alas for that beautiful black dress
coat—and, turning on his back, kicked out with his legs. But his
clothes were already wet and were a ponderous burden to him, and
he knew a moment of worry before his already weary limbs carried
him to the rocky bank. He crawled out, the water streaming from
his clothes, unwilling to move even while the mules came plunging
up out of the water beside him. Spendlove up above, still leaning
over the parapet, waved to him again.

Now it was a question of mounting a mule again. His wet clothes
weighed upon him like lead. He had to struggle up—the animal's
wet hide was slippery—and as soon as he settled himself astride he
realized that he was horribly saddlesore from the night before, and
the raw surfaces caused him agony. He had to brace himself to endure it; it was dreadfully painful as his mount plunged about, making his way over the irregular surface. From the river they made an
abrupt ascent into the mountains. They were retracing the path they
had taken the night before; hardly a path, hardly a track. They
picked their way up a steep gully, down the other side, up again.
They splashed across little torrents, and wound their way among
trees. Hornblower was numb both in body and mind by now; his
mule was weary and by no means as sure of foot as a mule should
be, stumbling more than once so that only by frantic efforts could he
retain his seat. The sun was sinking towards the west as they jolted

on, downhill at last. Passage through a final belt of trees brought them into open country upon which the sun blazed in tropical glory. This was savannah country, hardly rocky at all; there were cattle to be seen in the distance, and, beyond, a great sea of green—the vast sugar-cane fields of Jamaica stretching as far as the eye could see. Half a mile farther they reached a well-defined track, and there his escorts checked their mounts.

"Now you can go on," said one of them, pointing along the path winding towards the distant cane.

It was a second or two before Hornblower's stupefied brain could grasp the fact that they were turning him loose.

"That way?" he asked, unnecessarily.

"Yes," said his escort.

The two men turned their mules; Hornblower had to struggle with his, who disliked the separation. One of the escorts struck the brute on the rump, sending him down the path in a jerky trot acutely painful to Hornblower as he sought to retain his seat. Soon the mule eased to a leg-weary walk, and Hornblower was content to sit idly as it crawled along down the path; the sun was now clouded over and it was not long before, heralded by a brisk wind, a blinding rain began to fall, blotting out the landscape and slowing the mule even more on the slippery surface. Hornblower sat exhausted on the sharp spine of the animal; so heavy was the rain that he found it difficult to breathe as it poured upon his face.

Gradually the roaring rain ceased; the sky, while it remained overcast above him, opened to the west and admitted a gleam of the setting sun, so that the landscape on his left was made glorious with a rainbow which Hornblower hardly noted. Here was the first cane field; the track he was following became here a rough and narrow roadway through the cane, deeply rutted by cartwheels. The mule plodded on, eternally, through the cane. Now the road crossed another, and the mule pulled up at the crossroads. Before Hornblower could rouse himself to urge the mule onwards he heard a shout to his right. Far down the road he saw a group of horsemen illuminated against the sunset. With an urgent drumming of hoofs they came galloping towards him, and reined up at his side—a white man followed by two Negroes.

"It's Lord Hornblower, isn't it?" asked the white man—a young fellow; Hornblower noticed dully that, although mounted, he was still in full-dress clothes with his ruffled neckcloth all awry and bedraggled.

"Yes," said Hornblower.

"Thank God, you're safe, sir," said the young man. "Are you hurt? Are you wounded, my lord?"

"No," said Hornblower, swaying with fatigue on the back of the mule.

The young man turned to one of his Negro companions and issued rapid orders, and the Negro wheeled his horse round and went galloping full pelt down the road.

"The whole island has been turned out to seek for you, my lord," said the young man. "What happened to you? We have searched for you all day."

It would never do for an admiral, a commander-in-chief, to betray unmanly weakness. Hornblower made himself stiffen his spine.

"I was kidnapped by pirates," he said. He tried to speak nonchalantly, as if that was something that could happen to anyone any day, but it was difficult. His voice was only a hoarse croak. "I must go at once to the governor. Where is His Excellency?"

"He must be at Government House, I fancy," said the young man. "No more than thirty miles away."

Thirty miles! Hornblower felt as if he could not ride another thirty yards.

"Very well," he said stiffly. "I must go there."

"The Hough house is only two miles down the road here, my lord," said the young man. "Your carriage is still there, I believe. I have already sent a messenger."

"We'll go there first, then," said Hornblower, as indifferently as he could manage.

A word from the white man brought the other Negro from his horse, and Hornblower slid ungracefully from the mule. It was an enormous effort to get his foot up into the stirrup; the Negro had to help him heave his right leg over. He had hardly gathered the reins in his hands—he had not yet discovered which was which—when the white man put his horse into a trot and Hornblower's mount followed him. It was torture to bump about in the saddle.

"My name is Colston," said the white man, checking his horse so that Hornblower came up alongside him. "I had the honour of being presented to your lordship at the ball last night."

"Of course," said Hornblower. "Tell me what happened there."

"You were missed, my lord, after the supper march had been kept waiting for you to head it with Mrs. Hough. You and your secretary, Mr.—Mr.—"

"Spendlove," said Hornblower.

"Yes, my lord. At first it was thought that some urgent business was demanding your attention. It was not for an hour or two, I suppose, that your flag lieutenant and Mr. Hough could agree that you had been spirited away. There was great distress among the company, my lord."

"Yes?"

"Then the alarm was given. All the gentlemen present rode out in search for you. The militia was called out at dawn. The whole countryside is being patrolled. I expect the Highland Regiment is in full march for here at this moment."

"Indeed?" said Hornblower. A thousand infantrymen were making a forced march of thirty miles on his account; a thousand horsemen were scouring the island.

Hoofbeats sounded in front of them. Two horsemen approached in the gathering darkness; Hornblower could just recognize Hough and the messenger.

"Thank God, my lord," said Hough. "What happened?"

Hornblower was tempted to answer, "Mr. Colston will tell you," but he made himself make a more sensible reply. Hough uttered the expected platitudes.

"I must go on to the governor at once," said Hornblower. "There is Spendlove to think of."

"Spendlove, my lord? Oh, yes, of course, your secretary."

"He is still in the hands of the pirates," said Hornblower.

"Indeed, my lord?" replied Hough.

No one seemed to have a care about Spendlove, except Lucy Hough, presumably.

Here was the house and the courtyard; lights were gleaming in every window.

"Please come in, my lord," said Hough. "Your lordship must be in need of refreshment."

He had eaten yams and salt pork some time that morning; he felt no hunger now.

"I must go on to Government House," he said. "I can waste no time."

"If your lordship insists—"

"Yes," said Hornblower.

"I will go and have the horses put to, then, my lord."

Hornblower found himself alone in the brightly lit sitting room. He felt that if he threw himself into one of the vast chairs there he would never get up again.

"My lord! My lord!"

It was Lucy Hough fluttering into the room, her skirts flying with her haste. He would have to tell her about Spendlove.

"Oh, you're safe! You're safe!"

What was this? The girl had flung herself on her knees before him. She had one of his hands in both hers, and was kissing it frantically. He drew back, he tried to snatch his hand away, but she clung on to it, and followed him on her knees, still kissing it.

"Miss Lucy!"

"I care for nothing as long as you're safe!" she said, looking up at him and still clasping his hand; tears were streaming down her cheeks. "I've been through torment today. You're not hurt? Tell me! Speak to me!"

This was horrible. She was pressing her lips, her cheek, against his hand again.

"Miss Lucy! Please! Compose yourself!"

How could a girl of seventeen act like this towards a man of forty-six? Was she not enamoured of Spendlove? But perhaps that was the person she was thinking about.

"I will see that Mr. Spendlove is safe," he said.

"Mr. Spendlove? I hope he's safe. But it's you—you—you—"

"Miss Lucy! You must not say these things! Stand up, please, I beg you!"

Somehow he got her to her feet.

"I couldn't bear it!" she said. "I've loved you since the moment I saw you!"

"There, there!" said Hornblower, as soothingly as he knew how.

"The carriage will be ready in two minutes, my lord," said Hough's voice from the door. "A glass of wine and a bite before you start?"

Hough came in with a smile.

"Thank you, sir," said Hornblower, struggling with embarrassment.

"This child has been in a rare way since this morning," said Hough indulgently. "These young people— She was the only person in the island, I fancy, who gave a thought to the secretary as well as to the commander-in-chief."

"Er—yes. These young people," said Hornblower.

The butler entered with a tray at that moment.

"Pour his lordship a glass of wine, Lucy, my dear," said Hough, and then to Hornblower, "Mrs. Hough has been considerably prostrated, but she will be down in a moment."

"Please do not discommode her, I beg of you," said Hornblower. His hand was shaking as he reached for the glass. Hough took up carving knife and fork and set about carving the cold chicken.

"Excuse me, please," said Lucy.

She turned and ran from the room as quickly as she had entered it, sobbing wildly.

"I had no idea the attachment was so strong," said Hough.

"Nor had I," said Hornblower. He had gulped down the whole glass of wine in his agitation. He addressed himself to the cold chicken with all the calm he could muster.

"The carriage is at the door, sir," announced the butler.

"I'll take these with me," said Hornblower, a slice of bread in one hand and a chicken wing in the other. "Would it be troubling you too much to ask you to send a messenger ahead of me to warn His Excellency of my coming?"

"That has already been done, my lord," answered Hough. "And I have sent out messengers to inform the patrols that you are safe."

Hornblower sank into the cushioned ease of the carriage. The incident with Lucy had at least had the effect of temporarily driving all thought of fatigue from his mind. Now he could lean back and relax; it was five minutes before he remembered the bread and chicken in his hands and set himself wearily to eat them. The long drive was not particularly restful, for there were continual interruptions. Patrols who had not heard that he was safe stopped the carriage. Ten miles down the road they encountered the Highland battalion encamped at the roadside and the colonel insisted on coming and paying his respects to the naval commander-in-chief and congratulating him. Farther on, a galloping horse reined up beside the carriage; it was Gerard. The light of the carriage lamp revealed that he had ridden his horse into a lather. Hornblower had to listen to him say, "Thank God, you are safe, my lord"—everyone used those same words—and explain to him what had happened. Gerard abandoned his horse at the first opportunity and got into the carriage beside Hornblower. He was full of self-reproach at having allowed this to happen to his chief—Hornblower rather resented the implication that he was incapable of looking after himself, even though the event seemed to prove it—and at not having rescued him.

"We tried to use the bloodhounds they track runaway slaves with, my lord, but they were of no use."

"Naturally, since I was on muleback," said Hornblower. "In any case the scent must have been several hours old. Now forget the past and let me think about the future."

"We'll have those pirates dangling on ropes before two days are up, my lord."

"Indeed? And what about Spendlove?"

"Oh—er. Yes, of course, my lord."

Spendlove was very much of an afterthought with everyone, even with Gerard, who was his friend. But to Gerard must be given the credit at least for appreciating Hornblower's difficulty the moment it was pointed out to him.

"We can't let anything happen to him, of course, my lord."

"And how do we prevent it? Do we grant those pardons—do we persuade His Excellency to grant them?"

"Well, my lord—"

"There's nothing I would not do to set Spendlove free," said Hornblower. "Do you understand that? Nothing!"

Hornblower caught himself setting his jaw in grim determination; his ineradicable tendency to self-analysis revealed him to himself. He was cynically surprised at his own flow of emotion. Ferocity and tenderness intermingled; let those pirates touch one hair of Spendlove's head and—but how was he to prevent it? How to free Spendlove from men who knew that their lives, their actual lives and not merely their fortunes, depended on keeping him prisoner? How could he ever live with himself if anything were to happen to Spendlove? If the worst came to the worst he would have to go back to the pirates and yield himself up to them, as that Roman—Regulus—returned to death at the hands of the Carthaginians; and the worst seemed likely to come to the worst.

"Government House, my lord," said Gerard, breaking in upon this train of nightmare thoughts.

Sentries at the gates, sentries at the door. A brightly lit entrance hall, where aides-de-camp looked at him curiously, curse them. So did Gerard. He was ushered through into an inner room, where after only a moment another door opened to admit His Excellency, and the escorting aide-de-camp discreetly retired. His Excellency was an angry man, angry as a man can only be who has been badly scared.

"Now, what is all this, my lord?"

There was none of the usual deference displayed towards the man who had attained a peerage, the man of legendary fame. Hooper was a full general, far above a mere rear admiral; moreover, as governor he was absolute ruler throughout this island. His red face and bulging blue eyes—as well as the rage he was displaying—seemed to confirm the rumour that he was a grandson of the royal blood. Hornblower explained briefly and quietly what had happened; his fatigue —if not his common sense—prevented an angry reply.

"Do you realize the cost of all this, my lord?" blared Hooper. "Every white man who can sit a horse is out. My last reserve—the Highlanders—are bivouacked at the roadside. What that will mean in malaria and yellow fever I do not dare guess. For two weeks every man of the garrison except for them has been out guarding fishing boats and watching beaches at your request. The sick lists are enormous. And now this!"

"My instructions, and I believe Your Excellency's as well, laid the greatest stress on the suppression of piracy, sir."

"I don't need any whipper-snapper jumped-up rear admiral to interpret my instructions," roared Hooper. "What sort of bargain did you make with these pirates of yours?"

There it was. It was not an easy thing to explain to a man in this mood.

"I made no actual bargain, Your Excellency."

"Hard to believe you had that much sense."

"But my honour is pledged."

"Your honour pledged? To whom? The pirates?"

"No, Your Excellency. To my secretary, Spendlove."

"What was the pledge?"

"He was retained as a hostage when I was set free."

"What did you promise him?"

What? He had said something about thinking about him.

"I made no verbal promise, Your Excellency. But one was implied, undoubtedly."

"What was implied?"

"That I should set him free."

"And how did you think you could do that?"

Nothing for it but to take the bull by the horns.

"I was released in order that I might solicit from Your Excellency pardons under seal for the pirates."

"Pardons! Par—" Hooper could not even finish the word a second time. He could only gobble like a turkey for several seconds before, with a gulp, he was able to continue. "Are you insane, my lord?"

"That was why I was released. And that is why Spendlove is still retained."

"Then this Spendlove must take his chance."

"Your Excellency!"

"Do you think I could grant pardons to a gang of pirates? What d'ye mean? So that they can live like lords on their booty? Rolling in coaches round the island? A fine way that would be of suppressing piracy! D'ye want the whole West Indies in a turmoil? Have you lost your senses?"

The effect of this speech was in no way modified by the fact that Hornblower had guessed, long before, that Hooper would argue exactly along this line.

"I fully see the difficulty of the situation, Your Excellency."

"I'm glad you do. You know the hiding place of these pirates?"

"Yes, Your Excellency. It is a very secure place."

"No matter. It can be reduced, of course. A few hangings will quiet this island down again."

What in the world was there that he could do or could say? The sentence he framed in his mind was patently absurd to him even before he uttered it.

"I shall have to go back there before you take any steps, Your Excellency."

"Go back there?" Hooper's eyes almost came out of their sockets as the implications of what Hornblower was saying dawned upon him. "What new foolery do you have in mind?"

"I must go back and join Spendlove if Your Excellency does not see fit to grant the pardons."

"Rubbish! I can grant no pardons. I cannot. I will not."

"Then I have no alternative, Your Excellency."

"Rubbish, I said! Rubbish! You made no promise. You said yourself that you gave no pledge."

"I am the judge of that, Your Excellency."

"You're in no condition to judge anything at present, if ever you were. Can you imagine for one moment I'll let you tie my hands like this?"

"No one regrets the necessity more than I do, sir."

"Necessity? Are you dictating to me? I'll have you know that I'm your superior officer as well as governor of this island. One more word and you'll be under arrest, my lord. Let's hear no more of this nonsense."

"Your Excellency—"

"Not one more word, I said. This Spendlove is one of the King's servants. He must run the risks of his position, even though he is only a secretary."

"But—"

"I order you to keep silence, my lord. You have fair warning. To-morrow when you're rested we can plan to smoke out this wasps' nest."

Hornblower himself checked the protest that still rose to his lips. Hooper meant what he said when he threatened arrest. The massive discipline that permeated the armed forces of the Crown had Horn-blower in its grip as surely as if he were the least seaman. To dis-obey an order was hopeless from the start. The irresistible force of his own conscience might be driving him forward, but here he was up against the immovable barrier of discipline. Tomorrow? To-morrow was another day.

"Very well, Your Excellency."

"A night's rest will do you all the good in the world, my lord. Perhaps it would be best if you slept here. I will give the necessary orders. If you instruct your flag lieutenant as to the fresh clothes you will need I will send to Admiralty House for them to be ready for you in the morning."

Clothes? Hornblower looked down at himself. He had forgotten entirely that he was wearing his black full-dress. One glance was enough to tell him that never again could he wear that suit. Now he could guess about the rest of his appearance. He knew that his haggard cheeks must be sprouting a bristly beard, his neckcloth in wild disorder. No wonder that people had looked at him curiously in the anteroom.

"Your Excellency is very kind," he said.

There was no harm in being formally polite in the face of the temporarily inevitable. There had been that in Hooper's tone which told him that the invitation might as well have been an order, that he was as much a prisoner in Government House as if Hooper had actually carried out his threat of putting him under arrest. It was best to yield gracefully since he had to yield for the moment at least. Tomorrow was another day.

"Allow me to conduct you to your room, my lord," said Hooper.

The mirror in the bedroom confirmed his worst fears regarding his appearance. The bed, with its enormous mosquito net, was wide and inviting. His aching joints clamoured that he should allow himself to fall across that bed and repose himself; his weary brain demanded that he should sink into oblivion, forget his troubles in sleep as a drunkard might forget them in liquor. It was a relaxation to soap himself in a tepid bath, despite the smarting protests of the raw places on his body. And yet, bathed and relaxed, with one of His Excellency's nightshirts flapping round his knees, he could not give way to his weaknesses. His innermost ego refused to recognize them. He found himself hobbling barefooted about the room. He had no quarterdeck to pace; the candle-heated tropical air of the bedroom was not as conducive to inspiration as was a fresh sea breeze; mosquitoes buzzed about him, stinging his neck and his bare legs and distracting him. It was one of those dreadful nights; sometimes he relaxed so far as to sit on a chair, but within a few seconds a new train of thought brought him to his feet again, to limp up and down.

It was maddening that he could not keep his thoughts concentrated on the problem of Spendlove. He felt a contempt for himself that he should find his mind deserting his devoted secretary; there was a rival train of thought which was frequently successful in holding his attention. He knew, before the night was over, just how he would deal with the pirates' lair if his hands were free; he even knew satisfaction in recapitulating his plans, only to find the satisfaction replaced by sick despair at the thought of Spendlove in the pirates' hands. There were moments when his stomach turned over as he remembered Johnson's threat to dig out Spendlove's eyes.

Weariness took him by surprise in the end; he had sat down and rested his head on his hand, and then awakened with a start as he fell forward in his chair. The awakening was not complete enough; unconscious of what he was doing he settled himself back in his chair and slept in that fashion, the vast comfortable bed untenanted, until a knocking at his door roused him to blink about him wondering where he was before bracing himself to make it seem as if it were the most ordinary thing in the world to sleep in a chair when a bed was available.

It was Giles who came in, bearing clean linen and a uniform and razors; the business of shaving and of dressing carefully served to steady him and kept him from thinking too furiously about the problem he would have to solve in the next few minutes.

"His Excellency would be glad if his lordship would take breakfast with him."

That was a message conveyed through the door to Giles; the invitation must be accepted, of course, as it was the equivalent of a royal command. Hooper, apparently, was partial to a steak for breakfast; a silver dish of steak and onions was brought in almost as soon as Hornblower had uttered his formal good morning. Hooper looked at Hornblower oddly when he answered the butler's inquiry with a request for papaya and a boiled egg—that was a bad start, for it confirmed Hooper in his opinions of Hornblower's eccentricity that he should have these outlandish Frenchified notions about breakfast. Years of living on shore had not yet dulled the appetite for fresh eggs in their shells which Hornblower had acquired during decades at sea. Hooper daubed mustard on his steak and set about it with appetite.

"Did you sleep well?"

"Well enough, thank you, Your Excellency."

Hooper's abandonment of the formal "my lord" was a not too subtle indication that he was willing to forget last night's discussion and to act magnanimously as if Hornblower were a normal person with only a temporary lapse on his record.

"We'll leave business until we've eaten."

"As you wish, Your Excellency."

But not even a governor can be sure of his future. There was a bustle at the door, and a whole group of people came hurrying in, not merely the butler but two aides-de-camp and Gerard and—and— who was that? Pale and ragged and weary, almost unable to stand on tottering legs.

"Spendlove!" said Hornblower, his spoon clattering to the floor as he rose and hurried to him.

Hornblower clasped his hand, grinning with delight. Perhaps there had never been a moment in his life which had held so much sheer pleasure for him.

"Spendlove!" He could only repeat the name at first.

"Is this the return of the prodigal?" asked Hooper from the table. Hornblower remembered his manners.

"Your Excellency," he said, "may I take it upon myself to present my secretary, Mr. Erasmus Spendlove?"

"Glad to see you, young man. Take a seat at the table. Bring Mr. Spendlove some food! He looks as if a glass of wine would not come amiss. Bring the decanter and a glass."

"You're not wounded?" asked Hornblower. "You're not hurt?"

"No, my lord," said Spendlove, extending his legs cautiously under the table. "It is only that seventy miles on horseback have stiffened my unaccustomed limbs."

"Seventy miles?" asked Hooper. "From where?"

"Montego Bay, Your Excellency."

"Then you must have escaped in the night?"

"At nightfall, Your Excellency."

"But what did you do, man?" demanded Hornblower. "How did you get away?"

"I jumped, my lord. Into the water."

"Into the water?"

"Yes, my lord. There was eight feet of water in the river at the foot of the cliff; enough to break my fall from any height."

So there was.

"But—but—in the dark?"

"That was easy, my lord. I looked over the parapet during the day. I did when I said good-bye to your lordship. I marked the spot and I measured the distance with my eye."

"And then?"

"And then I jumped when it was fully dark, and raining hard."

"What were the pirates doing?" asked Hooper.

"They were taking shelter, Your Excellency. They were paying no attention to me, thinking I was safe enough there, with the ladder pulled up."

"And so—?"

"So I took a run, Your Excellency, and jumped the parapet, as I said, and came down feet first into the water."

"Unhurt?"

"Unhurt, Your Excellency."

Hornblower's vivid imagination conjured up everything about the feat, the half dozen strides through the dark and the roaring rain, the leap, the endless fall. He felt the hair at the back of his neck lifting.

"A most commendable deed," commented Hooper.

"Nothing for a desperate man, Your Excellency."

"Perhaps not. And then? After you were in the water? Were you pursued?"

"As far as I can tell, Your Excellency, I was not. Perhaps it was some time before they noticed my absence. Even then they would have to let down the ladder and climb down it. I heard nothing as I made off."

"Which way did you go?" asked Hornblower.

"I kept to the river, my lord, making my way downstream. It reaches the sea at Montego Bay, as we decided, if you remember, my lord, when we were making our first observations."

"Was it an easy journey?" asked Hornblower. Something was stirring in his mind, demanding his attention despite the strong emotions he was experiencing.

"Not easy in the dark, my lord. There were rapids in places, and the boulders were slippery. I fancy the main pass is narrow, although I could not see it."

"And at Montego Bay?" asked Hooper.

"There was the guard over the fishing boats, a half company of the West Indian Regiment, Your Excellency. I had their officer awakened, and he found me a horse, and I took the road through Cambridge and Ipswich."

"You got yourself remounts on the way?"

"I claimed I was on a mission of the greatest importance, Your Excellency."

"You made good time even then."

"The patrol at Mandeville told me his lordship was on his way to Your Excellency, and so I rode straight to Government House."

"Very sensible."

To the picture in Hornblower's mind of the leap in the darkness were now added others, of a nightmare journey down the river, falling over slippery boulders, tumbling into unexpected pools, struggling along invisible banks; then the endless weary ride.

"I shall represent your conduct to the Lords Commissioners, Mr. Spendlove," he said formally.

"I must thank your lordship."

"And I shall represent it to the Secretary of State," added Hooper.

"Your Excellency is too kind."

To Hornblower it was not the least of Spendlove's achievements (guessed at from a glance at his plate) that Spendlove had contrived somehow to gulp down a whole plateful of steak and onions while making his report. The man must have learned to dispense with chewing.

"Enough of compliments," said Hooper, mopping up his gravy with a piece of bread. "Now we have to destroy these pirates. This lair of theirs—you say it is strong?"

Hornblower let Spendlove answer.

"Impregnable to direct assault, Your Excellency."

"M'm. D'ye think they'll make a stand there?"

For the past several minutes Hornblower had been debating this point with himself. Those leaderless men, dazed now by the complete failure of their scheme—what would they do?

"They could scatter all over the island, Your Excellency," said Spendlove.

"So they could. Then I'll have to hunt them down. Patrols on every road, movable columns in the mountains. And the sick list is high already."

Troops exposed to the weather and the night air for long in the West Indies died like flies, and it might well take weeks to run the outlaws down.

"Maybe they'll scatter," said Hornblower, and then he committed himself, "But in my opinion, Your Excellency, they will not."

Hooper looked at him sharply.

"You think not?"

"I think not, Your Excellency."

That gang had been despairing as well as desperate when he had been among them. There was something childlike about them, leaderless as they were. On the cliff they had shelter, food—they had a home, if the expression could be tolerated. They would not readily leave it.

"And you say this place is impregnable? It would mean a long siege?"

"I might reduce them quickly with a naval force, Your Excellency, if Your Excellency would give me leave to try."

"Your lordship is welcome to try anything that will save lives." Hooper was looking at him curiously.

"Then I'll make my arrangements," said Hornblower.

"You'll go round to Montego Bay by sea?"

"Yes."

Hornblower restrained himself from saying "Of course." Soldiers always found it hard to realize the convenience of the sea for rapid and secret movements.

"I'll maintain my patrols in case they bolt while you smoke out the nest," said Hooper.

"I think Your Excellency would be taking a wise precaution in doing so. I trust my plan will not take long in execution. With Your Excellency's leave—"

Hornblower rose from the table.

"You're going now?"

"Every hour is of importance, Your Excellency."

Hooper was looking at him more inquisitively than ever.

"The navy displays its notorious reserve," he said. "Oh, very well, then. Order his lordship's carriage. You have my leave to try, my lord. Report to me by courier."

There they were, in the warm morning air, sitting, the three of them, Hornblower, Spendlove, and Gerard, in the carriage.

"The dockyard," ordered Hornblower briefly. He turned to Spendlove. "From the dockyard you will go on board *Clorinda* and convey my order to Captain Fell to make ready for sea. I shall be hoisting my flag within an hour. Then it is my order to you that you get yourself some rest."

"Aye aye, my lord."

At the dockyard the captain superintendent did his best not to appear surprised at an unheralded visit from his admiral, who by the last news had been kidnapped.

"I want a boat mortar, Holmes," said Hornblower, brushing aside the expressions of pleased surprise.

"A boat mortar, my lord? Y-yes, my lord. There's one in store, I know."

"It's to go on board *Clorinda* at once. Now, there are shells for it?"

"Yes, my lord. Uncharged, of course."

"I'll have *Clorinda*'s gunner charge 'em while we're under way. Twenty pounds apiece, I believe. Send two hundred, with the fuses."

"Aye aye, my lord."

"And I want a punt. Two punts. I've seen your hands using 'em for caulking and breaming. Twenty foot, are they?"

"Twenty-two foot, my lord," answered Holmes; he was glad that he could answer this question while his admiral had not insisted on an answer regarding so obscure a matter as the weight of boat-mortar shells.

"I'll have two, as I said. Send them round to be hove on deck."

"Aye aye, my lord."

Captain Sir Thomas Fell had his best uniform on to greet his admiral.

"I received your order, my lord," he said, as the twittering of the pipes died away in a last wail.

"Very well, Sir Thomas. I want to be under way the moment the stores I have ordered are on board. You can warp your ship out. We are going to Montego Bay to deal with pirates."

"Aye aye, my lord."

Fell did his best not to look askance at the two filthy punts that he was expected to heave onto his spotless deck—they were only the floating stages used in the dockyard for work on ships' sides—and the two tons of greasy mortar shells for which he had to find space were no better. He was not too pleased when he was ordered to tell off the greater part of his ship's company—two hundred and forty men—and all his marine detachment for a landing party. The hands were naturally delighted with the prospect of a change of routine and the possibility of action. The fact that the gunner was weighing out gunpowder and putting two pounds apiece in the shells, a glimpse of the armourer going round with the admiral on an inspection of the boarding pikes, the sight of the boat mortar, squat and ugly, crouching on its bed at the break of the forecastle, all excited them. It was a pleasure to thrash along to the westward, under every stitch of canvas, leaving Portland Point abeam, rounding Negril Point at sunset, catching some fortunate puffs of the sea breeze which enabled them to cheat the trade wind, ghosting along in the tropical darkness with the lead at work in the chains, and anchoring with the dawn among the shoals of Montego Bay, the green mountains of Jamaica all fiery with the rising sun.

Hornblower was on deck to see it; he had been awake since midnight, having slept since sunset—two almost sleepless nights had disordered his habits—and he was already pacing the quarterdeck as the excited men were formed up in the waist. He kept a sharp eye on the preparations. That boat mortar weighed no more than four hundred pounds, a mere trifle for the yard-arm tackle to lower down into the punt alongside. The musket-men were put through an inspection of their equipment; it was puzzling to the crew that there were pike-men, axe-men, and even mallet-men and crowbar-men as well. As the sun climbed higher and blazed down hotter the men began to file down into the boats.

"Gig's alongside, my lord," said Gerard.

"Very well."

On shore Hornblower returned the salute of the astonished sub-altern commanding the detachment of the West Indian Regiment on guard over the boats—he had turned out his men apparently expecting nothing less than a French invasion—and dismissed him. Then he ran a final glance over the rigid lines of the marine detachment, scarlet tunics and white crossbelts and all. They would not be nearly as tidy by the end of the day.

"You can make a start, Captain," he said. "Keep me informed, Mr. Spendlove, if you please."

"Aye aye, my lord."

With Spendlove as guide the marines marched forward; they were the advanced guard to secure the main body from surprise. It was time to give orders to *Clorinda*'s first lieutenant.

"Now, Mr. Sefton, we can move."

The little river had a little bar at its mouth, but the two punts carrying the mortar and the ammunition had been floated in round it. For a mile there was even a track beside the water, and progress was rapid as they dragged the punts along, while the vegetation closed in round them. The shade was gratifying when they first entered into it, but they found it breathless, damp, stifling, as they progressed farther in. Mosquitoes stung with venomous determination. Men slipped and fell on the treacherous mudbanks, splashing prodigiously. Then they reached the first stretch of shallows, where the river came bubbling down a long perceptible slope between steep banks under the light filtering in through the trees.

At least they had saved a mile and more by water carriage even this far. Hornblower studied the grounded punts, the soil, and the trees. This was what he had been thinking about; it was worth making the experiment before putting the men to the toil of carrying the mortar up by brute force.

"We'll try a dam here, Mr. Sefton, if you please."

"Aye aye, my lord. Axe-men! Pike-men! Mallet-men!"

The men were still in high spirits; it called for exertion on the part of the petty officers to restrain their exuberance. A line of pikes driven head downward when the soil was soft enough to receive them formed the first framework of the dam. Axe-men felled small trees with a childish delight in destruction. Crowbar-men levered at stumps and rocks. A small avalanche came tumbling down into the river bed. The water swirled about the trash; already there was sufficient obstruction to hold it. Hornblower saw the level rise before his very eyes.

"More rocks here!" roared Sefton.

"Keep your eye on those punts, Mr. Sefton," said Hornblower— the clumsy craft were already afloat again.

Felled trees and rocks extended, heightened, and strengthened the dam. There was water spouting through the interstices, but not as much as was being held back.

"Get the punts upstream," ordered Hornblower.

Four hundred willing hands had achieved much; the water was banked up sufficient to float the punts two-thirds of the way up the shallows.

"Another dam, I think, Mr. Sefton, if you please."

Already they had learned much about the construction of temporary dams. The stream bed was choked in a twinkling, it seemed. Splashing knee deep in water the men dragged the punts higher still. They grounded momentarily, but a final heave ran them over the last of the shallows into a reach where they floated with ease.

"Excellent, Mr. Sefton."

That was a clear gain of a quarter of a mile before the next shallows.

As they were preparing to work on the next dam the flat report of a musket shot came echoing back to them in the heated air, followed by half a dozen more; it was several minutes before they heard the explanation, brought back by a breathless messenger.

"Captain Seymour reports, sir. We was fired on by someone up there, sir. Saw 'im in the trees, sir, but 'e got away."

"Very well."

So the pirates had posted a lookout downstream. Now they knew that a force was advancing against them. Only time would show what they would do next; meanwhile the punts were afloat again and it was time to push on. The river curved back and forth, washing at the foot of vertical banks, preserving, for a time, miraculously, enough depth of water to float the punts at the expense of occasionally dragging them up slight rapids. Now it began to seem to Hornblower as if he had spent days on this labour, in the blinding patches of sunlight and the dark stretches of shade, with the river swirling round his knees, and his feet slipping on the rocks. At the next dam he was tempted to sit and allow the sweat to stream down him. He had hardly done so when another messenger arrived from the advanced guard.

"Captain Seymour reporting, sir. 'E says to say the pirates 'ave gorn to ground, sir. They're in a cave, sir, right up in the cliff."

"How far ahead of here?"

"Oh, not so very fur, sir."

Hornblower could have expected no better answer, he realized.

"They was shooting at us, sir," supplemented the messenger.

That defined the distance better, for they had heard no firing for a long time; the pirates' lair must be farther than the sound could carry.

"Very well. Mr. Sefton, carry on, if you please. I'm going ahead. Come along, Gerard."

He set himself to climb and scramble along the river-bank. On his left hand as he progressed he noticed the bank was growing steeper and loftier. Now it was really a cliff. Another stretch of rapids at a corner, and then he opened up a fresh vista. There it was, just as he remembered it, the lofty overhanging cliff with the waterfall tumbling down it to join the river at its foot, and the long horizontal seam half-way up the cliff; open grassland with a few trees on his right, and even the little group of mules on the narrow stretch of grass between the cliff and the river. Red-coated marines were strung out over the grassland, in a wide semicircle whose centre was the cave.

Hornblower forgot his sweating fatigue and strode hastily forward to where he could see Seymour standing among his men gazing up at the cliff, Spendlove at his side. They came to meet him and saluted.

"There they are, my lord," said Seymour. "They took a few shots at us when we arrived."

"Thank you, Captain. How do you like the look of the place now, Spendlove?"

"As much as before, my lord, but no more."

"Spendlove's Leap," said Hornblower.

He was pressing forward along the river-bank towards the cave, staring upwards.

"Have a care, my lord," said Spendlove urgently.

A moment after he had spoken something whistled sharply just above Hornblower's head; a puff of smoke appeared over the parapet of the cave, and a sharp ringing report came echoing from the cliff face. Then, made tiny by the distance, doll-like figures appeared over the parapet, waving their arms in defiance, and the yells they were uttering came faintly to their ears.

"Someone has a rifle up there, my lord," said Seymour.

"Indeed? Perhaps then it would be best to withdraw out of range before he can reload."

The incident had made little impression on Hornblower until that moment. Now he suddenly realized that the almost legendary career of the great Lord Hornblower might have been terminated then and there, that his future biographer might have had to deplore the ironic chance which, after so many pitched battles, brought him death at the hands of an obscure criminal in an unknown corner of a West Indian island. He turned and walked away, the others at his side. He found he was holding his neck rigid, his muscles tense; it had been a long time since his life was last in danger. He strove to appear natural.

"Sefton will be up with the mortar before long," he said, after casting about in his mind for something natural to say; and he hoped it did not sound as unnatural to the others as it did to him.

"Yes, my lord."

"Where shall we site it?" He swung round and looked about him, measuring ranges with his eye. "It had better be out of range of that rifle."

His interest in what he was doing immediately erased the memory of his danger. Another puff of smoke from the parapet; another echoing report.

"Did anyone hear that bullet? No? Then we can assume we're out of rifle shot here."

"If you please, my lord," asked Spendlove, "what range can you expect with a boat mortar?"

"The encyclopedic Spendlove displaying ignorance! Seven hundred yards with a one-pound charge of powder, and a time of flight of fifteen seconds. But here we have to burst the shell sixty feet above the firing point. A nice problem in ballistics." Hornblower spoke with perfect indifference, confident that no one knew that at one o'clock that morning he had been studying those figures in the manual. "Those trees there will be useful when we come to sway the mortar up. And there's level ground within twenty feet of them. Excellent."

"Here they come, my lord."

The first of the main body appeared round the distant corner of the cliff, hurrying along the river-bank. As they took in the situation, they broke into a yell and a run, leaping and scrambling over the broken ground; Hornblower was reminded of hounds rushing up, clamouring at sight of their quarry at bay.

"Silence, there!" he roared. "You, midshipman, there, can't you keep your men under control? Mark their names for punishment, and I'll mention yours to Mr. Sefton."

Abashed, the seamen formed up quietly. Here came the punts, gliding like fate along the silent pool, towed by working parties scrambling along the bank.

"Orders, my lord?" asked Sefton.

Hornblower glanced finally round the terrain before issuing them. The sun was long past its zenith as eager men clambered up the trees to fix the tackles; soon the mortar hung dangling from a stout limb while the mortar bed was hoisted out and settled in a smooth spot, the gunner fussing over it with a spirit level to make sure it was horizontal. Then, with violent manual labor, the mortar was swung over and finally heaved up into position, and the gunner drove the keys through the eye bolts.

"Shall I open fire, my lord?" asked Sefton.

Hornblower looked over at the distant seam in the face of the cliff across the river. The pirates there would be watching them. Had they recognized this squat object, inconsiderable in size, undistinguished in shape, which meant death to them? They might well not know what it was; they were probably peering over the parapet trying to make out what it was that had occupied the attention of so considerable a body of men.

"What's your elevation, gunner?"

"Sixty degrees, sir—my lord."

"Try a shot with a fifteen-second fuse."

The gunner went carefully through the processes of loading, measuring the powder charge and wadding it down into the chamber, clearing the touch hole with the priming iron and then filling it with fine-grain powder from the horn. He took his bradawl and drove it carefully into the wooden stem of the fuse at the selected point—these were very newfangled fuses, graduated with ink lines to mark the time of burning—and screwed it into the shell. He lowered the shell down upon the wad.

"Linstocks," he said.

Someone had been chipping away with flint and steel to catch a spark upon the slow match. He transferred the glow to a second linstock which he handed to the gunner. The gunner, stooping, checked the pointing of the weapon.

"Fuse!" he said. His assistant touched his linstock down, and the fuse spluttered. Then the gunner thrust his glowing match upon the touch hole. A roar and a billow of powder smoke.

Standing far back from the mortar Hornblower already had his face turned to the sky to track the shell in its flight. Against that light blue there was nothing to be seen—no, there at the height of the trajectory there was a brief black streak, instantly invisible again. A further wait; an inevitable thought that the fuse had failed, and then a distant explosion and a fountain of smoke, down at the base of the cliff somewhat to the right of the cave. There was a groan from the watching seamen.

"Silence, there!" bellowed Sefton.

"Try again, gunner," said Hornblower.

The mortar was trained round a trifle on its bed. Its bore was sponged out and when the charge had been put in, the gunner took a gill measure from his pocket and added a measure of powder to the charge. He pierced the fuse again, lowered the shell into the bore, gave his final order, and fired. A wait; and then a bold puff of smoke hung in the air, seemingly right in line with the seam in the cliff. The wretched people there were watching their fate creeping up on them.

"Fuse a little short," said Hornblower.

"Range short, I fancy, my lord," said the gunner.

At the next shot there was a cloud of dust and a small avalanche from the cliff face high above the seam, and instantly afterwards the burst of the shell on the ground at the near edge of the river where it had fallen.

"Better," said Hornblower. He had seen the principles of ranging with a mortar—a huge thirteen-inch one—at the siege of Riga nearly ten years before.

Two more shots, both wasted—the shells exploded at the top of their trajectory, high, high up. Apparently those newfangled fuses were not quite reliable. Fountains spouted momentarily from the river surface as fragments rained into it. But the pirates must by now be fully aware of what the mortar implied.

"Give me that telescope, Gerard."

He trained the instrument on the seam in the face of the cliff. He could see every detail now, the rough stone parapet, the waterfall at one end, but he could see no sign of the garrison. They were at the back of the cave or crouching behind the parapet.

"Fire another shot."

Fifteen long seconds after the report. Then he saw fragments flying from under the overhang.

"Good shot!" he called, still watching. The shell must have fallen right into the cave. But as he uttered the words a dark figure appeared at the parapet, the arms swinging together. He saw the tiny black disk of the shell against the background of rock curving downwards and then a burst of smoke. Someone had seized the hot shell in his two hands and slung it over the parapet in the nick of time. A desperate deed.

"Pitch another shell there with a second's less fuse and it will be all over," he said, and then— "Wait."

Surely those helpless people must surrender, and not stay to be massacred. What must he do to persuade them? He knew perfectly well.

"Send a white flag forward, my lord?" asked Spendlove, voicing his thoughts.

"I was thinking about it," said Hornblower.

It would be a dangerous mission. If the pirates were determined not to surrender they would not respect a flag of truce, and would fire on the bearer of it. There were a score of muskets and at least one rifle up there. Hornblower wanted neither to order someone forward nor to ask for a volunteer.

"I'll do it, my lord," said Spendlove. "They know me."

This was the price he had to pay, thought Hornblower, for his lofty position, for being an admiral. He had to order his friends to their death. Yet on the other hand—

"Very well," said Hornblower.

"Let's have your shirt and your pike, my man," said Spendlove.

A white shirt tied by the sleeves to a pike staff made a fair white flag. As Spendlove went forward with it, through the cordon of red-coated marines, Hornblower was tempted to call him back. It was only unconditional surrender that could be offered, after all. He went as far as to open his mouth, but closed it again without saying the words he had in mind. Spendlove walked towards the river-bank, stopping every few seconds to wave the flag. Through the telescope Hornblower could see nothing up in the cave. Then he saw a flash of metal, and a line of heads and shoulders over the parapet. A dozen muskets were taking aim at Spendlove. But Spendlove saw them too, and halted, with a wave of his flag. There were long seconds of tension, and then Spendlove turned his back upon the muskets and began to retrace his steps. As he did so there was a puff of smoke from the parapet; the rifleman had fired as soon as he had seen there was no chance of luring Spendlove within musket shot. Spendlove came walking back, trailing the pike and the shirt.

"He missed me, my lord," he said.

"Thank God," said Hornblower. "Gunner, fire."

The wind may have shifted a little, or the powder was not consistent. The shell burst in the air just below the level of the cave—so that the fuse must have been efficient—but some considerable distance from the cliff.

"Fire again," said Hornblower.

There it was. A burst of smoke, a fountain of fragments, right in the cave. Horrible to think of what was happening there.

"Fire again."

Another burst right in the cave.

"Fire again— No! Wait."

Figures were appearing on the parapet—there had been some survivors, then, from those two bursts. Two figures—tiny dolls in the field of the telescope—seemed to hang in the air as they leaped. The telescope followed them down. One struck water in a fountain of spray. The other fell on the rocky shore, broken and horrible. He raised the telescope again. There was the ladder being thrown over from the parapet. There was a figure—and another figure—climbing down. Hornblower shut the telescope with a snap.

"Captain Seymour! Send a party forward to secure the prisoners."

He did not have to see the horrors of the cave, the mutilated dead and the screaming wounded. He could see them in his mind's eye when Seymour made his report of what he found when he ascended the ladder. It was done, finished. The wounded could be bandaged and carried down to the beach on litters to the death that awaited them, the unwounded driven along with them with their wrists bound. A courier could be sent off to the governor to say that the pirate horde had been wiped out, so that the patrols could be called in and the militia sent home. He did not have to set eyes on the wretched people he had conquered. The excitement of the hunt was over. He had set himself a task to do, a problem to solve, just as he might work out a longitude from lunar observations, and he had achieved success. But the measure of that success could be expressed in hangings, in dead and in wounded, in that shattered broken-backed figure lying on the rocks, and he had undertaken the task merely on a point of pride, to re-establish his self-esteem after the indignity of being kidnapped. It was no comfort to argue with himself—as he did—that what he had done would otherwise have been done by others, at great cost in disease and in economic disturbance. That only made him sneer at himself as a hair-splitting casuist. There were few occasions when Hornblower could do what was right in Hornblower's eyes.

Yet there was some cynical pleasure to be derived from his lofty rank, to be able to leave all this after curt orders to Sefton and Seymour to bring the landing party back to the shore with the least delay and the shortest exposure to the night air, to go back on board and eat a comfortable dinner—even if it meant Fell's rather boring company—and to sleep in a comfortable bed. And it was pleasant to find that Fell had already dined, so that he could eat his dinner merely in the company of his flag lieutenant and his secretary. Nevertheless, there was one more unexpected crumpled petal in his rose-leaf bed, and he discovered it, contrariwise, as a result of what he intended to be a kindly action.

"I shall have to add a further line to my remarks about you to Their Lordships, Spendlove," he said. "It was a brave deed to go forward with that flag of truce."

"Thank you, my lord," said Spendlove, who bent his gaze down on the tablecloth and drummed with his fingers before continuing, eyes still lowered in unusual nervousness. "Then perhaps your lordship will not be averse to putting in a word for me in another quarter?"

"Of course I will," replied Hornblower in all innocence. "Where?"

"Thank you, my lord. It was with this in mind that I did the little you have been kind enough to approve of. I would be deeply grateful if your lordship would go to the trouble of speaking well of me to Miss Lucy."

Lucy! Hornblower had forgotten all about the girl. He quite failed to conceal his surprise, which was clearly apparent to Spendlove when he lifted his glance from the tablecloth.

"We jested about a wealthy marriage, my lord," said Spendlove. The elaborate care with which he was choosing his words proved how deep were his emotions. "I would not care if Miss Lucy had not a penny. My lord, my affections are deeply engaged."

"She is a very charming young woman," said Hornblower, temporizing desperately.

"My lord, I love her," burst out Spendlove, casting aside all restraint. "I love her dearly. At the ball I tried to interest her in myself, and I failed."

"I'm sorry to hear that," said Hornblower.

"I could not but be aware of her admiration for you, my lord. She spoke of your lordship repeatedly. I realized even then that one word from you would carry more weight than a long speech from me. If you would say that word, my lord—"

"I'm sure you overestimate my influence," said Hornblower, choosing his words as carefully as Spendlove had done, but, he hoped, not as obviously. "But of course I will do all I can."

"There is no need for me to reiterate my gratitude, my lord," said Spendlove.

This pleading creature, this poor love-lorn fellow, was the Spendlove whose cool daring had risked a leap in the darkness down a sixty-foot precipice. Hornblower remembered Lucy's lips on his hands, remembered how she had followed him on her knees across the floor. The less he had to do with any of this the better, he decided. But the passion of a child hardly out of the schoolroom for a man of mature years was likely to be fleeting, transient, and the memory of her lost dignity would later be as painful to her as it was to him. She would find need to assert herself, to show him that he was not the only man in the world—and how could she demonstrate that more plainly than by marrying someone else? To use a vulgar phrase, there was quite a chance that Spendlove might catch her on the rebound.

"If good wishes can help," he said, "you have all mine, Spendlove."

Even an admiral had to choose his words with care. Two days later he was announcing his immediate departure to the governor.

"I'm taking my squadron to sea in the morning, Your Excellency," he said.

"Aren't you going to stay for the hangings?" asked Hooper in surprise.

"I fear not," answered Hornblower, and added an unnecessary explanation. "Hangings don't agree with me, Your Excellency."

It was not merely an unnecessary explanation; it was a foolish one, as he knew as soon as he saw the open astonishment in Hooper's face. Hooper could hardly have been more surprised at hearing that hangings did not agree with Hornblower than he would have been if he had heard that Hornblower did not agree with hangings—and that was very nearly as correct.

4

SHE WAS EXACTLY LIKE a British ship of war; naturally, perhaps, since she had been one most of her life until she was sold out of the service. Now, as she came up into the harbour, she could pass without question for a man-o'-war brig except that she flew the Royal Yacht Squadron burgee instead of a commission pendant. Hornblower put down the telescope through which he had been watching, curiously, her progress into Kingston harbour, and referred again to Barbara's letter, two months old now, which had arrived a fortnight ago.

MY DEAREST HUSBAND [wrote Barbara. She sometimes misused her superlatives; that "dearest," strictly, implied that she had at least three husbands, even though it also implied that Hornblower rated highest of the three],

You are shortly going to have a visitor, a Mr. Charles Ramsbottom, a millionaire, who has purchased an old ship of the navy to use as a yacht, which he has named the *Bride of Abydos,* and in which he proposes to visit the West Indies. He has only lately made his appearance in society, having inherited his father's fortune—Bradford wool and army clothing contracts! Yet despite this obscure origin he has succeeded in entering into society, perhaps because he is very young, very charming, unmarried, mildly eccentric, and, as I said, a millionaire. I have met him frequently of late, in very good houses, and I recommend him to you, dearest, if for no other reason than that he has won some small portion of my heart by a delightful mixture of deference and interest which I might have found irresistible were I not married to the most irresistible man in the world. He has, indeed, won golden opinions in society, both on the government side and with the opposition, and he might become an important factor in politics should he decide to enter into them. I have no doubt that he will bring you introductions from personages even more influential than your loving wife. . . .

Hornblower had to read the letter through to the end, although it contained no further reference to Mr. Charles Ramsbottom, but he returned to the opening paragraph. It was the first time he had ever seen this new word "millionaire," which occurred twice. He disliked it on sight. It was inconceivable that a man should have a mil-

lion pounds, and presumably not in broad estates but in factories
and in stocks and shares, probably with a huge holding in Consols
and an immense balance at the bank as well. The existence of millionaires, whether in society or not, was something as distasteful as
the word itself now called into existence. And this one had been
charming to Barbara—he was not too sure if that really constituted a
recommendation. He picked up the telescope again and watched the
brig come to an anchor. The rapidity with which she took in sail
showed that she carried a large crew. Hornblower, as a commander-
in-chief of a squadron and accountable to the niggardly Lords of the
Admiralty for every penny expended, knew perfectly well what this
sort of thing cost. This Mr. Ramsbottom, to indulge himself in his
naval toy, was expending enough money to maintain a thousand
families in bread and beer and bacon.

The brig rounded-to and anchored very neatly indeed; if she had
been a vessel included in his command he would have grunted with
grudging satisfaction. As it was he grunted with a mixture of envy
and derision and turned away to await the inevitable call in the se-
clusion of Admiralty House.

When it came he fingered the visiting card with its plain "Mr.
Charles Ramsbottom" and found some small satisfaction in deciding
that he had at last come across a name more unlovely than his own.
But the owner of the name, when he was ushered in, made a better
impression. In his very early twenties, he was small and slight and—
for what it was worth—strikingly handsome, with black hair and eyes
and what could only be described as "chiselled features" deeply
tanned after weeks at sea; not at all what might be expected of a
Bradford wool manufacturer, while his dark green coat and formal
white breeches were in quiet good taste.

"My wife wrote to me about you, Mr. Ramsbottom," said Hornblower.

"That was very kind of Lady Hornblower. But of course she is
kindness personified. May I present my letters of introduction from
Lord Liverpool and Bishop Wilberforce, my lord?"

Barbara was perfectly right, then, in predicting that Ramsbottom
would win favour with both political parties—here were letters from
the Prime Minister himself and a prominent member of the opposition. Hornblower glanced through them, and was conscious of an un-
dernote of cordiality despite their formal wording.

"Excellent, Mr. Ramsbottom," said Hornblower. He tried to adopt the tone which he presumed would be adopted by a man who had just read a letter of introduction from the Prime Minister. "Is there any way in which I can be of service to you?"

"None that I am aware of at present, my lord. I must complete with water and stores, naturally, but my purser is a capable man. I intend to continue my voyage through these charming islands."

"Of course," said Hornblower soothingly. He could not imagine why anyone should voluntarily spend any time in these waters where piracy was still smouldering, nor why anyone should wish to visit countries where malaria and yellow fever were endemic, and where civil war, revolution and massacre claimed even heavier toll.

"You find the *Bride of Abydos* a comfortable ship?" asked Hornblower.

Those eighteen-gun brigs of the Royal Navy were notoriously unpleasant craft, crowded and crank.

"Comfortable enough, my lord, thank you," answered Ramsbottom. "I lightened her by changing the armament; she mounts only twelve guns now—two long sixes and ten carronades, twenty-four-pounders instead of thirty-two-pounders."

"So you could still deal with a pirate?"

"Oh yes indeed, my lord. And with the reduction in weight on deck—a full ten tons—and modifications in her sail plan I have made a seaworthy craft of her, I believe and hope."

"I'm sure you have, Mr. Ramsbottom," said Hornblower. It was likely enough; the brigs of war were naturally crammed with guns and warlike stores to the limit of stability and human endurance, so that a moderate reduction in dead weight might produce profound results in comfort and handiness.

"It would give me the greatest pleasure," went on Mr. Ramsbottom, "if I could induce your lordship to visit me on board. It would indeed be an honour, and would gratify my crew. Perhaps I could even persuade your lordship to dine on board?"

"We can discuss that after you have dined with me, Mr. Ramsbottom," replied Hornblower, remembering his manners and his obligation to invite to dinner any bearer of a reasonable introduction.

"You are most kind, my lord," said Mr. Ramsbottom. "I must, of course, present my introductions to His Excellency at the earliest opportunity."

There was something quite winning about Mr. Ramsbottom's smile as he said this, an awareness and a tolerance of the rules of social etiquette. A visitor to Jamaica would normally be bound to pay his respects first to the Governor, but Ramsbottom was no ordinary visitor; as captain of a ship, his first call was due to the naval authorities, to Hornblower, in fact. A trivial point, as his smile implied, but, etiquette being etiquette, trivial points demanded strict attention.

By the time Ramsbottom took his leave he had made a very good impression on the reluctant Hornblower. He had talked sensibly about ships and the sea; he was easy and natural in his manner, and not in the least like Lord Byron, who was probably more responsible than anyone else for the growing fad for yachting among the wealthy. Hornblower was even prepared to forgive him for having "won some small portion" of Barbara's heart. And in the course of his several days' stay in Jamaica Hornblower really came to like the young man, especially after having lost two pounds to him in a desperate tussle at whist and then winning ten pounds back in another tussle where admittedly Ramsbottom encountered a run of bad luck. Jamaican society gave Ramsbottom a warm welcome; even the Governor looked on him with approval, and the Governor's wife, Lady Hooper, was loud in her praises of his excellent manners and considerate ways.

"I wouldn't have expected it of a Bradford manufacturer's son," said Hooper grudgingly.

"Are you dining on board the *Bride of Abydos*, sir?" asked Hornblower.

"I am going there to dinner," answered Hooper, who enjoyed food, "but seeing that it is only a yacht I have little hope of dining."

Hornblower arrived on board early, at Ramsbottom's suggestion, so as to have time to inspect the vessel. He was received in navy fashion with sideboys attending the side and a long flourish on boatswain's pipes as he stepped on board. He looked keenly about him even while he shook Ramsbottom's hand. He could not have said he was not in a King's ship, as his eye took in the gleaming white deck, the ropes coiled in perfect symmetry, the gleaming trophy of pikes and cutlasses against the bulkhead, the brass winking in the sunshine, the disciplined orderly crew in blue jumpers and white trousers.

"May I present my officers, my lord?" asked Ramsbottom.

They were two half-pay lieutenants, hard-bitten men; as Hornblower shook their hands he told himself that if it had not been for a dozen strokes of luck he himself might still be a lieutenant, perhaps eking out his half pay by serving in a rich man's yacht. As Ramsbottom led him forward he recognized one of the hands standing at attention by a gun.

"You were with me in the *Renown,* out here in 1800," he said.

"Yes, sir, my lord, so I was, sir." The man grinned with uneasy pleasure as he shyly took Hornblower's outstretched hand. "And Charlie Kemp, sir, my lord, over there, sir, 'e was with you in the Baltic. And Bill Cummings, up on the fo'c'sle, 'e was foretopman in the *Lydia* round the Horn with you, sir, my lord."

"Glad to see you again," said Hornblower. That was true, but he was equally glad that he had not been under the necessity of remembering names. He moved on.

"You seem to have a navy crew, Mr. Ramsbottom," he remarked.

"Yes, my lord. They are nearly all man-o'-warsmen."

In these years of peace and depression it would be easy enough to recruit a crew, thought Hornblower. Ramsbottom might be considered to be doing a public service in providing easy employment for these men who had deserved well of their country. Listening to the sharp orders given as the crew were put through their paces, Hornblower could not suppress a smile. It was a harmless enough fad, he supposed, for Ramsbottom to indulge himself in playing at commanding a ship of war.

"You have a most efficient ship and a well-trained crew, Mr. Ramsbottom," he said.

"It is a pleasure to hear your lordship say so."

"You have seen no service yourself?"

"None, my lord."

There was a certain degree of surprise still to be found in the fact that in this year of 1821 there were grown men, even heads of families, who nevertheless had been too young to see service in the wars that had devastated the world for a whole generation. It made Hornblower feel like a centenarian.

"Here come further guests, my lord, if you will pardon me."

Two planters—Hough and Doggart—and then the Chief Justice of the island. So the arrival of the Governor would make a dinner party of six, three officials and three men in private life. They gathered under the awning, which, stretched across the main boom, shaded the quarterdeck, and watched the reception of His Excellency.

"Do you think the dinner will come up to the ceremonial?" asked Doggart.

"Ramsbottom's purser bought two tons of ice yesterday," said Hough.

"At sixpence a pound that bids fair," commented Doggart.

Jamaica was the centre of a small trade in ice, brought down from New England in fast schooners. Cut and stored away in deep places during the winter, it was hurried to the Caribbean insulated in a packing of sawdust. At the height of summer it commanded fantastic prices. Hornblower was interested; he was more interested still in the sight of a seaman down in the waist steadily turning a crank. It did not seem a very hard labour, although unremitting. He could not for the life of him think of what function that crank could play in the life of the ship. The guests made their bows to His Excellency, and at his suggestion seated themselves in the comfortable chairs. A steward appeared at once passing round glasses of sherry.

"Excellent, by George!" exclaimed the Governor after his first cautious sip. "None of your Olorosos, none of your sweet sticky dark sherries."

The Governor, by virtue of his reputed royal blood as well as in consequence of his position, could make remarks that well might appear rude in another man. But the sherry was indeed delightful; pale, dry, infinitely delicate in flavour and bouquet, cool but not chilled. A new sound struck on Hornblower's ear, and he turned and looked forward. At the foot of the mainmast a small orchestra had struck up, of various stringed instruments whose names he had never bothered to learn except for the fiddle. If it were not for the intrusion of this horrible music there could be nothing more delightful than to sit under an awning on the deck of a well-found ship with the sea breeze just beginning to come in, drinking this excellent sherry. The Governor made a small gesture which brought a fresh glass promptly to him.

"Ah!" said the Governor. "You keep a good orchestra, Mr. Ramsbottom."

It was well known that the royal family inherited a taste for music.

"I must thank Your Excellency," said Ramsbottom, and the glasses went round again before he turned an ear to the murmured words of the steward. "Your Excellency, my lord, gentlemen, dinner is served."

They filed down the companion; apparently every bulkhead had been taken down in the after part of the ship to make a cabin spacious though low. The carronades on either side struck a subdued warlike note in a scene of luxury, for there were flowers everywhere; the dining table stood in the centre concealed under a glittering linen cloth. Wind scoops at the scuttles helped to deflect the trade wind into the cabin, which, under the double shade of the awning and the deck, was pleasantly cool, but Hornblower's eye at once caught sight of a couple of strange objects, like small wheels, set in two scuttles and ceaselessly whirling round. Then he knew why the seaman was turning that crank in the waist; he was driving these two wheels, which by some ingenious mechanism propelled currents of air from outside into the cabin, acting like windmill vanes but in the opposite sense.

Seated at the table in accordance with the courteous indications of their host, the guests awaited the serving of the dinner. The first course made its appearance—two ample dishes set in dishes even more amply filled with cracked ice. The inner dishes held a grey granular substance.

"Caviare!" exclaimed His Excellency, helping himself liberally after his first astonished stare.

"I hope it is to your taste, sir," said Ramsbottom. "And I hope you will accompany it with some of the vodka here. It is the same as is served at the Russian imperial table."

Conversation regarding caviare and vodka occupied the attention of all during the first course. The last time Hornblower had tasted the combination was during the defence of Riga in 1812; the experience enabled him to add his quota to the conversation. The next course made its appearance.

"You gentlemen are accustomed to this dish," said Ramsbottom, "but I need not apologize for it. It is, I believe, one of the delicacies of the islands."

It was flying fish.

"Certainly no need to apologize when it is served like this," commented His Excellency. "Your *chef de cuisine* must be a man of genius."

The sauce that came with it had the merest hint of mustard.

"'Ock or champagne, my lord?" murmured a voice in Hornblower's ear. Hornblower had already heard the Governor answer the same question with "I'll try the hock first." The champagne was dry and insidiously delicate, an ideal companion for the food. The great eaters of antiquity, Nero or Vitellius or Lucullus, had never known what it was like to partake of champagne and flying fish.

"You'll be living differently from this soon, Hornblower," said His Excellency.

"No doubt about that, sir."

Ramsbottom, between them, looked a polite inquiry.

"Your lordship's going to sea?"

"Next week," replied Hornblower. "I take my squadron to sea for exercises before the coming of the hurricane season."

"Of course that would be necessary to maintain efficiency," agreed Ramsbottom. "The exercises will last for long?"

"A couple of weeks or more," said Hornblower. "I have to keep my men accustomed to hardtack and salt pork and water from the cask."

"And yourself too," chuckled the Governor.

"Myself too," agreed Hornblower ruefully.

"And you take your whole squadron, my lord?" asked Ramsbottom.

"All I can. I work 'em hard to try to make no exceptions."

"A good rule, I should think," said Ramsbottom.

The soup that followed the flying fish was a fiery mulligatawny, well adapted to West Indian palates.

"Good!" was the Governor's brief comment after his first spoonful. The champagne went round again and conversation became livelier and livelier, and Ramsbottom deftly kept it going.

"What news from the mainland, sir?" he asked the Governor. "This fellow Bolívar—is he making any progress?"

"He fights on," answered the Governor. "But Spain hurries out reinforcements whenever her own troubles permit. The government at Caracas is looking for the arrival of more at this moment, I believe. Then they may be able to conquer the plains and drive him out again. You know he was a refugee here in this very island a few years ago?"

"Indeed, sir?"

All the guests at the table were interested in the desperate civil war that was being fought on the mainland. Massacre and murder, blind heroism and devoted self-sacrifice, loyalty to the King and thirst for independence—all these were to be found in Venezuela; war and pestilence were laying waste the fertile plains and depopulating the crowded cities.

"How will the Spaniards stand now that Maracaibo has revolted, Hornblower?" asked the Governor.

"It's not a serious loss, sir. As long as they have the use of La Guaira their sea communications remain open—the roads are so bad that Caracas has always made use of La Guaira to preserve contact with the outside world; it's only an open roadstead but it provides good anchorage."

"Has Maracaibo revolted, Your Excellency?" asked Ramsbottom mildly.

"The news came this morning. A feather in Bolívar's cap after his recent defeats. His army must have been growing disheartened."

"His army, sir?" This was the Chief Justice speaking. "Half his men are British infantry."

Hornblower knew that to be true. British veterans formed the backbone of Bolívar's army. The *llaneros*—the men of the Venezuelan plains—supplied him with a brilliant cavalry, but not with the material for permanent conquest.

"Even British infantry could grow disheartened in a hopeless cause," said the Governor solemnly. "The Spaniards control most of the coast—ask the Admiral here."

"That's so," agreed Hornblower. "They've made it hard for Bolívar's privateers."

"I hope you're not going to venture into that turmoil, Mr. Ramsbottom," said the Governor.

"They'll make short work of you if you do," added the Chief Justice. "The Dons will tolerate no interference. They'll snatch you up and you'll languish in a Spanish prison for years before we can extricate you from King Ferdinand's clutches. Unless jail fever carries you off first. Or they hang you as a pirate."

"I have certainly no intention of venturing near the mainland," said Ramsbottom. "At least not while this war continues. It is a pity, because Venezuela was my mother's country, and it would give me pleasure to visit it."

"Your mother's country, Mr. Ramsbottom?" asked the Governor.

"Yes, sir. My mother was a Venezuelan lady. There I would be Carlos Ramsbottom y Santoña."

"Most interesting," remarked the Governor.

And more grotesque than Horatio Hornblower. It was significant of the world-wide interests of British commerce that a Bradford woollen manufacturer should have a Venezuelan mother. At any rate it accounted for Ramsbottom's dark, almost swarthy, good looks.

"I can very well wait until peace is settled one way or the other," said Ramsbottom off-handedly. "There will be other voyages to make. Meanwhile, sir, let me call your attention to this dish here."

The main course had now arrived on the table, roast chickens and a leg of pork as well as the dish that Ramsbottom indicated. What lay in it was concealed by poached eggs covering the surface.

"A made dish?" asked the Governor doubtfully. His tone indicated that at this stage of the dinner he looked rather for a substantial roast.

"Please try it, sir," said Ramsbottom coaxingly.

The Governor helped himself and tasted cautiously.

"Pleasant enough," he decided. "What is it?"

"A ragout of preserved beef," answered Ramsbottom. "Can I persuade you gentlemen to try it? My lord?"

At least it was something new; it was like nothing Hornblower had ever tasted before—certainly not in the least like the beef preserved in brine which he had eaten for twenty years.

"Extremely good," said Hornblower. "How is it preserved?"

Ramsbottom made a gesture to the waiting steward, who laid a square box, apparently of iron, upon the table. It weighed heavy in Hornblower's hand.

"Glass serves equally well," explained Ramsbottom, "but it is not as convenient on shipboard."

The steward was now at work upon the iron box with a stout knife. He cut it open and prized back the top and offered it for inspection.

"A tinned box," went on Ramsbottom, "sealed at a high temperature. I venture to suggest that this new method will make a noticeable difference to the food supply on shipboard. This beef can be eaten cold on removal from the box, or it can be hashed as you have it here."

"And the poached egg?" asked the Governor.

"That was the inspiration of my cook, sir."

Discussion of this new invention—and of the excellent Burgundy served with this course—distracted attention from the troubles of Venezuela, and even from Ramsbottom's Venezuelan mother. Conversation became general, and somewhat disjointed as the wine flowed. Hornblower had drunk as much as he desired, and, with his habitual dislike of excess, contrived to avoid drinking more. It was noticeable that Ramsbottom remained sober as well, cool and quiet-voiced, while the other faces grew redder and redder, and the cabin echoed to the roaring toasts and the bursts of inconsequential song. Hornblower guessed that his host was now finding the evening as tedious as he himself found it. He was glad when at last His Excellency rose, supporting himself by the table, to take his leave.

"A damned good dinner," he said. "And you're a damned good host, Ramsbottom. Wish there were more like you."

Hornblower shook hands.

"It was very good of you to come, my lord," said Ramsbottom. "I regret that I must take this opportunity to say good-bye to your lordship."

"You are sailing soon?"

"In a couple of days, I expect, my lord. I trust you will find your squadron exercises satisfactory."

"Thank you very much. Where will you head for now?"

"I shall beat back through the Windward Channel, my lord. Perhaps I shall see something of the Bahamas."

"Be careful of your navigation there. I must wish you good luck and a pleasant voyage. I shall write to my wife and tell her of your visit."

"Please give Lady Hornblower my best wishes and respects, my lord."

Ramsbottom's good manners persisted to the end; he remembered to send round his cards "*Pour prendre congé*" before he left, and mothers of unmarried daughters much regretted his leaving. Hornblower saw the *Bride of Abydos* in the early dawn reaching to the eastward to round Morant Point with the land breeze, and then forgot about her in the bustle of taking his squadron to sea for exercises.

It never failed to raise a wry smile on his face when he looked about him at "His Majesty's Ships and Vessels in the West Indies" under his command. In wartime he would have had a powerful fleet; now he had three small frigates and a motley collection of brigs and schooners. But they would serve his purpose; in his scheme the frigates became three-deckers and the brigs seventy-fours and the schooners frigates. He had a van, a centre, and a rear; he cruised in formation ready to meet the enemy, with rasping reprimands soaring up his signal halliards when any ship failed to keep station; he cleared for action and he turned by divisions into fighting line ahead; he tacked to double on the imaginary enemy's line. In pitch darkness he would burn blue lights with the signal "Enemy in sight" so that a score of captains and a thousand seamen came tumbling from their beds to deal with the non-existent foe.

Without warning he would hang out a signal putting the most junior lieutenants in command of their respective ships, and then he would plunge into intricate manoeuvres calculated to turn the anxious substantive captains, looking helplessly on, grey with anxiety —but those junior lieutenants might some day be commanding ships of the line in a battle on which the destiny of England might depend, and it was necessary to steel their nerves and accustom them to handle ships in dangerous situations. In the middle of sail drill he would signal "Flagship on fire. All boats away." He called for landing parties to storm non-existent batteries on some harmless uninhabited cay, and he inspected those landing parties once they were on shore, to the last flint in the last pistol, and treated excuses with a disregard that made men grind their teeth in exasperation. He set his captains to plan and execute cutting-out expeditions, and he commented mordantly on the arrangements for defence and the methods of attack. He paired off his ships to fight single-ship duels, sighting each other on the horizon and approaching ready to fire the vital opening broadside; he took advantage of calms to set his men to work towing and sweeping in desperate attempts to overtake the ship ahead. He worked his crews until they were ready to drop, and then he devised further tasks for them to prove to them that they still had one more effort left in them, so that it was doubtful whether "Old Horny" was mentioned more often with curses or with admiration.

It was a toughened squadron that Hornblower led back to Kingston; but while *Clorinda* was still working up into the harbour a shore boat came pulling out to her, with on board an aide-de-camp of the Governor's with a note for Hornblower.

"Sir Thomas, would you have the kindness to call away my barge?" asked Hornblower.

There was much apparent need for haste, for the note from Government House said briefly:

My Lord,

It is necessary that your lordship should attend here at the earliest possible moment to offer an explanation regarding the situation in Venezuela. Your lordship is therefore requested and required to report to me immediately.

Augustus Hooper, Governor

Hornblower naturally had no idea of what had happened in Venezuela for the last two weeks and more. He made no guess while the carriage took him up to Government House at its best pace, and in any case if he had tried he would never have succeeded in coming near to the truth.

"What is all this, Hornblower?" were the Governor's opening words to him. "What authority have you for blockading the Venezuelan coast? Why was I not informed?"

"I've done nothing of the sort," replied Hornblower indignantly.

"But— Damn it, man, I've the proof here. I've Dutchmen and Spaniards and half the nations of the earth here all protesting about it."

"I assure you, sir, I have taken no action on the Venezuelan coast. I have not been within five hundred miles of it."

"Then what does this mean?" shouted the Governor. "Look here at this!"

He held some papers up with one hand and slapped wildly at them with the other, so that Hornblower had some difficulty in taking them from him. Hornblower was bewildered already; he was more bewildered still as he read. One paper was an official despatch in French, from the Dutch governor of Curaçao; the other was larger and clearer, and he read it first. It was a big sheet of paper with bold writing.

Whereas [it began] notice has been received by the Lords Commissioners for executing the office of the Lord High Admiral from the Right Honourable Viscount Castlereagh, one of His Britannic Majesty's Principal Secretaries of State, concerning the need to establish a blockade of the Coast of His Most Catholic Majesty's Dominion of Venezuela, and of the Islands pertaining to the Dominion of His Majesty the King of the Netherlands, namely and to wit Curaçao, Aruba, and Bonaire,

Therefore I, Horatio Lord Hornblower, Knight Grand Cross of the Most Honourable Order of the Bath, Rear Admiral of the White Squadron, Commanding His Britannic Majesty's Ships and Vessels in West Indian Waters,

Hereby Proclaim that

The Coast of the Continent of South America from Cartagena to the Dragon's Mouth and

The Dutch Islands aforesaid of Curaçao, Aruba, and Bonaire

Are now in a state of blockade, and that

Any vessel of whatever description, whether carrying materials of war or not, found attempting to enter any port, harbour, or roadstead within the Territory so defined, or

Hovering with the intent to enter any such port, harbour, or roadstead,

Will be boarded and sent in for adjudication under His Britannic Majesty's High Court of Admiralty and

Will be condemned and seized without compensation to owners, freight owners, charterers, captain, or crew.

Given under my hand this First Day of June 1821,

HORNBLOWER, REAR ADMIRAL

Having read this document, Hornblower was able to spare a second glance at the other. It was a vigorous protest from the Dutch governor at Curaçao demanding explanations, apologies, the immediate withdrawal of the blockade, and exemplary compensation. Hornblower stared at Hooper in astonishment.

"This is in legal form," he said, indicating the proclamation, "but I never signed it. This is not my signature."

"Then—?" spluttered Hooper. "I thought you might be acting under secret orders from London."

"Of course not, sir." Hornblower stared at Hooper for another long second before the explanation came to him. "Ramsbottom!"

"What do you mean?"

"He's been posing as me, or as one of my officers at least. Is the Dutch officer who brought this available?"

"He's waiting in the next room. There's a Spaniard there, too, sent over in a fishing boat by Morillo from La Guaira."

"Can we have them in, sir?"

The Dutchman and the Spaniard were men full of indignation, which was not abated in the least by their presentation to the admiral responsible, in their minds, for this trouble. The Dutchman spoke fluent English, and it was to him that Hornblower first addressed himself.

"How was this proclamation delivered?" he asked.

"By one of your ships. By one of your officers."

"What ship?"

"The brig of war *Desperate.*"

"I have no such ship. There's none in the Navy List. Who brought it?"

"The captain."

"Who was he? What was he like?"

"He was an officer. A commander, with epaulettes."

"In uniform?"

"In full uniform."

"Young? Old?"

"Very young."

"Small? Slender? Handsome?"

"Yes."

Hornblower exchanged a glance with Hooper.

"And this brig, the *Desperate*. About a hundred and seventy tons, bowsprit steved nearly level, mainmast stepped rather far aft?"

"Yes."

"That settles it, sir," said Hornblower to Hooper, and, to the Dutchman, "You've been fooled, I'm sorry to say. This man was an impostor. This proclamation is a forgery."

The Dutchman stamped with annoyance. He was unable to find words to express himself in a foreign tongue for some moments. Finally from his splutterings emerged a name, which he repeated until it was understandable.

"The *Helmond!* The *Helmond!*"

"What is the *Helmond*, sir?" asked Hornblower.

"One of our ships. Your ship—this *Desperate*—captured her."

"A valuable ship?"

"She had on board the guns for the Spanish army. Two batteries of field artillery, guns, limbers, ammunition, everything."

"Piracy!" exclaimed Hooper.

"It sounds like it," said Hornblower.

The Spanish officer had been standing by impatiently, apparently only half understanding the English conversation. Hornblower turned to him, and, after desperately trying to recapture his half-forgotten Spanish, entered upon a limping explanation. The Spaniard replied volubly, so volubly that more than once Hornblower had to ask him to speak more slowly. Ramsbottom had come sailing into La Guaira and had brought his precious proclamation with him. At the merest hint that the British navy was instituting a blockade no ship had dared to stir on the South American coast, except for the *Helmond*. She had been badly needed. Bolívar was marching on Caracas; a battle was imminent on which depended the entire Spanish control of Venezuela. Morillo and the Spanish army were in need of artillery. Now not only were they left destitute, but with this news it could be taken as certain that those guns, those two batteries of field artillery, were in Bolívar's hands. The Spanish officer wrung his hands in despair.

Hornblower translated briefly for the Governor's benefit, and Hooper shook his head in sympathy.

"Bolívar has those guns. No doubt about it. Gentlemen, I much regret this occurrence. But I must impress upon you that His Majesty's government assumes no responsibility for it. If your chiefs took no steps to detect this impostor—"

That touched off a new explosion. The British government should make sure that no impostor wore its uniform or posed as an officer in its service. It called for all Hooper's elephantine tact to quiet down the angry officers.

"If you will permit me to consult with the Admiral, gentlemen, we may reach some satisfactory conclusion."

Alone with the Governor again Hornblower struggled with a smile; he had never outgrown his tendency to laugh during a crisis. There was something amusing in the thought that a cocked hat and a pair of epaulettes should change the course of a war; it was a tribute to the power of the navy that a single tiny ship should exert such enormous pressure.

"Ramsbottom and his Venezuelan mother!" said Hooper. "It's not merely piracy, it's high treason. We shall have to hang him."

"M'm," said Hornblower. "He probably holds a privateering commission from Bolívar."

"But masquerading as a British officer? Forging official documents?"

"That was a ruse of war. An American officer deceived the Portuguese authorities in Brazil in much the same way in 1812."

"I've heard some things about you, too," added Hooper with a grin.

"No doubt, sir. In war a belligerent who believes what he's told is a fool."

"But we're not belligerents."

"No, sir. And we've suffered no loss. The Dutch and the Spaniards have only themselves to blame."

"But Ramsbottom's a subject of His Majesty."

"Quite true, sir. But if he holds a Bolívar's commission he can do things as an officer of the revolutionary forces which he could not do as a private person."

"D'ye mean to suggest we ought to allow him to continue this blockade of his? Nonsense, man."

"Of course not, sir. I'll arrest him, and I'll send his ship in for adjudication, at the first opportunity. But a friendly power has asked you, sir, the representative of His Majesty, if you have instituted a blockade. You must do everything in your power to demonstrate the truth."

"Now for once you're talking like a sensible man. We must send word at once to Curaçao and Caracas. That will be your immediate duty. You'd better go in person."

"Yes, sir. I'll sail with the land breeze. Have you any further instructions for me, sir?"

"None whatever. What goes on on the high seas is your affair, not mine. You're answerable to the Cabinet through the Admiralty. I don't envy you, frankly."

"No doubt I'll survive, sir. I'll sail for La Guaira, and send another vessel to Curaçao. Perhaps if Your Excellency were to write official replies to the inquiries addressed to you they would be ready by the time I sail?"

"I'll draught 'em now." The Governor could not repress one further outburst. "This Ramsbottom—and his corned beef and caviare!"

"He used a sprat to catch a mackerel, Your Excellency," said Hornblower.

So it came about that the crew of H.M.S. *Clorinda* did not spend that night in the debauchery of Kingston as they had expected. Instead they worked until dawn completing with stores and water, so hard that they had no breath to spare to curse the admiral who did these things to them. In the very first light of morning they warped their ship out with the aid of the faint puffs of the land breeze, and *Clorinda*, her admiral's flag flying at the mizzen, headed close-hauled to the southeastward on her thousand-mile voyage to La Guaira. She had on board Brigadier General Don Manuel Ruiz, Morillo's representative, to whom Hornblower had offered a passage back to his headquarters. The man was in a fever to return and put an end to Ramsbottom's blockade; it was clear that the royal forces in Venezuela were hard pressed. He had no thought for anything else during that voyage. The lovely sunsets meant to him merely that another day had gone by without his reaching his destination. The gallant way in which *Clorinda* held her course, close-hauled, shouldering the long rollers aside in showers of spray, held no fascination for him, for she was not flying before the wind at her best speed. At noon each day, when the ship's position was pricked off on the chart, he would look long and despairingly, estimating by eye the further distance to be traversed. He had not had sufficient experience at sea to acquire the knack of resigning himself to the influence of forces beyond human control. When the wind drew southerly and foul, as it did for two days consecutively, he was clearly on the verge of accusing Hornblower of being in league with his enemies, and made no attempt to understand Hornblower's soothing explanation that on the starboard tack on which *Clorinda* was compelled to lie they were making easting which might be invaluable in possible later eventualities. He resented the caution of Captain Fell which led to *Clorinda*'s shortening sail as they entered the dangerous proximity of Grand Cay, and at dawn next day he was climbing the foremast shrouds as high as he dared, looking out for the first sight of the mountains of Venezuela—and even then he did not recognize as land the blue streak which he saw.

A shore boat came out to them before ever they dropped anchor, and there was an urgent conference on *Clorinda*'s quarterdeck between Ruiz and the officer it brought out.

"My general is in Carabobo," said Ruiz to Hornblower. "A battle is going to be fought. Bolívar is marching on Puerto Cabello, and my general has taken the army to meet him."

"Where is Ramsbottom and his ship?"

Ruiz looked to the arrival for the information.

"Near Puerto Cabello."

That was of course the likeliest place, a hundred miles or less to the westward, a roadstead where supplies might possibly be landed, and an ideal situation for intercepting all communications between Curaçao and La Guaira.

"Then I shall head for Puerto Cabello," said Hornblower. "You can accompany me if you wish, Don Manuel. The wind is fair and I'll land you there quicker than a horse would carry you."

Ruiz hesitated for a moment; he knew all about horses and he was suspicious of ships. But the advantage was so obvious that he accepted.

"Very well then," said Hornblower. "Sir Thomas, we'll hoist that anchor again, if you would be so kind. Set a course for Puerto Cabello."

Now *Clorinda* had the lusty trade wind on her quarter, her best point of sailing; she had her studding sails out and every possible stitch of canvas set, and she flew along. A horse at full gallop might go faster, but no horse could do as *Clorinda* was doing and maintain full speed for hour after hour, nor could any horse ever attain full speed on the mountain tracks of the Maritime Andes. Naturally no amount of speed could satisfy Ruiz. With telescope to his eye he watched the distant coast go by until his weary eye was almost blind, and then he paced about the quarterdeck, trickles of sweat running down his forehead and cheeks as the sun, climbing to its noontide height, blazed vertically down on him. He turned a suspicious eye on Hornblower when the crew of *Clorinda* poured aloft to take in sail.

"We are going in to shore now, General," explained Hornblower soothingly.

The leadsmen were in the chains as *Clorinda* headed in towards the roadstead. In the middle of their chant Ruiz suddenly turned to Hornblower and stood rigid, listening to another, more distant, sound.

"Cannons!" he said.

Hornblower strained his ears. The faintest, almost imperceptible noise, and then silence, save for the sound of the ship through the water and the bustle of preparing to come to an anchor.

"Order the 'Still' for a moment, if you please, Sir Thomas."

Now the leadsmen ceased their chant, and every man in *Clorinda* stood silent, even though the wind still played through the rigging and the sea chattered alongside. A very distant, flat detonation. Another. Two more.

"Thank you, Sir Thomas. You may carry on now."

"Cannons!" repeated Ruiz, glaring at Hornblower. "They are fighting the battle."

Somewhere on the outskirts of Puerto Cabello Royalists and Republicans were locked in combat. And those guns that they had heard? They might well be those that the *Helmond* had carried, now in the hands of the insurgents and firing upon their legal owners. The fact that artillery was being employed indicated a pitched battle, no petty skirmish. Over there the fate of Venezuela was being decided. Ruiz was pounding his fist into his open palm.

"Sir Thomas, kindly have a boat ready to land the General without delay."

As the gig pulled away from *Clorinda*'s side Hornblower looked up at the sun, called up before his mind's eye the chart of the Venezuelan coast, and reached a further decision. As always in the service, a long dull interval had heralded a period of activity. As the gig came skimming back again he was ready with his next order.

"Will you be so good as to make sail again, Sir Thomas? We

can continue to search to the westward for Ramsbottom while daylight lasts."

It was desirable to obtain the earliest possible news of the result
of the battle, but it was also, or more, desirable to lay hands on
Ramsbottom as quickly as might be. They had not sighted him between La Guaira and Puerto Cabello; he could not be much farther
along the coast. The sun was descending now, dazzling the lookouts
as they peered towards it while *Clorinda* continued her course along
the shores of the province of Carabobo. Not so far ahead the land
trended abruptly northward to San Juan Point—a lee shore. It was
curious that Ramsbottom should have gone even this far to leeward,
unless he had put up his helm and headed clear away, guessing that
his period of grace was at an end.

"Deck, there!" The lookout at the fore topgallant masthead was
hailing. "There's summat on the port bow, just in sight. Right in the
eye of the sun. But it may be a ship, sir. A ship's masts an' yards,
sir, with no sail set."

It would be incredible that Ramsbottom had anchored here on
this dangerous lee shore. But incredible things have to be done in
war. *Clorinda* had long ago taken in her studding sails. Now after a
sharp order from Fell, and five minutes' activity on the part of her
crew, she was gliding along under topsails and headsails alone. The
sun sank into a bank of cloud, suffusing it with scarlet.

"Deck, there! Two ships, sir. At anchor. One of 'em's a brig, sir."

A brig! Ramsbottom almost for certain. Now with the sun behind
the cloud it was possible to train a telescope in the direction indicated. There they were, sharp and clear against the sunset, silhouetted in black against the scarlet cloud, the masts and yards of a ship
and a brig at anchor. Sir Thomas was looking to Hornblower for
orders.

"Approach as close as you consider advisable, if you please, Sir
Thomas. And a boarding party ready to take possession."

"An armed boarding party, my lord?"

"As you please. He'll never dare to oppose us by force."

The guns of the brig were not run out, there were no boarding
nettings rigged. In any case the little brig stood no chance in an
unsheltered anchorage against a frigate.

"I'll anchor if I may, my lord."

"Certainly."

That was the *Bride of Abydos,* without a doubt. No mistaking her at all. And the other one? Most likely the *Helmond*. With the revolt of Maracaibo this part of the coast had fallen into the power of the insurgents. The batteries of field artillery that she had carried could be rafted ashore here—there was a beach in that little cove where it would be possible—and delivered to the insurgent army gathering for its march on Puerto Cabello. Ramsbottom, his task completed, would presumably be prepared to brazen it out, pleading—as Hornblower had already guessed—some privateering commission from Bolívar.

"I'll go with the boarding party, Sir Thomas."

Fell shot a questioning glance. Admirals had no business boarding strange craft from small boats, not only when bullets might fly but when one of the infinite variety of accidents possible in small boats might lead to an elderly and not so active senior officer being dropped overside and never coming up again, with endless trouble later for the captain. Hornblower could follow Fell's train of thought, but he was not going to wait quiescent on *Clorinda's* quarterdeck until a report came back from the *Bride of Abydos*—not when a word would give him the power of finding out several minutes earlier.

"I'll get your sword and pistols, my lord," said Gerard.

"Nonsense!" said Hornblower. "Look there!"

He had kept his telescope trained on the anchored ships, and had detected a significant activity around them. Boats were pulling hastily away from both of them and heading for the shore. Ramsbottom seemed to be absconding.

"Come along!" said Hornblower.

He ran to the ship's side and leaped for the boat's falls; sliding down, clumsily, cost him some of the skin from his soft palms.

"Cast off! Pull!" he ordered as Gerard tumbled in beside him. "Pull!"

The boat swung away from the ship's side, soared giddily up a swell and down again, the men throwing their weight on the oars. But the boat that was leaving the *Bride of Abydos* was not being handled in the man-o'-war fashion one would have expected of Ramsbottom. The oars were being plied without any coordination; the boat swung round on the swell, and then, as somebody caught a crab, swung round again. In next to no time Hornblower found himself alongside the struggling craft. The men at the oars were not the spruce seamen he had seen on board the *Bride of Abydos*. They were swarthy men clothed in rags. Nor was that Ramsbottom in the sternsheets. Instead it was someone with a heavy black moustache wearing some vestiges of a blue and silver uniform. The reddening sunset glared down upon him.

"Who are you?" demanded Hornblower, and then repeated the question in Spanish.

The boat had ceased its struggles and was lying on its oars, rising and falling on the swell.

"Lieutenant Perez of the First Regiment of Infantry of the Army of Greater Colombia."

Greater Colombia. That was what Bolívar called the republic he was trying to establish by his rebellion against Spain.

"Where is Mr. Ramsbottom?"

"The Admiral has been on shore for the last week."

"The Admiral?"

"Don Carlos Ramsbottom y Santoña, Admiral of the Navy of Greater Colombia." An admiral, no less.

"What were you doing on board that ship?"

"I was taking care of her until Your Excellency came."

"Is there nobody on board, then?"

"Nobody."

The boats soared up a swell and sank down again. It was a sickly thing to do, not conducive to logical thought. He had been prepared to arrest Ramsbottom, but it would be another matter to arrest a lieutenant of infantry, in territorial waters.

"Where is the crew of the ship?"

"On shore with the Admiral. With the army."

Fighting for Bolívar, presumably. And presumably as artillery men serving the stolen guns.

"Very well. You may go."

It was sufficient to make sure of the *Bride of Abydos;* there was no purpose in laying hands on men of Bolívar's army who had only been obeying the orders of their superiors.

"Lay me alongside the brig."

In the fading light the deck of the *Bride of Abydos* was not in too great disorder. The departing crew had apparently left everything shipshape, and the caretaking party of South American soldiers had not disturbed anything—although below deck it would probably be a different story. But what would have happened if a gale had blown up in this perilous anchorage on a lee shore would not bear thinking about. Presumably Ramsbottom had not cared what happened to his little ship once he had brought off his coup.

"Ahoy! Ahoy!"

Someone was hailing through a speaking trumpet from the other ship. Hornblower took the speaking trumpet from its becket by the wheel and hailed back.

"I am Admiral Lord Hornblower of His Britannic Majesty's Service. I am coming aboard."

It was almost dark when he mounted to the deck of the *Helmond*, to be welcomed by the light of a couple of lanterns. The captain who greeted him was a thickset man speaking excellent English with a marked accent, Dutch, presumably.

"You have not arrived too soon, sir," was his uncompromising beginning, not the way to address any officer of the Royal Navy, certainly not an admiral and a peer.

"I'll thank you to be civil," snapped Hornblower, his temper frayed.

Two angry men faced each other in the wavering light, and then the Dutchman realized that it would be better to restrain his ill temper in dealing with someone who, after all, had the power on this lonely coast to enforce any orders he might issue.

"Please come below, sir," he said. "Perhaps a glass of schnapps—?"

It was a comfortable, well-furnished cabin in which Hornblower was offered a seat and a glass.

"I was glad when I saw your topsails, sir," said the Dutch captain. "For ten days I have been through misery. My ship—my cargo—this shore—"

The disjointed words conveyed the anxieties of finding himself in the hands of the insurgents, and of being compelled to anchor off a lee shore with an armed guard on board.

"What happened?" asked Hornblower.

"That damned little brig fired a shot across my bows with Bonaire still in sight. They boarded me when I hove to. Put an armed party on board. I thought she was one of yours, a ship of war. They brought me here and anchored, and the army came out to us. That was when I knew she was not a ship of war, not British."

"Then they took your cargo?"

"They did. Twelve nine-pounder field guns, with limbers and caissons and horse harness. One ammunition waggon. One repair cart with tools. Two thousand rounds of ammunition. One ton of gunpowder in kegs. Everything." The Dutchman was obviously quoting verbatim from his bill of lading.

"How did they get it ashore?"

"On rafts. Those Britishers worked like madmen. And there were seamen among them."

It was a handsome admission, hardly grudging. Presumably keg pontoons had been employed; Hornblower told himself that he would have tackled the problem of getting the cargo onto the beach in that way, at least. Presumably a good deal of unskilled labour had been provided on shore by the insurgent forces, but that hardly detracted from the achievement.

"And then every single man went off with the guns?" asked Hornblower.

"Every man. Not too many for twelve guns."

Not too many. The *Bride of Abydos* carried a crew of some seventy-five men—hardly sufficient, in fact, to man two batteries in action.

"And they left a Venezuelan guard on board?"

"Yes. You saw them go when you came. They kept me here, at anchor on a lee shore."

That of course was to prevent the Dutchman spreading the news of the fraud that had been practiced.

"Those—those brigands knew nothing about ships." The Dutchman was continuing his tale of tribulation. "The *Desperate* started dragging her anchor once. I had to send my own men—"

"You were lucky they didn't burn your ship," said Hornblower. "Luckier still they didn't plunder it. You're lucky not to be in some prison on shore."

"That may be so, but—"

"As it is, sir," said Hornblower, rising, "you are free. You can use the land breeze to make an offing. Tomorrow night you can anchor in Willemstadt."

"But my cargo, sir? I have been detained. I have been in danger. My country's flag—?"

"Your owners can take action as they please. I understand that Ramsbottom is a wealthy man. He can be sued for damages."

"But—but—" The Dutchman could find no words that would express adequately his feelings regarding both his recent treatment and Hornblower's scant sympathy.

"Your government can address protests, of course. To the govern-

ment of Greater Colombia, or to King Ferdinand." Hornblower kept
his face expressionless as he made the ridiculous suggestion. "I must
congratulate you, sir, on your escape from very serious dangers. I
trust you will have a prosperous voyage home."

He had freed the *Helmond,* and he had laid hands on the *Bride
of Abydos.* That much he had accomplished so far, said Hornblower
to himself as the boat took him back to *Clorinda.* The governments
at home could squabble over the legal details, if they cared to go to
the trouble. What the Cabinet and the Admiralty would think about
his actions he could not imagine; he was conscious of a slight chill
of apprehension when his mind dwelt upon that side of the situation.
But an admiral could not show apprehension to anyone, certainly
not to a captain as stupid as Sir Thomas Fell.

"I'll be obliged, Sir Thomas," he said, when he regained *Clorinda's*
deck, "if you will send a prize crew on board the brig. Would you
please be good enough to instruct the officer whom you put in command to keep company with us? We shall sail for Puerto Cabello
again as soon as it is convenient to you."

Fell might be stupid, but he was a capable seaman. Hornblower
could leave to him the anxious business of making his way back
along the coast at night; the land breeze, fluky and unpredictable
though it might be, afforded an opportunity which must not be
missed of regaining the precious miles that had been squandered to
leeward. Hornblower could go down into his stifling cabin and compose himself to sleep. It had been a busy day, and he was physically
weary. He lay on his cot with the sweat trickling irritatingly over
his ribs, trying to persuade his mind to cease from debating the situation. The British public was turning a kindly eye on the struggle
for liberty that was being waged in every corner of the world. British
volunteers were playing their part—Richard Church had been leading the Greek rebellion against the Turks for years now; Cochrane
was at this very moment fighting in the Pacific for South American
independence. For that matter, as he knew, thousands of British soldiers were serving in the ranks of Bolívar's army just over there on
the mainland. Private fortunes in England had been lavished in the
cause of liberty, just as Ramsbottom had been lavishing his.

But none of this was any indication as to how the British Cabinet
would react; national policy might well be at odds with national
opinion. And the Lords of the Admiralty could be counted upon to
be as unpredictable as ever. And that was equally true of His Maj-

esty King George IV; Hornblower suspected that the First Gentleman of Europe had long ago forsaken his half-hearted liberalism.
The near future might hold a severe reprimand for His Majesty's
commander-in-chief in the West Indies; it might even hold disavowal
and recall.

Hornblower's mind had now attained the comforting certainty
that the future was uncertain, and that nothing he could do during
the next few hours could change it. With that, he might well have
gone to sleep; he was, in fact, on the point of dozing off when he
brushed what he thought was a trickle of sweat from his bare ribs. It
was not sweat. A flurry against his fingers told him it was a cock-
roach crawling over his skin, and he started up in disgust. The Caribbean was notorious for its cockroaches, but he had never grown to
tolerate them. He walked across in the darkness and opened the door
to the after cabin, admitting light from the lamp that swung there,
and this revealed a dozen of the disgusting creatures scuttling about.

"My lord?" It was the faithful Gerard hurrying out of bed as soon
as he heard his admiral stirring.

"Go back to bed," said Hornblower.

He put on the silk nightshirt with the elaborate smocking down the
front which had been laid out for him, and went on deck. The moon
had risen now, and *Clorinda* was creeping steadily along with the
land breeze now blowing fresh abeam. Cockroaches had driven
away all thought of his troubles; he could lean against the rail and
contemplate the beauties of the beautiful night with placidity. It fell
calm at dawn, but half an hour later a fortunate slant of wind enabled *Clorinda,* and the *Bride of Abydos* a mile astern, to hold their
course for Puerto Cabello; the town on its peninsula was already in
sight through the telescope and *Clorinda* approached rapidly. There
were fishing boats setting out from the town, small craft which were
using oars to enable them to get to seaward despite the unfavourable
wind. Something about them appeared strange in the telescope, and
as *Clorinda* drew up to them it became apparent that they were
crowded with people, ridiculously overloaded. But they plied their
oars unceasingly, and boldly rounded the peninsula into the open
sea, turning eastward towards La Guaira.

"I think General Morillo has lost his battle," said Hornblower.

"Indeed, my lord?" said Fell deferentially.

"And I think there are plenty of people in Puerto Cabello who

have no desire to be found there when El Libertador comes marching in," added Hornblower.

He had heard that the war of independence was being waged
with Spanish ferocity, that even Bolívar's reputation had been
clouded by executions and massacres. Here was a proof of it. But
those crowded boats were also a proof that Puerto Cabello was expected to fall to Bolívar. He had won his battle of Carabobo; a victory in the open field so close to Caracas meant the certain collapse
of the royal cause. Carabobo would be the Yorktown of the South
American war of independence; no doubt about that. Presumably
Ramsbottom would consider the loss of the *Bride of Abydos* as a small
thing compared with the freeing of a continent.

It was necessary that all this should be confirmed without doubt,
however. The Cabinet would be anxious for early and firsthand information regarding the situation in Venezuela.

"Sir Thomas," said Hornblower, "I shall go ashore."

"You'll have an armed guard, my lord?"

"As you will," said Hornblower. A dozen seamen with muskets
would hardly save him from the clutches of a conquering army, but
agreement saved him from argument and reproachful looks.

By the time Hornblower set foot on the pier in the blinding sunlight the little harbour was deserted. Not a fishing boat was left, nor
was there a human being in sight. He pressed on, his guard tramp-
ing behind him and Gerard at his side. The long winding street was
not quite deserted; there were a few women, a few old men, a few
children to be seen, peering out of the houses. Then away to his right
he heard a brief rattle of musketry, the reports sounding flat in the
heavy damp air. Now here came a ghastly column of sick and
wounded, half naked, hobbling along the road; some fell down to
struggle to their feet again, and some, under Hornblower's very eyes,
fell not to rise again, and of these some managed to roll to the side
of the road and others lay still while their staggering comrades
stumbled over them. Wounded, half naked, barefooted, crazy with
fever or bending double with abdominal pains, they came reeling
along the road, while behind them the rattle of musketry came
nearer and nearer. At the heels of the last of the wounded came the
first of the rear-guard, soldiers whose rags were faintly reminiscent
of the blue and white of the Spanish royal army. Hornblower made
a mental note that the royal forces still could provide a disciplined
rear-guard, and so were not in total rout, but the rear-guard was

woefully small, a couple of hundred men, perhaps; they were not keeping good order, but they were fighting a steady fight, biting open their cartridges, ramming home their charges, spitting their bullets into their musket barrels, and waiting in ones and twos behind cover to get a fair shot at their pursuers. A dozen officers, their drawn swords flashing in the sun, were among them. The mounted officer in command caught sight of Hornblower and his party and reined round his horse in astonishment.

"Who are you?" he shouted.

"English," replied Hornblower.

But before another word could be exchanged the firing in the rear increased in intensity; not only that, but suddenly from out of a side lane level with the rear-guard appeared a dozen horsemen, lancers, their spear points reflecting the sun, and the rear-guard broke in disorder, running wildly down the road to escape being cut off. Hornblower saw a lance point enter between the shoulders of a running man, saw him fall on his face, sliding over the surface of the road for a yard before the lance point tore its way out again, leaving him struggling like a broken-backed animal. Over him swept the skirmishers of the insurgent advanced guard, a swarm of men of every shade of colour, running, loading, and firing. There was a moment when the air was full of bullets.

"My lord—" expostulated Gerard.

"That's all right. It's all over now," said Hornblower.

The fight had swept past them up the road; no one had paid them any attention save for the single question of the mounted Spanish officer. The small column of infantry marching in regular order behind the skirmishers saw them, however, saw the glittering gold, the epaulettes, and the cocked hats. Again a mounted officer wheeled towards them with the same question to receive the same answer from Hornblower.

"*Ingleses?*" repeated the officer. "English? Why—you're a British admiral!"

"Commanding the British squadron in West Indian waters," said Hornblower.

"A pleasure to see you, sir. William Jones, late Captain, Twenty-third Foot, now Major commanding a battalion in the army of Greater Colombia."

"Delighted to make your acquaintance, Major."

"Pardon me, but I must attend to my duties," said Jones, wheeling his horse again.

"Hooray for England!" yelled someone in the marching ranks, and he was answered by a thin cheer; half of these ragged scarecrows must have been British, mingled indiscriminately with Negroes and South Americans. The cavalry followed them, regiment after regiment, a flood of men and horses filling the road like a river brimming its banks. Lancers and light-horse, sore-backed horses and lame horses; most of the men had coiled ropes at their saddle bows, and they were all ragged and drooping in their saddles with fatigue; from the appearance of both men and beasts they had marched far and fought hard, and now they were pressing on to the limit of their strength after their defeated foe. A thousand men had passed, estimated Hornblower, judging the column as well as he could, when a new sound came to his ears through the monotonous trampling of the horses' hoofs. A thumping and a jingling, loud and irregular. Here came the guns, dragged along by weary horses; at the heads of the horses walked men ragged and bearded—they were wearing the remains of blue jumpers and white trousers. It was the crew of the *Bride of Abydos*. One of them lifted his weary head and recognized the party at the roadside.

"Good old Horny!" he shouted; his voice was thin with fatigue and sounded like an old man's.

In the mounted officer riding alongside Hornblower recognized one of Ramsbottom's lieutenants; he sat his plodding horse like a sailor, and raised his arm in a weary salute. One gun clattered by, and another followed it. The guns of Carabobo, which had won the independence of a continent.

Hornblower realized that he had not yet seen Ramsbottom, whom he would have expected to be at the head of the artillery column, but as the realization came to him he saw something now beside the second gun. It was a horse litter, extemporized from two poles and some sheets of canvas. It was slung from two horses, one fore and one aft; the bight of canvas between the poles was shaded by an awning spread above it, and lying in the trough was a man, a smallish man, black-bearded, lying feebly against pillows behind his back. A seaman walked at the head of each horse, and with the plodding step of the animals the litter lurched and rolled, and the black-bearded man lurched and rolled at the same time. Yet he was able to take note of the group by the roadside, and he made an effort to sit up, and he called an order to the seamen leading the horses which caused them to turn out of the road and stop by Hornblower.

"Good morning, my lord," he said; he spoke shrilly, like someone hysterical.

Hornblower had to look twice and more to recognize him. The black beard, the feverish eyes, the shocking dead pallor upon which the tan looked like some unnatural coating, all made identification difficult.

"Ramsbottom!" exclaimed Hornblower.

"The very same but a little different," said Ramsbottom, with a cackling laugh.

"Are you wounded?" asked Hornblower; at the moment the words passed his lips he perceived that Ramsbottom's left arm was concealed in a roll of rags—Hornblower had been looking so intently at the face that the arm had escaped his notice until then.

"I have made my sacrifice in the cause of liberty," said Ramsbottom, with the same laugh—it might have been a laugh of derision or a laugh of mere hysteria.

"What happened?"

"My left hand lies on the field of Carabobo," cackled Ramsbottom. "I doubt if it has received Christian burial."

"Good God!"

"Do you see my guns? My beautiful guns. They tore the Dons apart at Carabobo."

"But you—what treatment have you received?"

"Field surgery, of course. Boiling pitch for the stump. Have you ever felt boiling pitch, my lord?"

"My frigate is anchored in the roadstead. The surgeon is on board—"

"No—oh no. I must go on with my guns. I must clear El Libertador's path to Caracas."

The same laugh. It was not derision—it was something the opposite. A man on the edge of delirium keeping a desperate hold on his sanity so as not to be diverted from his aim. Nor was it a case of a man laughing lest he weep. He was laughing lest he should indulge in heroics.

"Oh, you can't—"

"Sir! Sir! My lord!"

Hornblower swung round. Here was a midshipman from the frigate touching his hat, agitated by the urgency of his message.

"What is it?"

"Message from the cap'n, my lord. Ships of war in sight in the offing. A Spanish frigate an' what looks like a Dutch frigate, my lord. Bearing down on us."

Desperate news indeed. He must have his flag flying in *Clorinda* to meet these strangers, but it was a maddening moment in which to be told about it. He turned back to Ramsbottom and back again to the midshipman, his customary quickness of thought not as apparent as usual.

"Very well," he rasped. "Tell the captain I'm coming immediately."

"Aye aye, my lord." He turned again to Ramsbottom.

"I must go," he said. "I must—"

"My lord," said Ramsbottom. Some of his feverish vitality had left him. He was leaning back again on his pillows, and it took him a second or two to gather his strength to speak again, and when he did the words lagged as he uttered them. "Did you capture the *Bride,* my lord?"

"Yes." He must end this; he must get back to his ship.

"My bonny *Bride.* My lord, there's another keg of caviare in the after lazarette. Please enjoy it, my lord."

The cackling laugh again. Ramsbottom was still laughing as he lay back with his eyes closed, not hearing the hurried "Good-bye" which Hornblower uttered as he turned away. It seemed to Hornblower as if that laugh followed him while he hastened to the pier and down into the boat.

"Shove off! Put your backs into it!"

There lay *Clorinda* at anchor, with the *Bride of Abydos* close to her. And there, undoubtedly, were the topsails of two frigates heading in towards them. He scrambled up the ship's side with hardly a moment to spare for the compliments with which he was received. He was too busy taking in the tactical situation, the trend of the shore, the position of the *Bride of Abydos*, the approach of the strangers.

"Hoist my flag," he ordered curtly, and then, recovering his poise, with the customary elaborate politeness, "Sir Thomas, I'd be obliged if you'd get springs on the cable, out of the after ports on both sides."

"Springs, my lord? Aye aye, my lord."

Cables passed through the after ports to the anchor cable; by hauling in on one or the other with the capstan he could turn the ship to bring her guns to bear in any direction. It was only one of the many exercises Hornblower had put his crews through during the recent manoeuvres. It called for heavy, closely coordinated labour on the part of the hands. Orders were bellowed; warrant and petty officers ran at the heads of their different parties to rouse out the cables and drag them aft.

"Sir Thomas, please order the brig to kedge closer in. I want her in shore of us."

"Aye aye, my lord."

Now it became apparent that there was some time in hand. The approaching frigates, hull up now when a glass was trained on them from the quarterdeck, were shortening sail, and then, even while Hornblower held them in the field of his telescope, he saw their main topsails suddenly broaden as they were swung round. They were heaving-to, and a moment later he saw a boat lowered from the Dutch frigate and pull to the Spanish one. That would mean a consultation, presumably. Thanks to the difference of language they could hardly be expected to agree on a course of action by signal or even by speaking trumpet.

"The Spaniard's wearing a commodore's broad pendant, Sir Thomas. Will you please be ready to salute it as soon as he salutes my flag?"

"Aye aye, my lord."

The consultation took some little time, the second half of one sand-glass and the beginning of the next. A monstrous creaking down below, and a clanking of the capstan, told that the springs were being tested. *Clorinda* swung a trifle to starboard, and then a trifle to port.

"Springs are tested and ready, my lord."

"Thank you, Sir Thomas. Now will you be good enough to send the hands to quarters and clear for action?"

"Clear for action? Aye aye, my lord."

It was a detestable nuisance to take this precaution. It meant that his bedding and books and personal equipment down below would be swept away in a horrible muddle that might take days to straighten. But on the other hand, if those frigates came down determined to fight, his reputation would never survive being unready for them. It would be chaos to try to clear away the guns and bring up cartridges while actually under fire; the battle—if there were to be a battle—would be lost before it was begun. And there was something of the old thrill about these preparations; the pealing of the whistles, the hoarse cries of the petty officers, the orderly rush of the men to the guns, the tramp of the marines to the quarterdeck and the sharp order of their officer as they dressed into a rigid line.

"Ship cleared for action, my lord."

"Thank you, Sir Thomas. Stand by, if you please."

There would have been just time even if the strangers had come instantly down and gone into action without parley. By a rapid use of his springs he would have raked the first comer thoroughly enough to have made her captain wish he had never been born. Now he must wait, and the ship's company, standing by their guns, must wait with him, the matches smouldering in their tubs, the fire parties standing by with their buckets, the powder boys, cartridge carriers in hand, waiting to start their race from powder magazine to guns and back again.

"Here they come, my lord!"

Those topsails were narrowing again; those masts were coming into line. Now the frigates' bows were pointed straight at *Clorinda* as they came towards her. Hornblower held them steady in his telescope; no guns were run out, he could see, but it was impossible to tell if they were cleared for action. Nearer and nearer; now they were almost within extreme random cannon shot. At that moment there was a puff of smoke from the Spaniard's starboard bow, and for the life of him Hornblower could not check a gulp of excitement. The breeze blew the puff away, and then the puff was replaced by another; as the second appeared, the heavy thud of the first discharge came to Hornblower's ears. There was a momentary temptation to plunge into the luxury of mental arithmetic, involving the speed of sound conveyed over water, and the five seconds' interval between saluting guns, and the distance between the ships, but it had to be foregone.

"You may return the salute to the broad pendant, Sir Thomas."

"Aye aye, my lord."

Thirteen guns for a rear admiral's flag; eleven for a commodore; twenty-four guns, one hundred and twenty seconds, exactly two minutes; those ships, approaching at four miles in the hour, would be a cable's length closer at the end of the salutes, within distant gunshot.

"Sir Thomas, I would be glad if you would take several turns upon the starboard spring."

"Aye aye, my lord."

The violent creaking made itself heard again, and *Clorinda* turned herself to present her broadside towards the newcomers. No harm whatever in letting them know that a hot reception was awaiting them if they intended mischief; it might save much trouble later.

"They're taking in sail, my lord!"

So he could see for himself, but there was nothing to be gained by saying so. The two ships obviously had heavy crews, judging by the rapidity with which sail was got in. Now round they went, up into the wind. Hornblower believed he could hear the roar of the cables as they anchored. It seemed like a decisive moment, and Hornblower was about to mark it by shutting up his telescope with a snap when he saw a boat lowering from the Spaniard.

"I fancy we'll be having a visitor shortly," said Hornblower.

The boat seemed to fly over the glittering water; the men at the oars were pulling like madmen—presumably the eternal desire of the men of one navy to show another navy what they could do.

"Boat ahoy!" hailed the officer of the watch.

The Spanish officer in the sternsheets, conspicuous by his epaulettes, hailed back; Hornblower could not be sure of what he said, but the letter that was waved at the same time told the story.

"Receive him on board, if you please, Sir Thomas."

The Spanish lieutenant looked sharply round him as he came over the ship's side; no harm in his seeing the men at quarters and the preparations made. He picked out Hornblower at once, and with a salute and a bow presented his letter.

Su excellencia el Almirante Sir Hornblower, said the superscription.

Hornblower broke the seal; he could read the Spanish of the letter easily enough.

The Brigadier, Don Luiz Argote, would be honoured if His Excellency Sir Hornblower would accord him the opportunity of an interview. The Brigadier would be delighted if he could visit His Excellency's ship and would be equally delighted if His Excellency would visit His Most Catholic Majesty's ship.

In Spanish naval usage, Hornblower knew, "brigadier" was equivalent to "commodore."

"I'll write a reply," said Hornblower. "Sir Thomas, please make this gentleman welcome. Come with me, Gerard."

Down below, with the ship cleared for action, it was a nuisance to hunt up writing paper and ink; it was even more of a nuisance to have to compose a letter in Spanish, for in writing, misspellings and bad grammar would be far more evident than in speech. Luckily the brigadier's letter itself supplied most of the spelling and the tricky conditional form.

Rear Admiral Sir Horatio Hornblower would be delighted to receive the Brigadier Don Luiz Argote in his flagship whenever the Brigadier wishes.

Sealing wax and seal and candle had to be discovered; it would never do to appear careless about these formalities.

"Very well," said Hornblower, giving grudging approval of the second impression after the failure of the first attempt. "Take a boat to the *Bride of Abydos* as quick as lightning and see if there's any of that sherry left which Ramsbottom served at his dinner party."

The brigadier, when he came up *Clorinda*'s side, to be received with the appropriate compliments, was followed by another figure in cocked hat and epaulettes. Hornblower bowed and saluted and introduced himself.

"I took the liberty of asking Captain Van der Maesen, of the Royal Netherlands Navy, to accompany me," said the brigadier.

"It is with much pleasure that I welcome Captain Van der Maesen on board," said Hornblower. "Perhaps you gentlemen will accompany me below. I regret very much that we will not be very comfortable, but, as you see, I have been exercising my crew in their duties."

A screen had been hurriedly run across the after part of the frigate, and the table and chairs replaced. The brigadier sipped with increasing and astonished appreciation at the glass of wine offered him. Inevitably several minutes passed in desultory conversation—Spanish was the one language the three had in common—before the brigadier began to discuss business.

"You have a beautiful ship here, milord," he said. "I regret much to find you in company with a pirate."

"You mean the *Bride of Abydos*, señor?"

"Naturally, milord."

Hornblower saw a trap opening before him.

"You call her a pirate, *señor?*"

"What do you call her, milord?"

"I am waiting to hear your opinion, *señor*." It was important not to commit himself.

"Her actions call for explanation, milord. She has captured and plundered a Dutch ship. That can be interpreted as an act of piracy.

On the other hand it might be said she is operating under a so-called commission issued by the rebels in Venezuela. In the one case Captain Van der Maesen will seize her as a pirate. On the other, if she is a privateer, I will seize her as an enemy of my country."

"In neither case, *señor*, has a court of law determined her status. In the meanwhile, gentlemen, she is in my possession."

Hats were in the ring now. Hornblower met the eyes of the others with the least expression he could manage. Of one thing he was certain, that whatever might be eventually decided regarding the *Bride of Abydos* neither the British government nor the British public would approve of his tamely allowing her to be taken out of his hands.

"Milord, I have assured Captain Van der Maesen of my support in any action he may decide to take, and he has given me the same assurance."

The Dutch captain confirmed this with a nod and a half-intelligible sentence. Two to one, in other words; odds that *Clorinda* could not hope to face.

"Then I hope, gentlemen, I hope very sincerely indeed, that you decide upon approving of my course of action."

It was the politest way of defying them that he could think of.

"I find it very hard to believe, milord, that you extend the protection of His Britannic Majesty's navy to pirates, or to privateers in a war in which His Majesty is neutral."

"You may have noticed, *señor*, that the *Bride of Abydos* is flying His Britannic Majesty's flag. Of course you understand that as a naval officer I cannot permit that flag to be hauled down."

There it was, the ultimate defiance. Ten minutes from now and the guns might be firing. Ten minutes from now and this deck might be littered with dead and wounded. He might be dead himself. The Spaniard looked at the Dutchman and back to Hornblower.

"We would much regret taking strong action, milord."

"I am delighted to hear that, *señor*. That confirms me in my decision. We can part the best of friends."

"But—"

The brigadier had not intended his last sentence to be interpreted as a sign of yielding. He had been uttering, he thought, a further threat. Hornblower's interpretation of it left him speechless for a moment.

"I am overjoyed to find that we are in agreement, gentlemen. Perhaps we can drink the healths of our sovereigns in another glass of this wine, *señor*—and may I take this opportunity of acknowledging the debt the rest of the world owes to your country for such an exquisite production?"

By taking their withdrawal for granted he was giving them a chance of withdrawing gracefully. The bitter moment of admitting that they had been outfaced had come and gone before they had realized it. Once more the Spaniard and the Dutchman exchanged unavailing glances, and Hornblower seized the opportunity to pour more wine.

"To His Most Catholic Majesty, *señor*. To His Majesty the King of the Netherlands."

He held his glass high. They could not refuse that toast, even though the brigadier's mouth still opened and shut as he struggled to find words for his emotions. Common politeness forced the brigadier to complete the toast, as Hornblower waited, glass in hand.

"To His Britannic Majesty."

They drank together.

"This has been a delightful visit, gentlemen," said Hornblower. "Another glass? No? It cannot be that you are leaving so soon? But I expect you have many duties calling for your attention."

As the sideboys, white-gloved, formed up at the entry port, and the bosun's mates pealed upon their whistles, and the ship's company, still at their guns, stood to attention, in compliment to the departing visitors, Hornblower could spare a moment to glance round. Those sideboys and bosun's mates and gun's crews might be facing imminent death at this moment if that interview had taken a more stormy course. He deserved their gratitude, but of course he would never receive it. Shaking hands with the brigadier, he made the final clarification of the situation.

"A prosperous voyage, *señor*. I hope I shall have the pleasure of meeting you again. I shall be sailing for Kingston as soon as the land breeze serves."

One of Barbara's regular letters, received months later, helped to round off the incident.

MY DEAREST HUSBAND [wrote Barbara as usual, and, as usual, Hornblower read those words with a smile. There were several sheets to the letter, and the first sheet contained much of interest to Hornblower, but it was not until the second sheet that Barbara began her usual society and professional gossip],

Last night the Lord Chancellor was my left-hand partner at dinner, and he had much to say about the *Bride of Abydos,* and in consequence, to my great pleasure, much to say about my dear husband. The Spanish and Dutch governments, through their ambassador and minister, have naturally lodged protests with the Foreign Secretary, who has only been able to acknowledge receipt of the notes and to promise a further reply when the legal aspects of the case are made clear. And, in all the history of Admiralty law, said the Lord Chancellor, there never was a case as complicated as this one. The insurers plead negligence on the part of the assured (I hope that I have these technical terms right, my very dearest) because the captain of the *Helmond* took no steps to verify the *bona fides* of the *Bride of Abydos,* and they further plead negligence on the part of the Dutch government because the capture took place within Dutch territorial waters off Bonaire, and the Dutchmen deny hotly both that they were negligent and that the capture was really within their territorial waters. Further, the actual plundering and detention took place in Spanish territorial waters. And there seem to be untold complications arising from the fact that you found the *Bride of Abydos* abandoned by her crew—did you know, dearest, that it seems a matter of great legal importance as to whether her anchor was actually touching bottom or not? In any case, there has been no legal action in any court so far because no one seems to be able to decide which court has jurisdiction in the matter (I hope, dearest, you will give your wife all credit for listening attentively and taking note of these difficult expressions). Taking one thing with another, and allowing four months on the average for each necessary round trip to the West Indies to take evidence on commission, and taking into account demurrers and rebuttals and surrebuttals, the Lord Chancellor thinks that it will be thirty-seven years before any case reaches the House of Lords, and he went on to say, cackling into his soup, that our interest in the case will be greatly diminished by then.

This is by no means all the news, dearest. There is something further which would greatly distress me if it were not for the fact that I know my husband the Admiral will be delighted. Taking tea today with Lady Exmouth (I know how your dear eyes will open wide with horror at women being in possession of such secrets), I heard that Their Lordships take a most favourable view of your attitude towards the Spanish and Dutch naval authorities—dearest, I am so delighted even though I could never doubt it. It has already been decided to extend your command for the extra year, and my pleasure in knowing how pleased you will be at this compliment almost—quite—allays my sorrows at the thought of our further separation. Dearest, there is no woman who could love you—there is no woman on earth who could love any man as much as I love you, the truest, the bravest, the boldest, the cleverest— I must not write like this because there is still further news to add.

This is that the government has always, apparently, looked with favour at the attempt of the Spanish colonies to attain their independence, and with the greatest disfavour upon the decision of the Spanish government to attempt their reconquest with troops sent out from Europe. There have been hints that the other. powers, uneasy at the movement towards liberty, have been meditating giving military assistance to Spain in Spanish America. The victory at Carabobo, where poor Mr. Ramsbottom and his guns played such a part, has made this intervention more unlikely. It is a great state secret, so great that over the teacups it is mentioned only in whispers, that the British government meditates making a declaration that it will not permit military intervention in Spanish America. And it appears that our government is in accord with the Americans over this, for it is believed that President Monroe is planning to issue a declaration regarding a similar doctrine, and discussions regarding it are taking place. So that my dearest husband finds himself at the centre of world affairs, as he has always been at the centre of his wife's fondest affections.